TOXO

TOXO

Medical Kidnap Files #4

P.D. WORKMAN

ISBN: 9781989080542 (IS Hardcover)

ISBN: 9781989080535 (IS Paperback)

ISBN: 9781989080504 (KDP Paperback)

ISBN: 9781989080511 (Kindle)

ISBN: 9781989080528 (ePub)

ALSO BY P.D. WORKMAN

YOUNG ADULT FICTION:

Medical Kidnap Files:

Mito

EDS

Proxy

Toxo

Pain (Coming soon)

Between the Cracks:

Ruby

June and Justin

Michelle

Chloe

Ronnie

June, Into the Light

Tamara's Teardrops:

Tattooed Teardrops

Two Teardrops

Tortured Teardrops

Vanishing Teardrops

Breaking the Pattern:

Deviation

Diversion

By-Pass

Stand Alone YA novels

Stand Alone

Don't Forget Steven

Those Who Believe

Cynthia has a Secret

Questing for a Dream

Once Brothers

Intersexion

Making Her Mark

Endless Change

Gem, Himself, Alone

MYSTERY/SUSPENSE:

Reg Rawlins, Psychic Detective

What the Cat Knew

A Psychic with Catitude

A Catastrophic Theft

Night of Nine Tails

Telepathy of Gardens

Delusions of the Past

Fairy Blade Unmade

Web of Nightmares

A Whisker's Breadth

AND MORE AT PDWORKMAN.COM

*For those whose needs are different
Whose differences are needed*

Mrs. Bradshaw touched Caleb on the shoulder. He looked up at her through the fringe of brown hair that hung in his face. Mrs. Bradshaw spoke, but Caleb's sound processor clicked and buzzed. He tapped it, frowning and focusing on her face to try to understand what she was saying. She wore very red lipstick and made a weird fish-face when she was trying to make it easier for him to read her. It didn't help.

She asked him something. Caleb tapped on his sound processor, trying to make it work properly. The battery shouldn't have been dying already. His school day was not even over. Mrs. Bradshaw touched Caleb's hand lightly to make him be still and spoke again. He thought she was talking to him about catching the bus.

"Bus?" Caleb repeated. "Catch the bus after school?"

She nodded, making a motion toward the bus loading zone and repeating her instructions to catch the bus.

Caleb nodded impatiently. He tapped his sound processor again, trying to make sense of the bursts of noise. Mrs. Bradshaw nodded and moved on, walking down the aisle between the desks, toward the back of the room. Caleb put his head back down to puzzle through his math questions.

He heard the buzzing in his ear when the school bell rang, felt it through his fingers on the desk, and saw the other students moving to put away their books and pack up to go. Caleb closed his book, stacked everything up, and headed for the door. Mrs. Bradshaw made a motion to get his attention. He waved his acknowledgment and went to his locker to pack his backpack.

———

When he got out to the bus loading zone, the crowds of students were already thinning, the earlier buses having already loaded up and left. Caleb looked for his bus, scanning the window placards for bus D. He couldn't see it in the line. Had it already left without him? He'd taken longer than he'd intended to at his locker, the noise of the students around him buzzing angrily in his head, making it impossible to concentrate on sorting out his books. He'd eventually turned the sound processor off to silence it, but then Jenny C had tapped him on the shoulder and tried to talk to him about the English essay they had been assigned. Caleb had turned it back on, tried to listen to her, turned it off again, and had done his best to read her speech and answer her questions. Eventually, Jenny C had shaken her head, thrown up her hands in disgust, and walked away from him without even saying goodbye.

But Caleb didn't think the bus would have left without him. Usually, even if he were late, Mrs. Mills still waited. There were not that many kids on his bus, and she knew to wait. Caleb paced up and down the street, looking for bus D, until most of the buses had pulled out.

It was obvious that Bus D wasn't there. Maybe there was a substitute driver and she didn't know to stay and wait for Caleb if he took too long like Mrs. Mills did. Caleb headed back to the school to go to the office and tell them that he'd missed the bus, but when he reached the doors, they were all locked.

Caleb bit the side of his hand, trying to decide what to do. His bus wasn't there and he couldn't get back into the school. He would have to walk home. It would take longer, but he knew the way. He'd walked that far before. Not by himself, usually. But he knew the way. He would just walk.

He swung his backpack up over both shoulders and snugged the straps so that it was properly balanced on his back. If he'd known he was going to be walking, he would not have taken so many books. The backpack was heavy, weighing on him even after the few minutes he'd been looking for the bus. Mom said sometimes his backpack weighed as much as he did, but that's because he was skinny.

Caleb started walking down the street.

His brain was whirling with thoughts and worries. Mom would be worried when he didn't get off the bus. She always said to go back in the school and call her, but he couldn't. She would be mad.

He snapped his fingers beside his head. Even though he couldn't hear the sound with his processor turned off, it was still calming. He rubbed his eyebrow with the other hand and shaded his eye from the direct sun. Some of the anxiety eased, but he was still worried. Mom would call Dad. Dad would be mad. They would both want to know where he was and why he'd missed the bus and why he hadn't called. If he hurried, maybe he wouldn't be too late. He picked up his pace, but in doing so, tripped over a crack in the sidewalk, and the heavy backpack prevented him from regaining his balance. He fell down, smashing his chin on the pavement and getting the wind knocked out of him by thirty pounds of books landing in the middle of his back.

Caleb groaned. He rolled over and picked himself up slowly, his whole body vibrating with the impact. He swiped at his chin to see if it was bleeding, but his fingers were dry. He readjusted the backpack and started to walk again, his regular pace, not trying to hurry. Caleb knew he was going to take longer getting home, and anxiety flooded through his whole body, making his stomach hurt and his muscles move jerkily like he was a robot that hadn't been programmed properly.

He snapped his fingers rapidly. He pulled his hood up over his head so that it blocked some of the sun from his eyes. He smoothed his eyebrow. He started to count. He snapped his fingers as fast as he could beside his face.

He covered one block at a time, focused on his goal of getting home. He tried to structure a script in his head to explain to Mom what had happened and why he was late getting home.

Someone grabbed Caleb's shoulder and he tried to jerk away, startled by the contact. With his hood up and his hands by his face, his peripheral vision was cut off and he hadn't seen anyone approaching. He tried to jerk away a second time, dropping his left hand to widen his field of vision.

It was a big, blue-uniformed policeman. Caleb knew he could go to a policeman if he needed help. But he didn't need help. He was just walking home and he knew the way.

"No," he told the man. "Go home."

The policeman's grip on Caleb's shoulder tightened and he gave Caleb a hard shake. Caleb watched his face and read, "Where are you going?"

"Go home," he insisted. "Caleb go home."

He tried to pull away and the officer pushed him hard into a big tree with deep, craggy, rough bark. Caleb was walking on the pathway through the park. That was the way home. That was the way Mom always took him home if they were walking. Caleb stopped snapping his fingers and flapped his hand beside his face.

"Let go!" He struggled to pull away. He didn't need help. He knew the way home.

———

Purnell took the tweaker to the ground, tripping himself in the process and landing hard on top of the boy. The boy struggled to get away, shouting incoherently in his cracking adolescent voice.

"Hold still!" Purnell shouted, trying to get control of him. "Give me your hands! Stop fighting!"

But the boy kept thrashing wildly, too far gone to understand a word Purnell was saying. The heavy backpack was in the way, and Purnell fought to jerk it off of him. He had his billy out and smacked the addict several times in the arms and shoulders to subdue him.

"Just hold still. Stay down and quit fighting me! You want to get tased?"

The boy kept shouting. Purnell was aware that they were attracting the attention of the park users. The kid could have friends and Purnell was there alone. He succeeded in getting the backpack off the boy and pinned him down. He fumbled with his radio, calling for backup while the boy bucked and screamed incoherent curses, completely off his head. Purnell grabbed one of the wildly flapping hands and twisted it up behind the boy's back. He shoved his baton back into his belt and managed to grab the other hand.

Like other tweakers Purnell had dealt with, the boy was surprisingly strong for his slight frame, immune to any pain while high. On amphetamines, a skinny man could fight off several cops with seeming inhuman strength, breaking his own bones in the process without even noticing. Purnell twisted the boy's second arm hard, hoping that he wouldn't break anything, but knowing that he had to get the boy under control before he could hurt Purnell and before any of his friends decided to help out. Purnell finally managed to get both hands close enough together to ratchet the handcuffs into place.

The boy howled and bucked, still trying to escape. Purnell did his best to pat down the thrashing junkie and search his pockets for more drugs. He didn't have anything on him. He must have taken his whole buy at once.

Two more units rolled up and, with the help of the other officers, Purnell managed to get the kid locked up in the back of his car for transport. He wiped his forehead with the back of his hand, sweating in spite of the chilly temperature. Officer Jacobs, in one of the backup units, laughed. "Quite a workout, hey?"

"Stupid tweakers. It doesn't seem like it matters how many times we tell them to stay out of the park, they just gotta come here to shoot up."

"This one's pretty young." Jacobs peered through the window at the boy, howling and crying in the back seat, trying to tell the whole world his woes. "Probably not shooting yet."

"Well, whether he's popping or shooting, he's high as a kite. Gonna take some time before he comes down."

After having a coffee to decompress, Purnell returned to the cool-down room to see how his arrestee was doing. Kristen Oakes, supervising in his absence, looked up from the monitors when he entered the control room.

"How's my guy?" Purnell asked. "Coming down yet?"

"I don't think your tweaker is a tweaker," Kristen advised.

"You wouldn't say that if you'd seen him in action. Classic signs."

He looked at the two monitors showing his subject in the cool-down room. The boy was sitting in the corner, back against the wall, knees drawn up to his chest, rocking back and forth. Kristen touched the audio dial to turn up the volume and he could hear the boy humming or moaning to himself. He shrugged.

"Still looks like a tweaker to me."

"Well, he's calmed down, so why don't we see if we can get anything coherent from him?"

Purnell agreed and they went together to the cell, barely bigger than a caretaker's closet, the wall and floors rubberized to cushion against injury. There was not much space for socializing.

"Hey," Purnell said, when the boy didn't look at him. "Time to talk. You want to tell me your name and what you were doing in the park today?"

The boy continued to hum and rock. Purnell could see they were going to have to clean him up. He had a number of scrapes and smudges on his face and his bare knees and shins. His hoodie covered his arms and most of his head and face.

"Are you going to behave yourself?" Purnell demanded. "If I take the handcuffs off of you, will you behave?"

The boy continued to rock and paid him no attention.

Purnell raised an eyebrow at Kristen, wondering if she still thought that he was just a regular kid, not high at all.

"Let's give it a try," she agreed. She moved toward the boy.

"You'd better let me do it," Purnell warned. "He was pretty violent at the park. He's crazy strong on whatever he took."

"Do you think I can't handle myself?" Kristen challenged.

She was medium height and compact, but he knew she was no marshmallow. He'd seen her boxing at the gym and she had a reputation as someone who didn't put up with any nonsense. Soft when she was dealing with a victim or a remorseful perp, but hard as nails when confronted by a disrespectful or violent detainee.

"Sorry. Go ahead, if you want."

She nodded and went over to the boy. She crouched in front of him, directly in his line of sight, and murmured something comforting. His eyes rolled up and away from her, avoiding eye contact. She reached up to pull back his hoodie, and he jerked away from her, his hum going shrill. She pulled her hand back.

"I'm going to take the cuffs off," Kristen told him in an even, reassuring voice. She squished herself up against the wall to try to get them unlocked without moving him. It required some contortion, but she managed to get the handcuffs off.

The boy immediately had both hands up beside his face, flapping one hand back and forth beside his eye, and smoothing his eyebrow with the other, folding in on himself, blocking out the rest of the world.

"You see?" Purnell pointed out. "He's tweaking bad."

Kristen nodded. "I see," she agreed. She reached again for his hood, and though he flinched away from her, the boy didn't block her from pulling it back.

At first, Purnell didn't see anything out of the ordinary. The boy had longish, shaggy, light brown hair, wavy, disordered from having had his hood over it, a fringe falling over his eyes. Then Purnell saw the odd plastic circle and the wire running down to a bulky hearing aid wrapped around the boy's ear.

"He's hearing impaired?"

Kristen tapped the boy's shoulder. "Can you hear me?"

He stopped tweaking for long enough to motion her away. He tapped the hearing aid and made a noise that might have been speech, but was too slurred to understand.

"Not hearing impaired," Kristen said. "Deaf. This part," she pointed to the plastic disk but didn't touch it, "is a cochlear implant. It feeds electronic impulses directly into his cochlear nerve, which the brain interprets as sound."

The boy tapped his ear and grunted again, then went back to tweaking.

"I don't think it's working properly," Kristen said. "I think that's what he's saying."

"He can talk. When I first stopped him, he told me to go home."

"Some of his speech may be clear and some of it may not be. He might need to be able to hear his own voice to be comprehensible."

"Being deaf doesn't mean he isn't tweaking."

Kristen caught the bottom of the boy's hoodie and lifted it slightly. He didn't move at first, but as she tugged it up, he moved automatically to withdraw his arms through the sleeves and allowed Kristen to pull it up over his head. Kristen handed it behind her to Purnell, and he double-checked the pockets to make sure they were empty. With his face fully visible and the bulk of his hoodie not hiding his skinny frame, Purnell could see that the boy was even younger than he had originally estimated. He couldn't have been even fifteen.

Kristen again tried to talk to the boy, making gestures as she spoke. "Do you sign? Can you read my lips?"

He remained remote, rocking, flapping his hand, shielding his eyes from her.

"He didn't have any kind of identification on him?" Kristen asked.

"Nothing on his person. I'm ready to inventory his backpack now. Might be something in it."

"Okay." Kristen looked at the boy for a minute. "I guess leaving him in here is the easiest for now. I'll continue to monitor. You want to bring his backpack into the control room so I can see what he's got too?"

Purnell felt a stab of resentment at her taking such an interest in his collar, but there was no reason for him to feel possessive about it. Not like he'd broken open an organized crime ring. All he'd done was pick up a kid tweaking in the park. Trying to keep the streets clean. The kid would be in jail for a few days, they'd release him until his trial date, and he'd be back at the park shooting up again. At his age, it was likely his first offense, and he'd get nothing more than a slap on the wrists.

"Sure," he agreed. "I'll be right back."

The backpack was heavy, full of textbooks and binders. That was the first dissonance. If the kid was a tweaker, why was he taking so many books home? He planned on getting high and then doing his homework? Or were the books a cover, something to convince his parents that everything was normal and he was still doing fine at school? *Leave me alone, Mom, I'll be in my room doing my homework.*

He stacked the schoolbooks neatly in a pile. Opening the cover of the first textbook, he found a name neatly printed on the inside.

"Caleb Hibbert," he told Kristen. "Unless it's a second-hand textbook and that's the previous owner's name." He opened each textbook. They all had the same name in the same neat printing. "Yep, looks like that's our tweaker's name."

She frowned, but didn't correct him.

Purnell dug back into the backpack, pulling out odds and ends; pens and pencils, mashed up permission forms, snack wrappers. He checked the front and side pockets and found a thin wallet, stiff, obviously used little. He opened it to find Caleb's student ID card and a business card printed on a home inkjet printer, streaky and a worn. He read the first few lines on the business card and swore, his gut clenching.

Kristen looked away from the monitor to see what was wrong. "What is it?" she asked, looking at the information card he held in his hands.

"He's autistic."

———

Riley Hibbert looked up from her computer and out the window, pushing her straight brown hair back behind her ear. Something was wrong. Her ears, well-attuned to the sound, caught the noise of the engine of the school bus. It didn't stop in front of the house, but continued to trundle on down the street. She rushed to the door and stepped out, hurrying down to the city sidewalk. She expected the bus to stop a little farther down the street when the driver realized she had missed her stop. Probably a substitute bus driver. The kids would shout at her that she had missed his stop and she would be sure to pull over and let Caleb disembark. Even if Caleb was lost in thought and didn't notice he'd missed his stop, there were enough other students on the bus who would notice as soon as there was a change in the usual routine.

But the bus didn't stop. Riley hurried after it, waving both arms, trying to get the driver's attention. But it was moving too fast, and in a few seconds, was making a turn at the corner and disappearing from sight. Riley hurried after it, pulling her phone out of her pocket.

She wasn't the most well-coordinated person, and chasing the bus while trying to operate her phone was more than she could manage. She stopped where she was and searched for the school's phone number. The office number rang through to voicemail. She tried again, with the same results. She tried a third time, not giving up. There was bound to still be someone in the office. It was just a matter of persistence. Someone would pick up the phone.

Riley looked at the time on the phone, startled to see how late it was. Had something happened? If something had disrupted Caleb's routine, he would be frantic. Even if someone had taken the time to explain it to him, he was likely to be upset.

She dialed the office again, growling at the office staff under her breath to pick up the phone. As if they had heard her, the phone was picked up, and there was a pause before she heard Mrs. Beauvais's calm, even voice.

"Central Middle School. How may I help you?"

"It's Riley Hibbert. Caleb's bus didn't stop to drop him off. Can you get ahold of the driver?"

"Oh, we were informed she was running late today, Mrs. Hibbert. The bus should be there shortly."

"It was here. It just went by the house. But it didn't stop. Caleb must still be on the bus and he'll be upset when he realizes he missed his stop."

"Oh…" Mrs. Beauvais considered this. "I see. I'll have to call the bus company and get their dispatcher. They'll give the driver instructions to keep Caleb on the bus until she can return and drop him at your house."

"They'd better not just let him out…" It seemed like at least once a year, some driver let a kindergartner or special needs student off at the wrong stop, leaving them to wander aimlessly until someone stopped to help them or they reached home in tears, hysterical over having to walk five miles home.

"I'll get right on it. Can I reach you back at this number, Mrs. Hibbert?"

"Yes. Please call me back as soon as you know what's going on. I'm really worried."

"I'll call back as soon as I can."

Mrs. Beauvais disconnected. Riley went back to the house. She packed everything she needed in her purse, put on a jacket, and went to the door, watching for any sign of Caleb and waiting for the return phone call. Every minute that passed was excruciating. Finally, the phone rang.

"Hello?"

What she wanted to hear from Mrs. Beauvais in her calm, reassuring voice was that Caleb was still on the bus, which would loop around back to her house once it had finished the rest of the drop-offs. Instead, Mrs. Beauvais's voice was higher than usual, anxious and staccato.

"Mrs. Hibbert… I've talked to the bus driver… Caleb was not on the bus today."

"What do you mean, he wasn't on the bus? Where else would he be?"

"We're trying to find out now if anyone saw him or talked to him. I'm so sorry."

"Sorry?" Riley tried to stem the flow of words before she said something she would regret later. She knew this was going to happen. She'd always worried about Caleb being able to ride the bus on his own, but the school had assured her that Caleb was capable of managing it. He didn't need someone to walk him to the bus and see him on, as he had in the younger grades. He was used to the routine. There was no danger whatsoever. "Did you talk to the bus driver directly? Or was this relayed through the dispatcher? Did they even talk to the right bus driver?"

"I talked to her directly. It was Maria Mills, his usual driver. She said that Caleb didn't get on. She asked the other kids, and they said they hadn't seen him. So she assumed he wasn't riding today."

"You said the bus was delayed. What happened?"

"Maria called to say she was going to be late. There was a traffic delay on the freeway. All of the kids were told that the bus would be late and to wait in the resource room."

"Caleb was told to wait in the resource room?"

"Yes. All of the children were told."

"Did you talk to Mrs. Bradshaw? She confirmed she told him?"

"No… I'm still trying to get her. She's left for the day and I haven't been able to reach her yet. But I will. I'll confirm that she told him."

"Well, it doesn't matter whether she told him or not," Riley said impatiently. "Because he didn't go to the resource room to wait there, did he? Or he would have been waiting there with the other children."

"Yes… I'm afraid that's true," Mrs. Beauvais admitted. "For some reason, he didn't go to Resource and he wasn't there to catch the bus."

"So he walked home?"

"I… suppose so. Unless he might have gotten on one of the other buses."

Riley rubbed the middle of her forehead, where pain was burrowing in like a maggot. "I don't think he would have, but you're going to have to call the bus dispatcher back and tell them to check with each driver to see if they ended up with an extra kid. And you need to have someone search the school. I'll have to get someone to watch the house in case he shows up here, and drive our usual route to the school looking for him. Hopefully, he just decided to walk, and I'll find him along the way. If not…"

"I'll talk to the dispatcher and we'll make a search," Mrs. Beauvais agreed immediately. "I'm so sorry, Mrs. Hibbert. We've never had something like this happen before…"

Riley hung up. She didn't believe for a minute that they'd never had a bus mishap before. Not when she saw them in the news every year. She'd told them that Caleb wasn't ready to take the bus himself. She'd told Wes, but he'd said that she needed to give Caleb a chance to develop some independence. Caleb needed to learn to do things on his own without his mother or a teacher or mentor hanging over him all the time. He needed to develop his own confidence.

Well, that had worked out well, hadn't it?

She hurried across the street to Mrs. Fields's house. She had known Caleb ever since he was a toddler and she was always home. Mrs. Fields came to the door. She made a show of rubbing her arms to demonstrate to Riley how cold it was, inviting her to come inside and shut the door. Riley stepped into the overly warm house.

"Mrs. Fields, could I ask you a favor? I need someone to watch the house in case Caleb gets home. He wasn't on the bus and I'm going to drive back to the school and hopefully find him somewhere along the way. But if I miss him and he comes home, would you look after things until I get back?"

"Of course!" the old woman patted Riley's arm. "I'd be happy to. You must be scared to death! Just leave the door unlocked, and I'll watch and go over if Caleb shows up."

She knew better than to suggest she bring Caleb back to her own house while they waited for Riley to return. Caleb would go ballistic if she tried to drag him away from home, where he was supposed to be after school, especially when Riley hadn't arranged it with him ahead of time.

"Thanks so much. I appreciate it."

Back across to her own side of the street, Riley jumped in the car and pulled out. She made a U-turn and headed over to the school, watching the sidewalk like a hawk for any sign of Caleb. She was sure she would see him two-thirds to three-quarters of the way home, trudging along in his shorts, hoodie, and overloaded backpack. If she had known he was going to end up walking home, she would have insisted on long pants; it was too cold for shorts. But she hadn't known and Caleb would have had a meltdown over it.

When she reached the halfway point, she was starting to panic. She should have seen him before that. Unless he left the school very late or was walking very slow, she should already have intersected with him. A red Taurus cut in front of her and she came within an inch of hitting it. She slowed down even more and ground her teeth. Getting in another car accident would not help matters. She needed to stay alert and she needed to find Caleb.

———

Caleb had settled down enough in the cool-down room that they were able to move him to an interview room, where he sat in one of the plastic chairs and they gave him a can of pop to help make him comfortable. He was still flapping his hands around, but not as frantically, and he stopped occasionally to take a drink.

Stimming is what Kristen called the hand movements that Purnell had taken for tweaking. She had a nephew who had autism and she told Purnell she'd had suspicions about Caleb when she saw him rocking and stimming in the cool-down room. When she suggested that she should be the one to keep him company while they waited for DFS, he was happy to pass the duty off to her.

He could already see the headlines. He'd made a righteous arrest, taken down a tweaker in the park, with all kinds of people watching, only to find that the boy wasn't high, but had autism. How many of those people had taken pictures or video on their phones? How long before they were online, proclaiming him an abusive cop trampling all over the civil rights of a defenseless, disabled child? He knew he had to get his reports written up immediately and talk to his superiors to explain what had happened before it was all over the internet. Give them a chance to mitigate the damage.

"Why get DFS involved?" Pete McMillan asked, as Purnell relayed the required information to him. "Why not just call the mother to come pick him up?"

"There are some concerns. He's out wandering by himself, apparently without any supervision. There's no missing report on him. He has a lot of cuts and bruises. His hearing thing isn't working. He's thin. Maybe it's nothing. But maybe it's neglect and abuse."

"Probably just wandered off from wherever he was supposed to be. These kids are like that, you know. Prone to wandering."

"Then maybe he should have better supervision. Or an ankle tracker. If he can't communicate his own needs, he shouldn't be alone."

McMillan nodded his agreement and logged the request for DFS.

CHAPTER THREE

Caleb was feeling better, but didn't know where Mom was. He knew that they must have called her to tell her where he was, so why wasn't she there yet? He needed to tell her that his sound processor wasn't working and he had to tell her about what had happened before the police told her that he had done something wrong. He hadn't done anything wrong, he had just been trying to walk home. He couldn't get the bus and he couldn't get back into the school, so he had to walk home.

The woman policeman who had brought him the pop smiled a lot and moved slowly. She didn't hit him or yell at him like the policeman who had stopped him in the park. She seemed gentle and safe, the kind of person Mom would have asked to watch him while he was waiting for her.

Caleb didn't like the flickering of the fluorescent lights overhead. He motioned to his hoodie.

"Put it back on."

She shook her head and made calm-down motions with her hands, but Caleb wasn't getting upset or overly excited. He was just asking for his hoodie.

"Not yet."

He didn't know why she was saying 'not yet.' He needed his hoodie and he shouldn't have to wait to put it back on again.

"Now." Caleb thumped his hand on the table. "Put back on now."

He watched her face, squinting in the flashing light. "Wait, Caleb. You can put it back on in a while. Are you cold?"

Caleb was not cold. He wanted the hood over his head to block out the visual overload. He shook his head and stimmed, watching the way his fingers appeared to strobe in the flickering light. The policewoman touched his arm to stop him and tried to say something to him, but then the door opened, distracting both of them.

A new man walked in. It wasn't the policeman who had arrested Caleb. Instead, it was a tall man in a suit. His shirt was yellow instead of white. He looked like the principal at the school or one of the vice principals. They always wore suits, and sometimes wore shirts that were not white. The man nodded at the policewoman and greeted her. Caleb looked back at his hand, flapping it up near his eyes.

He could feel both of them looking at him and stared harder at his hand. They spoke to each other for a few minutes. Maybe the man was her husband or her boss. The policewoman tapped Caleb's shoulder and he slid his eyes away from his hand to her face to see what she wanted. He thought she told him to stop moving his hand. Caleb shook his head and continued to stim. She put her arms out in front of her, forearms and palms up, like she was showing her mother her hands were clean. She nodded at Caleb. "Like this," she repeated several times, keeping her arms out.

Reluctantly, Caleb held out his hands and arms for inspection. The woman and the policeman from the park had already used wipes to clean up the dirt that had gotten on them when the policeman had pushed him down and hit him in the park. She knew that his hands and arms had been clean when she gave him his pop. The new man studied Caleb's arms, making notes in his notebook.

The woman turned her arms over, palms and forearms down. Caleb obediently mimicked her. The man studied them for a moment and then looked under the table at Caleb's legs. The woman said something to Caleb, then stood up and pulled his chair back from the table. They looked at his legs. Caleb knew his mother said it was too cold outside for shorts, and that he had bruises and scraped knees from various accidents. He didn't even know where some of them were from. They just seemed to magically appear from day to day.

The man motioned for Caleb to stand up. Caleb looked over at the woman, confused as to why they had changed roles. She nodded and gave him a 'get up' motion as well. Caleb got to his feet.

They both moved around him. Caleb tried to track their movements and keep them in front of him where he could see them both. The woman grasped him by the arm and held him still, her face calm and reassuring. But Caleb didn't like the man walking around behind him and tried to pull free. She tightened her grip, commanding him to stay still. Caleb kept his body in place, but brought his hands back up to his face, stimming to block out the discomfort of having someone behind him looking at him. The policewoman didn't try to stop his movements. Behind him, the man pulled up Caleb's t-shirt, making him stiffen in surprise. The woman kept him from turning around or striking out and, after a moment, the man lowered his shirt again. The woman gave Caleb a little tug toward the chair and Caleb sat back down, drawing his feet up onto the chair, his knees forming a barrier between him and the strangers.

"Do you want your hoodie, now?" The woman slid the shirt across the table toward him.

Caleb snatched it up and had it on in seconds. He pulled the hood down low over his eyes, making it his warm, safe cave to shelter inside.

———

Riley was sitting in her car, on the phone with Wes when the call came through. It was a blocked number.

"That might be someone," Riley said hurriedly. "I'll call you back."

She hung up the phone before he had a chance to answer and switched to the waiting call.

"Hello?"

"Is this Mrs. Hibbert?"

"Yes."

"Mrs. Hibbert, this is Kristen Oakes, with the police department."

Riley breathed open-mouthed, waiting for the news.

"We have your son, here, Mrs. Hibbert."

"Oh, thank goodness! I'll be right there to pick him up."

"You're welcome to come in and talk with us, but there is an ongoing investigation and you will not be able to pick him up."

Riley's foot pressed the gas pedal all the way down in a reflexive reaction.

It was a good thing she was in park and only revved the engine. She stared at the school through her windshield.

"What do you mean, I can't pick him up?"

"Why don't you come in and talk with us? It's better if I can explain everything face to face."

"There must be some kind of misunderstanding. You can't have arrested Caleb for something. He's... he has autism. If he did something, it's a misunderstanding. He couldn't have done anything."

"No, Caleb is not under arrest. We can discuss it when you get here." Kristen relayed the address of the police station and made sure that Riley understood where it was and who to ask for before hanging up the call.

Riley took a few deep breaths before putting the car into reverse and carefully pulling out of the parking space. She called Wes back, and confused him just as much as, if not more than, the officer's call had confused her.

"Can you meet me there? I don't want to be there alone, Wes. You can talk to them."

He would feel a lot more comfortable talking to the police than Riley would. She knew he'd had a certain amount of contact with the police growing up, certainly more than she had ever had. He was much more comfortable talking to police officers. Riley always felt like they were up on a pedestal, almost a different race from what she was, and judging her for all of her shortcomings.

"Where is it? I'll be there."

Riley gave him the details, trying to ignore the honks of the cars around her as she switched lanes without signaling, distracted by the conversation.

"Okay, I'll see you there, Riles."

He hung up. Riley focused on her driving, trying not to think about what was going on and why the policewoman would say that she wouldn't be able to pick Caleb up.

CHAPTER FOUR

Riley looked for Wes's car in the parking lot at the police station, hoping that he had made it there before her. She didn't want to have to go in without him, but she also didn't want to have to wait. She couldn't just sit in the parking lot while Caleb was inside wondering where his mother was and what was going on.

She couldn't see his black Jeep in the rows of parked vehicles, but then she saw it pull in from the street. He found a parking stall near hers and got out. He had a long stride and his usually-studious face had given way to concern.

He pulled her into an embrace without a word. Riley held her husband tightly for a minute, trying to absorb his strength, then finally pulled back from him.

"They said he's okay and that he hasn't been arrested," Wes summarized.

"Yes. I think so. Yes."

"Then everything is fine. It's just a matter of finding out what's going on and getting it straightened out. He's okay. We're all okay." He ran his fingers through his spiky black hair.

Riley nodded. "I've been so scared. Ever since the bus didn't stop… I've just been getting more and more panicked."

"You can stop worrying. You know he's safe. He hasn't been kidnapped, he isn't out there hurt or lost. He's safe here."

"Okay." Riley breathed out. "Okay. He's fine. He's safe. Let's go see what's going on. We'll sort it out."

They went in together and asked for Kristen Oakes as instructed. In a few minutes, the dark-haired, small-framed woman with a neat bun came to the reception area to greet them.

"Mr. and Mrs. Hibbert? Good to meet you. Come with me."

She led them to a small meeting room and had them sit down. Riley looked around nervously. She had hoped that they would be taken to see Caleb immediately, and didn't like the idea of being interrogated while he waited somewhere else, not understanding what was going on.

"First, let me assure you that Caleb is fine," Kristen told them. "There was a little confusion when he was brought in, due to his communication issues, but that was all smoothed out."

"Communication issues?" Riley repeated.

Kristen's brow wrinkled for a moment, then smoothed. "Because of his autism and his deafness," she said. "It makes proper communication a bit of a challenge."

"But Caleb can talk. He can get a little garbled sometimes, but unless he's melting down over something…"

"He *was* very upset when he was brought in, and not being able to hear us—"

"He can hear with his cochlear."

"Apparently, it's on the fritz today." Kristen's brows went up as if she'd asked a question.

Riley was taken aback. "Oh. I didn't know that. It was fine this morning, and the school didn't say that he'd had any trouble…"

"Is there somewhere you would take it for repair? Or a doctor that you would go to…?"

"The auditory lab. I'll call and see if we can get him in tomorrow." Riley looked at the time as she pulled out her phone. "They're going to be closed right now. But maybe I can leave a message…"

"If you want to just give me that information, I'll make sure that we get Caleb in."

Riley stiffened. She looked at Wes. He turned to Kristen, giving her a puzzled frown. "I don't understand. Caleb will be coming home with us."

"As I told your wife, that won't be happening. Not today."

"Caleb is our son. He hasn't done anything wrong. Why wouldn't we be taking him home?"

"There is a DFS investigation."

It took a few moments of silence for the words to sink in.

"A DFS investigation," Wes repeated. "You mean… into abuse?"

Kristen studied them each in turn before saying anything. "Yes. Into possible abuse or neglect."

"Of Caleb?" Riley demanded. "But that's ridiculous! Do you know how much time and attention we put into looking after Caleb's needs and making sure that he has everything he needs and all of the opportunities and educational supports that he requires? Do you have any idea how many doctors and therapists we have had to deal with over the years? Abuse or neglect of Caleb? That's nonsense!"

Wes put his hand on Riley's arm to quiet her. Riley looked at him in shock and disbelief. "They can't think that we would do anything to hurt Caleb!"

"I'm sure it's just a misunderstanding."

Riley turned back to Kristen Oakes. "Whatever would make you people think something like that?"

"I'll have the investigator come in to speak with you. I wanted to give you the news first and to let you know that Caleb is okay. He'll be well-taken-care of during the course of this investigation, and I'm sure that if you cooperate with the DFS investigator, everything will be resolved quickly."

She gave a smile that seemed forced and stood up.

"Can't we see Caleb?" Riley asked, standing up and taking a step or two after her.

"Not right now, Mrs. Hibbert. Perhaps later. You'll have to ask Mr. Searle."

She shut the door behind her. Riley turned and looked at Wes. "How could this be happening? What's going on?"

"We'll straighten it out," he soothed. "It's not like we haven't run into bumps in the past. When he was a baby and wasn't growing properly. All of the people who think they know more about how to care for him and what diagnosis and therapies he should have. If one person makes a complaint, we have to defend against it even if it's ridiculous."

Riley rubbed the center of her forehead. "Like Mrs. Sailor, complaining about how he was always crying."

Wes nodded. "When actually, he was having a blast hearing his own voice on the cochlear."

Riley took a deep breath and let it out again. "I just thought we were past that point. That people would finally stop interfering and pay attention to what a great young man he is growing into. If we were abusing him, don't they think someone would have figured it out before now?"

Wes frowned. Riley realized that she had overstepped. In some cases, no matter how many complaints there were, the abuse continued to go on until the child was able to escape the home. Wes had left home at the tender age of sixteen and never returned. He hadn't even gone to his mother's funeral.

"I'm sorry."

He scratched at his goatee, his frown turning to a blank mask. "No need. I think things are a lot different now. People are more aware. It isn't accepted that 'sometimes a boy just needs a good thrashing, and it's nobody's business but the parents'.' Things have changed."

"I hope so."

Riley sat back. They waited in silence, holding hands, the seconds ticking by with agonizing slowness.

Eventually, the door was opened by a tall man in a dark, pressed suit. He gave them both a nod, but no smile.

"Mr. and Mrs. Hibbert. I'm Andrew Searle, Department of Family Services. Thank you for coming in. Before I talk to you, there are some forms I would like to get your signature on."

He spread several documents on the table in front of them. Riley picked one up, reaching for a pen from her purse. "What is all of this?"

"Waivers that you understand you are not required to talk to me. That you understand this is not a police investigation and you haven't been charged with anything. Declarations that you have been in charge of Caleb's care since… his birth?"

"Of course." Riley nodded. She started scribbling her name on each document and passing them to her husband.

Wes put his square-framed glasses on to look at the papers, then took them back off again, a nervous tic.

"We've always been his caregivers," Riley said. "Caleb never even had a babysitter when he was younger. I didn't trust anyone else to take care of him."

Searle watched them sign the forms and collected them into a neat stack.

"Thank you. That's most helpful." He settled into the seat across from them. "I'm sure this has all come as a shock to you, but if you'll work with me, we'll get it straightened out just as quickly as we can."

Riley and Wes nodded together, synchronized.

"I gather you are the primary caregiver, Mrs. Hibbert?"

"You can just call me Riley. Yes. I'm the primary caregiver. But we're married, we both have custody. Wes is the breadwinner and I'm a stay-at-home mom, but we both are very involved in Caleb's care."

"So, you got Caleb ready for school this morning?"

Riley hesitated. "Y-yes."

Searle raised one eyebrow. "That didn't sound too definite," he said with the hint of a laugh.

"Well… Caleb is thirteen. He is mostly in charge of getting himself ready for school. I'm there to help with anything he needs, of course, but… he's a big boy. We have tried to teach him independent living skills. So that he can take care of himself as much as possible."

"I see." He wrote something down. "So what does he do for himself and what do you help him with?"

Riley looked at Wes uncertainly. He said nothing, letting her take charge. "Well… his alarm is set, and he's supposed to get himself out of bed. If he doesn't get up, then I'll get him up. Most days he gets himself up. Today he got himself up. Sometimes if he's really tired or worn out, or coming down with something, he needs a hand waking up in time."

Searle nodded.

"He has a shower and dresses. He gets his breakfast. If he's really running late, I'll get his breakfast out for him, but he usually only has cereal, so it's not like it takes more than a minute to get everything out. He eats, brushes his teeth, and gets his books together." Riley hesitated again. "Usually, I end up helping him get his books together. So that I can be sure everything ended up in his bag and I'm not going to have to run something over to the school later on. Then I can make sure I sign any forms and see any notices that have been sent home with him."

"I see." Searle made notes. Riley couldn't imagine what he had found interesting enough to write down.

"Then… I make sure he's at the door by the time the bus gets there.

Sometimes he dawdles. He's pretty much mastered his morning routine. He knows what to do."

"So Caleb chooses his own clothes. Do you make sure he's appropriately dressed for the day?"

Riley sighed. "I suppose you're talking about the shorts. I told him it was getting to be too cool for shorts and he needed to wear long pants. But he wasn't supposed to be outside for any length of time, just getting on and off the bus. So rather than having a fight over it… I let him get away with shorts, even though it was a chilly day. He doesn't feel the cold, so he doesn't understand why it's not appropriate."

"He wasn't supposed to be walking today."

"No. There was a bust-up at the school about the bus. It got stuck in traffic. The teacher was supposed to tell Caleb to wait in the resource room. He didn't get the message, so I guess he headed home on his own instead of going back to the office for help. We've told him to go back into the school if there are any problems, but sometimes he panics and does something impulsively."

"Caleb doesn't have his own cellphone so he can call you if he has a problem?"

"No. I know a lot of the kids his age do have their own phones, but Caleb isn't great at taking care of his possessions and I haven't seen the need to get him one. He's either at home or at school, he doesn't go out on his own."

"Except when something like this happens."

"Nothing like this has ever happened before. He's supposed to go back into the school if he runs into problems. And the school is supposed to ensure that he gets on the bus. They know his challenges. Someone should have made sure that he got to the Resource Room and understood he was supposed to wait there until the bus arrived."

Searle didn't agree or disagree. "I notice that Caleb has a number of cuts and bruises."

Riley rolled her eyes. "Boys always have cuts and bruises. He's a sensory seeker. He's impulsive and doesn't always have a good sense of cause and effect. And he doesn't have good proprioceptive sense."

Searle blinked at her, then his eyes slid over to Wes, soliciting his opinion.

"Riley's right," Wes said. "He doesn't look before he leaps, and he's forever walking into things or tripping over cracks in the sidewalk. He always seems to have bruises from one thing or another."

"You look at his medical record," Riley said. "It's one thing after another."

Wes gave her a warning look, but Riley was unconcerned. Anyone looking at Caleb's medical records would see that they had always taken good care of him and made sure he had everything he needed.

"Does he self-harm?" Searle asked.

Riley exchanged a look with Wes, unsure how to handle the question. Searle raised an eyebrow. "Mrs. Hibbert…?"

"I don't think—no, not in the way that you're thinking. He doesn't cut and he isn't suicidal."

"But…?"

"Kids with autism sometimes stim in ways that they hurt themselves. Banging their heads when they're upset, hitting themselves, picking their skin, pulling out eyelashes or hair. It isn't because they're intentionally harming themselves. It's just… an autistic thing."

"And Caleb does those things?"

"Like I said, he's a sensory seeker. So he crashes into things for sensory stimulation. He sometimes hits himself when he's upset about something not going the right way, especially if he caused it. And he picks at scabs and his cuticles, bites himself, so sometimes he makes himself bleed or gets an infection. But like I say, it's not intentional self-injury."

"I see. I suppose you know he has a big bruise on his back."

Riley frowned. "No." She looked at Wes. "Did you notice a bruise on his back?" She shook her head at Searle. "What kind of bruise? Can you tell what it is from?"

"A big bruise in the middle of his back. Like someone punched him."

Wes and Riley both shook their heads, baffled. "No. Did you ask him what happened? Maybe someone at school is bullying him. He's had problems with that before."

"Caleb is not responsive to questions. Is he usually… verbal?"

"Yes! He can be hard to understand sometimes, but…"

"Maybe it's the problem with his hearing aid, then. Thank you for the number of the auditory clinic. We'll follow up with them tomorrow."

"Can we see him? Please can we talk to him and make sure he's okay?" Riley choked up as it started to sink in that Caleb wasn't going to be coming home with them. He was going to be going somewhere unfamiliar in a foster or respite home where nobody knew him and his particular quirks.

Searle closed his notebook and considered the request. "If we're going to move things along quickly, I'm going to need access to each of you for individual interviews, a home visit, the school teachers and administrators…"

"I'll do whatever I can. When do you want to do the home visit?"

Searle considered, as if mentally reviewing his very busy schedule. "Would I be able to see it tonight?"

Riley wanted to backpedal and suggest he at least wait until the next day. She wouldn't have any time to tidy up and make sure the house was properly set to receive visitors. But that was probably exactly what he wanted. To get in and see it before she had a chance to change anything.

"Uh… yes. Sure. Tonight is fine."

Wes pressed his lips together, but didn't disagree. Searle considered the two of them.

"You can see Caleb for a few minutes, but you will be supervised and you will not be able to take him home. Please don't make him any promises, like that he'll be home with you tomorrow. That will just make things harder for him and make him less cooperative."

Riley swallowed the lump in her throat along with any protests. She tried to keep the tears out of her voice. "Where is he going to go tonight? He doesn't adjust well to new situations. He has a routine and when he can't follow it…"

"I can't tell you where he'll be tonight. We'll look after him. He'll be okay."

Riley squeezed Wes's hand, trying to keep her emotions under control. He squeezed back gently. His eyes were steady and clear, encouraging her to stay strong. She didn't want Caleb to see her crying. That would just upset him and, as Searle said, it would make it harder for them to deal with Caleb, which would make him even more unhappy. She took a long, deep breath and tried to keep her heart rate and respiration normal.

"Okay. If we could see him… then you could come do the home visit… Unless you have to take him to wherever he is going first…"

"I'll have another social worker take him where he'll be staying tonight. Come with me and I'll give you a chance to see him for a couple of minutes. Please do whatever you can to keep him calm and don't make him any promises."

Riley and Wes nodded and followed Searle out of the room. He took them through the winding corridors, eventually leading them into the room Caleb was waiting in.

Caleb looked up as the door opened and his face broke into a huge grin. "Mom!" he shouted, and he ran toward her. Riley turned her body slightly to absorb the impact, not wanting to get knocked over or have his head hit her face. Then she put her arms around him.

"Oh, baby. Caleb. Are you okay?" She gave him a hard squeeze and rubbed his back, then remembered what Searle had said about the bruise on his back and pulled her hand away. She kissed Caleb, then held his face away from hers so that he could see her mouth.

"Caleb. Are you okay?"

He nodded vigorously. "Okay, Mom."

"Did you get hurt?"

He shook his head. But he did have a bruise on his face that hadn't been there before, and looking at the parts of his body not covered by his favorite black hoodie, Riley could see that he'd skinned his knees and had a number of old and new bruises. She gestured to her own back.

"Show me your back."

Caleb looked back over his shoulder, frowning.

"Your back." Riley made a twirling motion to him. "Turn around and let me see."

Caleb spun in a circle, but didn't stop with his back to her. Riley took him by the shoulders and turned him around, then lifted up his shirts to have a look. There was a big, dusky-colored bruise below his shoulder blades. Riley touched it gently, and turned Caleb again.

"How did you hurt yourself there? Did someone hit you?"

Caleb looked past Riley to Wes. "Dad!" He held out his arms for a hug. Riley moved out of the way to let the two of them hug. Wes also avoided the bruise. He kissed Caleb on the cheek and held him close.

Riley tried to get Caleb's attention again. She motioned to her head, the mirror position of Caleb's cochlear implant.

"What's wrong with your cochlear?"

He threw his hands up and grunted in disgust. He tapped the sound processor a few times with his finger and shook his head. He made a noise that Riley guessed was his imitation of repeated bursts of static.

"The audiologist will look at it tomorrow. He'll fix it for you."

Caleb nodded. "Go home."

Riley looked at Wes, afraid that if she told Caleb he couldn't go home, she would burst into tears.

Wes took a deep breath. He motioned to Searle. "You are going to go on a sleepover tonight. You can't come home. Tomorrow—" he caught himself, "—not coming home today."

Caleb looked at him blankly, shaking his head.

Wes pointed to Searle. "Mr. Searle will tell you where to go."

Caleb frowned. He grabbed Riley's arm tightly. "Go home, Mom."

"No, Caleb."

His face crumpled. He let go of her to stim, flapping his hand beside his face.

"Home, home, home!" he insisted.

Riley's heart was breaking. She tried to calm him. "I'm sorry, Caleb. You'll be home soon. It's okay. I promise, it's going to be okay."

"No, no, no!" Caleb started to hit himself in the head, drumming on it with both fists.

Riley positioned herself behind Caleb and put her arms around him. He was getting too big for the hold, but she reached up and grabbed his arms, crossing them and hugging him to her. He folded over and they both sat down on the floor, Riley holding Caleb still to keep him from hitting himself, holding him safe in her arms, her boy who was almost as big as she was. She knew he couldn't hear her, but she still murmured to him, trying to calm him like she always did. He could still feel the vibrations as she spoke, he would know what she was saying because of every other time she had done it.

"No," he whimpered.

"It's okay, baby. It will be okay. We'll get it all straightened out. Shh…"

Riley was so totally focused on Caleb and his emotional state that she completely blocked out Wes and Searle. When Caleb started to rock and his body relaxed, she released him slowly, withdrawing the hold until they were no longer touching and he was sitting by himself and self-regulating.

"I'm going to have to ask you to leave now," Searle said. His voice was harder than it had been earlier, and she wondered whether his friendliness and apparent consideration toward them before had just been a mask.

She looked at Caleb. She wanted to hug him again and tell him good-bye, but she knew she couldn't. They needed to leave while he was calm and inwardly focused. If he lashed out again, he might really hurt himself or one of them.

Wes held his hand out toward Riley. She finished getting to her feet and went to him. They exited the room. Searle followed them, but motioned a woman in a skirt-suit toward the room. "Stay with him."

His face was hard. Riley sensed that he was furious, but she couldn't figure out why. He had just witnessed a tender scene between parents and child. He had watched Riley transition Caleb from a distressed, destructive state to a calm, safe one, a feat that, if he knew Caleb and his history, he would understand was gargantuan. Something that no professional in thirteen years could have taught her. Something that had to come from inside her, originating from her love for Caleb.

Wes gave Riley a comforting squeeze around the shoulders. He knew that she had done what he could never do. What none of the experts could do.

"It should take about fifteen minutes to get from here to your home," Searle said, his voice flat.

"Yes, that's about right."

"I'll be right behind you. Don't make any stops along the way, I don't expect to have to wait once I get there."

CHAPTER FIVE

ndrew Searle paused for a minute after turning off the engine and before getting out of the car to go up to the house. He needed to get himself into a good place before seeing Caleb Hibbert's home. He needed to be an unbiased, dispassionate observer and not get wrapped up emotionally in what he saw. Home visits were one of the most difficult parts of his job, especially when they brought back memories of his own childhood.

There was no proof yet that Riley and Wes Hibbert were abusive. They put on a good show. But Wes was obviously trying to hide something and keep a tighter rein on his wife, and she had no trouble with being physical with her son and self-righteously justifying everything she did, even when she blatantly broke the rules he had just given her.

He felt his notebook in his pocket and his ID around his neck to ensure that everything was in place, then got out of the car.

Wes Hibbert opened the door. Of course he was watching for Searle, knowing he would be there just minutes after they arrived home. Riley was moving around the house, trying to tidy up and make it presentable for company. But he knew she didn't have time to do much and he would still be able to see the red flags, despite any superficial attempt to hide what was going on with the family. He was well-trained and had plenty of experience in that area.

"Can I get you a drink?" Riley suggested. "Tea or a soft drink…?"

"I'm not here to drink," Searle told her. "You can show me to Caleb's room. I'll start there."

She froze for an instant. Just a fraction of a second while she thought about Caleb's room and realized she had no chance to sanitize whatever he was going to find there. Then she nodded and led him to Caleb's bedroom in the back of the little bungalow.

Caleb's room was claustrophobically close. Searle looked around slowly, taking in the shelves and storage bins that lined the walls. Caleb was a hoarder. He had rows upon rows of rocks, bottle caps, pinecones, and other treasured collections. Riley stood behind Searle and gave a little laugh.

"Sorry, I didn't get a chance to tidy up before you came…"

"That was the idea," Searle agreed. "If you could please leave me alone to look around…?"

"Uh…" She hesitated, looking around the room. She wanted to explain things away. She didn't want him to stay in the room alone. Which was exactly why Searle needed to. He gave her a warning look. Riley put up her hands in surrender. "Okay. Of course. Sorry."

She withdrew and went to talk to her husband or to clean up the other rooms. Searle started to go through the bins, methodically going through each one, looking not just at what was on top, but what was buried beneath.

Caleb Hibbert was not just a hoarder of collections. He was also food hoarder. There was food secreted in just about every hiding place in the room. In the bins, the dresser, the closet, under the bed, under the covers of the bed. And of course, not all of it was shelf-stable. The room smelled of mold and rot.

Food hoarding was a big red flag for neglect. Kids who didn't know where their next meal was coming from hoarded food when it was plentiful to cover for the lean times, knowing that there wouldn't always be food there when they needed it. Even kids who had been in stable foster homes for years felt the compulsion to save food for periods of starvation. Searle noted the details in his pad and starred a reminder to ask the school about food. Did Caleb go to school hungry? Did he steal or barter for food from other students? He had already noticed Caleb's bony frame. He would need a trip to the doctor to confirm whether he was malnourished.

The lock on the door to Caleb's room had been reversed so that he could be locked inside. A typical measure for children who wandered, but also a red flag for abuse and neglect. There were no additional locks. No scratches in the paint on the inside of the door to indicate that Caleb had tried to claw his way out.

Searle left Caleb's room. Riley appeared briefly in the hallway, her expression worried, wanting to explain things to him.

"I work best when I can just have a look around on my own," Searle advised, shooing her back away. Riley mumbled an apology and again withdrew, leaving Searle to look through the combination guest room/home office and the master bedroom. Both were neat and well-organized. Nothing Riley needed to explain or apologize for. The parents appeared to be sleeping together, the sheets on the guest room bed still creased from being folded in the linen closet.

They kept a central laundry basket in the bathroom. Searle went through it, examining all of Caleb's clothing for blood or anything else suspicious. There didn't appear to be more than a couple of days' worth of clothing in the basket, and it all looked clean, the typical first-world wear-once-and-wash. Nothing that indicated Caleb was left in squalor.

He ignored Wes and Riley as he crossed through the living room to check out the kitchen. Well-stocked cupboards and fridge. Nothing obviously rotten. No fast food containers or junk food. No more than half a day's dishes in the dishwasher. Searle found the stairs to the basement and went down without asking permission.

Basements always made him a little queasy, especially unfinished basements, which the Hibberts' was. A laundry room and cold room had been drywalled. Piles of dirty and clean laundry sat waiting to be dealt with. Everything else was framed but unfinished. Not a living space. Maybe an entertainment room and a dedicated home office to be built sometime in the future.

There were no false walls or crawlspaces. Some random boxes of clothes, Christmas decorations, and other miscellany stored for later use or donation. Some old toys or broken items that might be repaired, but most likely would just be thrown away after being underfoot for a year or two.

The rooms that had been drywalled didn't have any doors. Therefore no locks. No sign that Caleb had ever been locked in the basement as punishment for some perceived misdeed.

Searle returned upstairs. He took a quick glance around the living room, but wasn't too concerned with it. That was the room the public saw. It would hold few secrets.

"Is there anything you would like to tell me?" He always gave parents the opportunity to explain what he had observed.

"Caleb's room…" Riley started awkwardly. "We try to keep it clean, but as you can see, he holds on to everything. I know it's hard to believe, but I'm through there at least every week to get rid of whatever junk I can." Searle could tell it had been at least a couple of weeks since she had done so. Unless she had no concerns about leaving rotting food where it was, growing mold and attracting bugs. "He's diagnosed with OCD. There isn't really an accepted treatment for hoarding. No medication or therapy. Just trying to teach him to let things go, and trying to keep it from getting out of control…"

"I see."

"He's just… he gets attached to things. If you try to clean things out, he has a meltdown. I try to do what I can when he's at school, but he always knows when I've touched things…"

Searle nodded. "Anything else?"

"I don't know…" Riley looked at Wes for guidance. "Is there anything else?"

Wes looked down at her. Clearly, he was used to letting her do most of the talking. But he was also the one who was aware when she was saying too much. He swallowed and considered.

"The lock on the door?" he said finally. "Caleb has autism… sometimes he gets up in the night. The lock is just there to keep him safe."

"The lock will have to go," Searle said. "You may have been told that it was okay to lock him in his room, but that is incorrect. You'll have to look at alarms or other measures. Locks and cages are completely unacceptable."

"Cages?" Riley repeated, outraged. "We would never put him in a cage!"

"If you did, you wouldn't be the first one. No restraints of any kind are acceptable."

Riley flushed pink. "Are you saying that I can't hold him? I can't stop him when he's hurting himself?"

"Only in a certified therapeutic setting where they have been properly trained in safe holds can they manually restrain him."

"I'm his mother! Are you saying that a parent can't pick their child up or hold them back from running into the street? That's ridiculous."

"Caleb is a teenager. He is nearly as big as you are. It is too dangerous for you to be restraining him. Even the police officer who brought him in had a difficult time getting him under control and needed backup. He's too big for you to physically control him. One of you will get hurt, and my concern is for his safety."

Riley sputtered and opened her mouth to argue with him. Wes put his hand on her shoulder from behind, trying to keep her quiet. Searle was mildly disappointed not to be able to hear what she wanted to say to him. Parents said interesting things when they were upset. Things that they wouldn't say if they thought it through.

"I will need to have an interview with each of you individually. Are you available tomorrow?"

They looked at each other and weighed their answers. While they would probably rather avoid individual interviews altogether, they had to know that they wouldn't get Caleb back if they didn't cooperate. The longer they put it off, the longer it would be before they would get their son back.

———

The next day, Searle was able to talk to Mrs. Bradshaw during a break. She was obviously upset about the sequence of events. Her eyes were red-rimmed.

"I just can't believe all of this," she fussed, after giving him her limp hand to squeeze. "I feel so awful for what happened to Caleb. I should have walked him to the Resource Room. I thought he understood."

"Have a seat, please."

They both sat down in armchairs in a student conference room. A room that was supposed to be more like a family living room than a guidance counselor's office, and thus encourage comfort and the sharing of feelings.

"This investigation is not specifically in regard to Caleb missing the bus," Searle reassured her. "But why don't we start there, anyway. What was it that happened yesterday?"

"We got a call from the bus driver that she was going to be delayed because of traffic. I guess there was a big accident on the highway. Because she drives the special-needs bus, the office asked us to have the kids wait in the Resource Room, so that they would all be in one place and not wandering around or getting confused." She gave a helpless shrug. "But then… I thought Caleb understood me. He was nodding and repeating phrases. He's usually good at following simple instructions."

"It turns out that his cochlear implant was malfunctioning. He couldn't hear."

"Why didn't he tell me that? Why didn't he tell me he didn't understand?"

Searle refrained from pointing out that she knew why. He had not just one, but two communication disabilities. She had been tasked with making sure he waited in the Resource Room; she should have walked him there.

"Is this the first time he's had problems with the bus?"

"As far as I know. He's okay as long as everything is the same. He gets upset if his mom comes and picks him up instead of him taking the bus. But I don't know of any time he's missed it."

"How often does she pick him up?"

"Oh… maybe once a week. For doctor's appointments or that kind of thing."

"He goes to the doctor once a week?"

"No, I didn't mean that. Different doctors, therapists, evaluations. There's always something."

Searle nodded and made a note of it. Seeking medical attention could be a red flag.

"Do you have any concerns about Caleb?"

"He's a sweet boy. He has his difficulties, but he's a hard worker and he finishes his assignments. I do my best to accommodate him. Make sure he's at the front of the class, give him extra instruction, keep an eye out for any bullying. He's often late; I know his mom has a hard time getting him moving in the morning. He misses the bus and she has to bring him in herself."

"He dresses for the weather?"

"Oh," she rolled her eyes, "no thirteen-year-old boy dresses for the weather. You should see them in the middle of the winter with no hats, no gloves, half of them just in sweatshirts. Freezing their little butts off because they think they're too cool to dress warmly."

"Caleb no more so than anyone else? He was wearing shorts yesterday."

"It's a sensory thing. Even when he wears long pants to school, half the time he switches to shorts partway through the day. He puts them in his backpack or puts on his gym shorts. When he wears pants, he's shimmying all over the place trying to get comfortable. It makes it pretty hard to concentrate on his work."

"So he's allowed to change once he gets here."

"If we didn't let him change, he'd be sitting there in his underwear!" She paused. "That's assuming he wears underpants. I never asked."

Searle made some notes. "Have there ever been issues with food? Him forgetting his lunch or coming to school hungry…?"

Mrs. Bradshaw bit her lip, not answering immediately.

"This remains confidential," Searle encouraged, studying her closely. "I won't be telling Mrs. Hibbert that you said anything."

"Well… we're not supposed to talk about which kids use the free breakfast or lunch programs. We're not even supposed to notice. It's open to all kids, no need to prove income level, and there's no limit on how many times they're allowed to use it."

"You can't very well not notice, just because they say so."

"No. You do notice. And you do… judge. Whether someone should be able to afford to feed their kids better. Wondering if a family is going through a rough time or the parents are out of work. Being more lenient on discipline for kids who are using the lunch program because you figure things must be pretty tough for them on other fronts and they're just acting out…"

Searle nodded his understanding. Of course the teachers would notice who was less fortunate. As would the other students. There was supposed to be no stigma attached, but how could there really be no judgment about it? Searle could remember what it was like to go to school hungry and to try to concentrate on the teacher and getting his work done. Kids needed lunch programs. But the only way they could ever truly be non-stigmatizing was if everyone was required to participate.

"So did you notice Caleb using the breakfast and lunch programs?"

"Yes. Now, I know his mother is very strict about what he's allowed to eat. No junk food, all whole, healthy foods and all that. I know kids function better when they're not eating junk, so I can't fault her for that. Maybe Caleb was only eating here so he could have food that he wasn't allowed at home, I don't know." She held up her hands in a helpless gesture. "You're not allowed to ask."

So Caleb's intake at home *was* being restricted, despite full cupboards and a well-stocked cold room. The doctor would determine whether or not he was malnourished, but Mrs. Bradshaw's observation was a nail in the Hibberts' coffin.

Withholding food was always abuse, no matter what excuse Riley Hibbert gave.

CHAPTER SIX

Gabriel heard Renata swear under her breath. He slid his eyes over to her computer to see what she was looking at. A video was playing across the screen. Choppy, amateur, obviously taken with a phone camera. It bounced all over the place, but the cameraman had attempted to keep it pointed at the hooded figure being accosted by a police officer. Gabriel winced at the way the cop was beating him down, trying to force him to be still and submit to being handcuffed. Something that, as a black teenager, Gabriel always worried about. Sure, he'd seen the same thing on *Cops* a dozen times, but the policeman was so much bigger than the hooded figure that the reaction seemed way out of proportion to the provocation.

"Who is that?" he asked, as the video ended.

Renata pointed to the title of the video. *Autistic Teenager Endures Beat-down by Police.*

Gabriel's stomach tightened. "Play it again."

Watching from the beginning this time, he saw the teen walking along the pathway in the park, bothering no one, stimming as he walked. The audio track played snickers and an indecipherable comment from the person recording him. The camera caught a sliver of the boy's face; very young, no facial hair or masculine definition. Then the cop appeared, shouting at him, asking him questions. The boy acted as if he wasn't even there.

Then physical contact. The boy jolted. He said a few words, trying to pull away. The cop smashed him into a tree. Threw him on the ground and jumped on top of him. Kept hitting with his baton until he managed to get the boy's backpack off and the handcuffs on. Other police arrived. As a group, they managed to manhandle him into one of the cars.

"Can you believe it?" Renata demanded. "That's police brutality. Even if it had been a real drug addict—that's what the cop is saying he thought— that's still brutality. Throwing him down? Beating him like that? They can't get away with that!"

Gabriel shook his head. "I hope not. What did the police department say? Are they investigating?"

Renata followed a few links and scrolled through bulletin boards. "They say that there was no excessive force. The cop said he tripped. You can bet they'll change their tune about it being a measured response when they realize it's gone viral!"

"Yeah. I hope he's okay. Poor kid."

"We should do something about this."

Gabriel hesitated. "It's not exactly our wheelhouse," he pointed out. "We've got enough to do focusing on kids being taken away from their families because of their medical conditions rather than abuse. There are so many kids suffering through this because doctors want them for medical research or they don't understand there is an underlying medical condition rather than abuse. This is bad—" he gestured at the screen, "—but I don't think we can spread ourselves any thinner."

Renata's angry look softened a little. She knew that Gabriel was just as invested in helping the victims of medical kidnap as she was. They'd been through enough together that she couldn't deny his dedication to the cause.

"You are looking a little too thin," she admitted, playing on his words.

Gabriel brushed his somewhat-baggy clothes self-consciously. "I didn't mean that."

"I know. But you are."

"You're one to talk."

Renata drew herself up. Her arch expression made her vaguely Hispanic features seem more prominent. "My formula is perfectly balanced to provide me exactly the nutrients I need. I'm not too thin. I'm perfectly balanced."

Gabriel chuckled. He caught the eye of one of the librarians on them.

"We'd better be quiet, or she's going to bust us."

While they did their best to be clean and tidy and look like students working on a research project so they didn't stand out, it was hard not to look homeless when they actually were. Their backpacks held necessaries of life rather than textbooks, and they were both suspiciously gaunt.

Renata put her head down and stared at the computer screen seriously. Gabriel looked back at his research, monitoring the librarian's position in his peripheral vision until she finally stopped watching them and walked away.

———

Caleb's appointment with the doctor was before his appointment with the audiology clinic, so when Searle took him to the doctor's office, he still couldn't hear. Searle had seen from the night before that he could read lips, but he seemed to misunderstand more than he got right when Searle tried to talk to him. Maybe it was easier for him to read his parents because he was familiar with them and had learned speech from them in the first place. It made sense that a different face, and someone who formed his words a different way, would be harder for Caleb to read. And since he usually had the cochlear implant to help him hear sounds, he wasn't used to relying solely on lipreading.

Caleb clearly recognized the doctor's office for what it was as soon as they walked in. He shook his head.

"No," he grumbled. "Go home. Caleb go home."

Searle made sure that Caleb was facing him and spoke slowly. "You can't go home right now. You need to see the doctor. He's just going to make sure everything is okay."

"Not sick. Go home." Caleb shook his head, moaning.

Searle took him over to the corner and showed him the stack of books and magazines he could look at while they waited. Caleb shook his head and plonked himself down in the middle of the small tot toys, starting to put together a train track. Searle sat down and watched him.

When they were taken into an exam room, Caleb's hearing impairment made it easier for Searle to talk openly with the nurses and doctors instead of having to meet with them privately. The nurse carefully took Caleb's height and weight and wrote them on the chart.

"What percentile is his weight? Is he underweight?"

The nurse looked at Caleb, but seeing that he had no interest in the conversation, looked at her charts and nodded. "He's just a hair into the underweight category. It's not unusual for teenagers. They lengthen out before they fill in."

"Were you able to access his medical history? Has he been consistently at a low weight?"

"If you can give me a minute on the computer, I'll make sure we got them loaded. The doctor will be with you in a minute."

Searle nodded and she left them alone. Caleb obviously knew the routine in a doctor's office and boosted himself up onto the examining table. He stared up at the ceiling, making popping noises with his mouth that Searle tried to ignore.

When the doctor came in some time later, he had his glasses perched low on his nose as he scanned through the chart the nurse had prepared for him.

"So, you have concerns about possible abuse and neglect, is that right?"

"We're investigating the possibility."

The doctor nodded. He put the clipboard aside, jammed his glasses into his lab coat pocket, and approached Caleb.

"How are you feeling today, Caleb?"

He looked puzzled when Caleb didn't answer.

"His cochlear implant isn't working. We're going to have that looked at next," Searle explained, even though the nurse had already put it on the chart.

"Oh, I see." The doctor began with palpitating the lymph nodes behind Caleb's jaw. "Does he read lips?"

"Not reliably."

"That's one of the problems with these devices. They really need to be used in conjunction with other measures. So that the patient has something to fall back on when they suddenly stop working. Can you imagine suddenly being deaf and not being able to understand what anyone around you was saying?"

"It would be a challenge."

Caleb remained indifferent, slouching, staring up at the ceiling, making liquid noises with his mouth. The doctor grimaced, but continued his examination, listening to Caleb's chest and back with his stethoscope, examining his face, limbs, and torso.

"He has quite a few scrapes and bruises. Was he in a fight?"

"He had an altercation with the police," Searle admitted. "So some of the fresh marks may be from that."

"Pretty hard for me to make a determination on abuse when he's been in a fight," the doctor pointed out.

"I'm just asking you to do your best."

The doctor grunted. He put his fingers over Caleb's protruding ribs and walked his fingers up them slowly. Caleb jolted and struck out, hitting the doctor in the chest and making him step back.

"Whoa, there," the doctor soothed, even though Caleb couldn't hear. He stepped up to Caleb again, and adjusted Caleb's head position so that he was looking into the doctor's face. "Show me where it hurt."

Caleb just looked at him for a minute. The doctor tapped Caleb's side lightly. "Where does it hurt?"

Caleb fingered his ribs experimentally. Eventually, he stopped, wincing. He kept his fingers where they were.

"There?" The doctor put slight pressure on the spot, and Caleb again jolted. But he didn't hit the doctor a second time. He just nodded. "We'll want an x-ray. See if he broke a rib. He hasn't been complaining about it?"

Searle shrugged. "The group home said he didn't sleep last night. Wouldn't lay down and stay in bed. But he never said he was hurt."

"It can be hard to tell with kids who... have challenges. They don't always act the same way as typical children who are hurt." The doctor peered at the bruise on Caleb's back. "You saw this one already, I assume?"

"Yes."

The doctor continued his examination for a few minutes and checked Caleb's eyes and ears with some difficulty, as Caleb kept shying and pulling away.

He patted Caleb on the shoulder. "Good job. All done for now."

Caleb watched the doctor sit down on the small, round stool and pull himself up to his computer, then stared up at the ceiling again, mouth open.

"Did you get his historical records?" Searle asked.

The doctor tapped away for a few minutes. He nodded. "Looks like we got a pretty comprehensive history. Can't guarantee this is everything—it can be hard if parents jump around between doctors. But it looks pretty extensive."

"How far back?"

More tapping. The doctor put his glasses on again and peered at the screen. "Labor and delivery," he said. "Any further back, we'll need mom's records."

"Was it a normal labor and delivery? Healthy baby?"

The doctor pushed his glasses up and Searle watched them slowly slide back down again.

"No. Low birth weight and jaundice. Poor suck, feeding problems. Unexplained bruising at birth." The doctor tapped the down arrow, reading through the log. "He was in NICU for some time. Several seizures in his first few days of life. They put him under the lamps for jaundice, but he continued to be fussy."

"Was he tested for drugs or alcohol at birth?"

The doctor looked up briefly, then back down at the computer. "No, not that I can see. If he was an addicted baby, he was never identified as such. But the symptoms fit. He could have been."

"What about his other issues?" Searle looked over at Caleb, but the boy was ignoring their conversation. "His hearing impairment and autism. Could that be from mom's substance abuse?"

"It's a possibility. It could be related to prematurity or low birth weight, to mom's substance abuse, an infection, something genetic. Hard to put your finger on it without knowing more."

"How about after he got out of NICU and the hospital? Did he continue to have problems?" Searle was sure the answer would be yes. The teacher had said that Riley took him to doctor's appointments weekly.

"Yes, looks like he was a pretty challenging baby. Diagnosed with Failure to Thrive. Wasn't growing properly or meeting milestones. Language development was slow, but of course that's to be expected with being deaf. He got his cochlear implant in good time, but didn't show the expected progression. Had some infections. One of the risks of surgery. The doctors attributed his slow language development to that."

"Was there a DFS investigation in connection with his Failure to Thrive?"

"That probably wouldn't make it to his medical records. But a social worker is often called in cases where they can't find a physical cause. Even if they don't open an investigation, they might advise mom and dad, recommend classes or other resources."

"Were they doctor shopping?"

The doctor paged more quickly through the lists of records.

"No, I wouldn't say so. They mostly stayed with the same few doctors. A ped, a GP, a ped with a developmental focus. Some referrals out to gastro, neuro, and other specialties. Lots of doctors, but not bouncing from one to the next. They stayed with the same core team."

CHAPTER SEVEN

For a long time after Riley hung up the phone, she just sat there, her world falling down around her. She had expected the call with DFS Searle to go completely the opposite direction to what it had. She should have known after the personal interviews that things were going to go sideways. His analysis of their family and theories about their lives and challenges were so ridiculous it was almost funny. She had known that the tests would vindicate them and then Searle would have to file a favorable report and return Caleb to them. Then they could get on with being a family.

But Searle had called to give her the results of the test and to inform her that they would not be getting Caleb back in the near future. If they complied with his directives, they might be able to get Caleb back sometime in the future, but he didn't even sound encouraging about that. Riley knew without Searle actually putting it into words that, as far as he was concerned, she was the worst mother and he would do everything in his power to prevent Caleb from being returned to them again.

Finally, Riley stirred. They would fight it. She would take it to the press and show them what an injustice had been done. They would bring pressure to bear on DFS to have someone else review the file and reconsider their decision.

Riley knew her friends and supporters would be just as outraged about the situation as she was. She had worked tirelessly to provide Caleb with every advantage she could. She had fought the medical system to get him properly diagnosed and to get him the therapies and accommodations he needed. He was doing work at almost grade level, held back only by his language difficulties. He was attending a regular school. He might not be indistinguishable from his peers, but he had come so far from the uncommunicative little boy he had once been, isolated in his own world. He was happy. He showed others love and concern. He shared his problems with them. He'd overcome so many barriers, just to be stolen away from them by an overenthusiastic social worker who invented abuse where there was none.

Riley opened her laptop and started to jot down the things she would need to do:

Update her blog and social media pages to keep everyone up to date on what was happening with Caleb and the investigation. Plugins would automatically cross-post her blog entries to each of her social media accounts to get the word out.

Start a crowdfunding campaign to raise the money they would need to hire a lawyer and whatever experts they needed to prove their innocence.

She would need to go through hundreds of photos to pick out just the right ones to show Caleb's journey from a sickly baby the doctors warned her would never be normal to the confident, happy young man he had become.

If Searle thought she was going to crawl under a rock and cry about what he had done, he had better think again. Riley was not going to give up so easily.

———

Gabriel read the text on his phone and frowned, thinking it through. He looked up at Renata. She was scanning the restaurant for any sign of trouble, looking for anyone who was paying them too much attention or who might be police, a private investigator, or some paid thug for a doctor or clinic who thought the organization was cutting into their profits by getting children who were victims of medical kidnap out of their experimental medical studies and back to their parents. Things had been quiet recently, but that didn't mean they weren't still in danger. Renata knew better than anyone how vigilant they had to be, making sure they didn't stay in one place for too long or frequent any one establishment too many times. Even McDonald's would notice the pair of them eating there regularly, with Renata's feeding tube.

Renata caught him looking at her. "What? I'm just checking…"

Gabriel nodded. "I didn't say anything."

"No, but you're giving me that look."

Gabriel glanced down at his phone. Renata straightened. "Who is it?"

"Carmel."

Her nostrils flared. Gabriel wasn't sure why Renata had such animosity toward Carmel. It was true that he had suspected her of informing on them at one point, but Carmel had proven her worth to them and Gabriel was sure she was one-hundred-percent loyal. Renata remained unconvinced. "What does blondie want?"

"She said Judge Dee-Dee wants to get in touch with you."

Renata scowled. "What does *she* want?"

"Maybe she has a case she wants us to look into."

"I didn't think she was going to get involved again after what happened with Seth."

Gabriel shrugged. "I can't think of any other reason she would want to get us, can you?"

Renata fiddled with her feeding tube, making a show of looking for kinks. "Why would she contact you to ask for me?"

"Because I'm easier to get ahold of."

"She reached out through Carmel. She could have told Carmel to get me instead of you."

"Maybe she did. Have you turned on your phone lately?"

Renata glared. But after a few seconds, she delved into her backpack and pulled out her current burner. She pressed the power button, and she and Gabriel both watched the splash screen as it booted up. Renata tapped her password into the unlock screen and went immediately to the text app. They waited for any pending text messages to arrive. Renata gave it about two minutes, with no results, then powered the phone back off again.

"Carmel knows I check mine more often than you do," Gabriel said. "That's probably why."

"She wouldn't even know if we would be together." Renata watched the street and parking lot outside the windows. They were sitting in a corner booth so that they had a good view in both directions.

Gabriel found himself looking for any suspicious vehicles; tinted windows, extra antennas, a vehicle that might have passed by a couple of times. He forced himself to look away. Renata would spot any trouble. He didn't need to be as vigilant when he was with her.

"So do we go see her?" he asked.

"Carmel?"

"Judge Dee-Dee."

"Bad idea. She shouldn't be making contact with us."

"She's helped us before. She's trustworthy."

Renata shook her head. "She's high risk. What if there's a warrant out on one of the cases we've been involved in? She'd feel obligated to enforce it."

"She kept me out of jail before. She wouldn't."

"She would." Renata disconnected her tube and buttoned her shirt. "You want to meet her, go ahead. I'm not."

"It's you she wants to talk to."

"If it's a kid for us to look into, you can handle it."

Gabriel realized it was true. Judge Dee-Dee had dealt with him directly before. Why was she asking for Renata?

"We could go together," he suggested. "I could keep guard for you."

Renata didn't answer. Gabriel let it go. He'd let Renata think about it. If he tried to push her into something, she would just get suspicious and oppositional. Given the chance to think it through and make her own decision, Renata might come up with a solution that she felt comfortable with.

CHAPTER EIGHT

Caleb walked into his bedroom and stopped. He looked around, his stomach getting tight and sick. All of his things were on his bed instead of in the drawers. Who had moved his things? Nobody was supposed to touch his things. Mrs. Hill had promised that nobody else would touch his things. She promised she would make sure that no one touched them.

"Mrs. Hill!" Caleb shouted. He flapped his hands by his face. "No! My stuff!"

She came into the room right behind him, holding her hands up. "It's okay, Caleb—"

"No!" He pointed to the bed. "All Caleb's stuff!"

"I know. I know. I got it out, but none of the other boys have touched it. Mr. Searle asked me to get you ready to move today."

Caleb concentrated on her words. "Move? Move out?"

"Yes. I was just going to get a bag to put everything in."

Caleb's heart was beating very fast. "Am going home?" A smile stretched his face. He hadn't been able to smile for a long time.

"No." There was no happiness on Mrs. Hill's face. "Not back to your mom and dad. I'm sorry. But DFS has agreed to let your uncle look after you."

Caleb mouthed DFS. The letters always tripped him up and made him miss the rest of the sentence. "DFS… where?"

"At your uncle's house. Do you know your uncle?"

"Uncle Kris?"

"I don't know his name. I just know that he lives in town and Mr. Searle said that's where you were going."

Caleb tried to decide what he thought about that. He did *not* like living at the group home. They wouldn't let him keep any of his things, but kept throwing them out. Anything that they did let him keep, like his clothes and his toothbrush, the other boys touched. They teased him and made fun of him and even though Mrs. Hill said they were bad boys, they still had to live there and Caleb had to live there and put up with them.

He liked Uncle Kris. He was tall and dark-haired like Dad. He came over for holidays and birthdays and sometimes just to watch football on the TV. He ruffled Caleb's hair and called him 'buddy' and sometimes brought him a present or a treat. He was Dad's brother, and although they were very different, Dad liked to have him over. Even though Dad didn't like football the rest of the time, he would put it on when Uncle Kris was there, and they would sit down and talk and watch it together.

Maybe if Caleb went to live with Uncle Kris, he'd be able to visit Mom and Dad on holidays or to watch football like Uncle Kris.

"Where is the bag?"

Mrs. Hill brushed a lock of her graying hair off of her forehead. "I'll go get it, Caleb."

———

When she had said 'a bag,' Caleb thought she meant a backpack or a duffel bag, but what she came back with was a garbage bag. Caleb's mouth dropped open.

"Not garbage!"

"I know it's not, Caleb. But this is what I have. It's just a bag to put them in to take them to your uncle's. It doesn't mean we're throwing them out."

He hit his head with his fist. "Can't put Caleb's things in garbage!"

"I promise, we're not putting it in the garbage. We're just putting it in a bag to carry it. You can't carry everything in your arms."

"Not in garbage!"

"Caleb. Sit down." She pushed him to sit down on the bed, next to his clothes. She grabbed his hands and held them down in his lap. "You need to stop shouting."

"Not shouting!"

"Yes, you are. You need to be calm and respectful. You may be leaving here, but you still need to show me respect while you're here. There is no shouting!" She pointed her finger in his face, like he was a disobedient dog.

"Not—"

"Caleb!" Her own shout vibrated the sound processor and made a painful ringing in Caleb's head. Caleb squeezed his eyes closed and held his head. She tried to talk to him. She touched his shoulder to get his attention and Caleb shrank back from her.

"No," he murmured, keeping his voice very low. "No touching."

She stood there for another minute. He could feel her beside him and could hear her trying to get his attention. But he blocked her out and eventually she walked away.

———

Most of the other boys had things they did after school; sports, getting together with friends, special tutoring, or other activities. Caleb didn't have to go anywhere after school unless he had a doctor's appointment, so he always just went straight to the group home after school.

Tyson came home and Caleb heard him jeering about Caleb sitting on the bed crying like a little baby, but he ignored the taunts, and eventually Tyson got whatever it was that he needed from his drawers and left Caleb alone again. At least Tyson didn't hit or pinch him.

Caleb was still on the bed when Mr. Searle got there.

"Caleb."

Caleb didn't move.

"Caleb." Mr. Searle nudged his shoulder. Caleb pulled back, but didn't look at Mr. Searle.

"Caleb, look at me." Mr. Searle pulled Caleb's hands away from his face, grasped Caleb's chin, and forced him to look up. Caleb could have kept his eyes closed, but Mr. Searle would persist until Caleb did what he was told. So he stared sulkily at Mr. Searle's chin, waiting for him to speak.

"Mrs. Hill told you that you're going to your Uncle Kris's. Don't you want to go live with your Uncle Kris? Your parents said that you like him."

Caleb shrugged.

"I'm going to take that as a yes. Then you need to stop pouting and get your butt in gear."

Mr. Searle stood there with his arms folded across his chest.

"Do you really think he should be with this uncle?" Mrs. Hill asked. Caleb shifted his gaze to her face to understand her words better. "It isn't a therapeutic foster home. He doesn't have any training in dealing with a boy with Caleb's needs. He has no parenting experience at all."

"Family members are not required to have the same training as a licensed foster home," Mr. Searle said. "We will be monitoring the situation. I think it will be better to have Caleb away from all of these other boys."

"He does tend to get cross-threaded with them. And he doesn't need the same rules to keep him out of trouble with the law."

"I think a less restrictive environment and having one-on-one care will be better for him. The prevailing opinion is that children should be kept with relatives if possible. We'll provide supports and opportunities for training."

"I suppose." Mrs. Hill approached Caleb. "It's time to go, now, Caleb."

Caleb still stubbornly refused to move. Mrs. Hill picked up Caleb's pile of clothes and slid it into the garbage bag.

Caleb reached for his possessions. "No! Not garbage!"

She gathered up his toothbrush and the case for his sound processor and put them into the bag.

"No!"

Mrs. Hill avoided Caleb's grasp, tossing the final few items into the bag. Mr. Searle caught Caleb by the wrist and jerked him to his feet. He took the garbage bag from Mrs. Hill in his other hand.

"Time to go. If you want your things, you'd better come."

Caleb did.

CHAPTER NINE

Gabriel looked around the cafe for anyone who seemed out of place. He was pretty familiar with how people looked when they were just sitting down for a bite to eat or to visit with friends, and how they looked when they were watching for a suspect or conducting surveillance. He was pretty good at picking out plain clothed store security. He and Renata were in agreement that if there were anyone in the cafe who looked out of place, they wouldn't stay around. Judge Dee-Dee was too powerful to take risks with. If she decided to come after them, she would bring in the big guns.

He spotted Judge Dee-Dee on his first scan of the interior and, thinking that he had missed her, she raised her hand to wave at him. Gabriel ignored her hand for a moment and continued to examine the clientele. Then he finally looked back at her and gave a smile and nod to confirm he had seen her and was on his way over.

He looked behind him. No big, shifty-looking dudes with dark glasses. No one with too-bulky clothes that could be hiding weapons. No one who looked official or was looking down at a warrant or a picture of Gabriel in order to be able to identify him. Just the normal, everyday crowd.

"Party of one?" asked a waitress, who apparently decided that Gabriel didn't understand the sign that said to be seated and was going to find a table for him.

"No, I'm here to meet someone. Gabriel nodded toward Judge Dee-Dee. "There she is. Thank you."

He didn't engage with the waitress any more, drifting away from her without a backward glance. She wouldn't remember him in ten minutes, let alone a few days down the line if someone made inquiries.

Gabriel still didn't head straight for Judge Dee-Dee's table. He veered as if he were going to the restroom and took a glance down the little, dimly-lit corridor for anyone hanging around. He walked down the length of the room, glanced out the window like he was checking to see if his ride was there to pick him up, and then finally approached Judge Dee-Dee, swiveling his head around one more time for anything that might set off his internal alarms. He sat down across from her.

"Gabriel."

"Your Honor."

The gray-haired little woman gave a little smile. "We're not in the courtroom. Judge Dee-Dee is fine."

Gabriel nodded. Judge Dee-Dee leaned forward a little.

"That was quite the performance. Is this Renata's paranoia, or have you developed your own?"

Gabriel didn't let her bait him. "Considering that people have tried to kill us or arrest us in the past, I don't think you can call it paranoia."

There was silence between them for a few minutes.

"How are you, Gabriel?" Judge Dee-Dee eventually asked.

"I'm okay. Hanging in there."

"Your health? Are you feeling okay?"

"Doing the best I can. We try to take care of each other." He somehow found it easier to look after his own physical needs when he was with Renata, which seemed counterintuitive, because then he had to worry about Renata's needs as well as his own, and they didn't always need the same thing. But somehow, it balanced out so that having Renata to talk to and to remind him to eat and to get enough sleep ended up being a net gain.

"She hasn't had any more… episodes?"

"You know I'd take her to the hospital if she needed treatment."

"Yes, but I don't know if we would hear about it. The two of you are able to use other names, get other identification. You might be able to keep anyone from figuring out who you are."

"We haven't had to find out."

"Good."

A waitress came by to give them each a glass of ice water, inquiring if they were ready to order.

"I'm not staying," Gabriel said.

"You might as well have something," Judge Dee-Dee protested. "I'm picking up the tab. You need to eat sometime."

"I'm not staying," Gabriel repeated. "Either Renata will come over and I'll keep watch, or we'll have to leave."

Judge Dee-Dee put her small, wrinkled hand over Gabriel's. His black skin made her white complexion look almost blue. Her skin seemed thin and translucent.

"Gabriel. There's no danger. I'm not going to do anything and I haven't brought anyone with me. It's just you and me."

"And Renata. And whoever drove you. Your security. People must know where you are."

"No one is going to bother you. You can both come over and have a bite to eat."

Gabriel shook his head. The waitress raised her eyebrow at Judge Dee-Dee to see if she was going to order. The judge placed her lunch order. "And if you could come back over, my other guest may want something—"

"Renata doesn't eat," Gabriel reminded her. "She can't. If she ate something off the menu, she'd be sick. All she can have is her formula."

"Oh—how stupid of me! I don't know how I could forget that. I guess I thought... maybe she had grown out of it. Maybe she found something else she could eat. DFS suggested that it was her mother making her sick and that she'd be able to eat normally if Elena was out of the picture."

"No. I've never seen her eat anything. Just the tube feeding."

Judge Dee-Dee shook her head. "I can't imagine living that way. When I think about all you kids have to put up with…"

Gabriel took a quick glance around the cafe. He was getting nervous with her small talk.

"Can we get down to business? Why do you want to see Renata?"

"I do have a situation that the two of you might like to look into. I'm not telling you to, obviously. I can't do that. But you might be interested, like to see what's going on, just to make sure everything is okay."

"Alright… Do you have any details? Or do you want to drop them somewhere?"

"Did you two see a viral video some weeks ago? An autistic teenager who had a run-in with a police officer?"

"Oh, yeah." Gabriel remembered watching it with Renata in the library. "Poor guy. Renata was pretty wound up about it. But we're focused on medical kidnap. We can't split our focus worrying about educating the police about the difference between a kid who's high and one who is stimming. That will have to be someone else's mission."

"Oh, I understand that. I wasn't thinking you would look into the police."

"Then, what…?" Gabriel studied her, trying to divine what she wasn't saying. What she wasn't allowed to say. "You're saying he is a medical kidnap victim?"

Judge Dee-Dee took a sip of her water. "I couldn't say. It certainly seems like I am seeing more and more cases where DFS simply jumps to the conclusion that parents are abusive."

Gabriel slid his phone out. He knew it wasn't polite for him to text at the table in the middle of the conversation, but it was the only way he was going to be able to reach Renata.

Come talk with us.

Not both of us together. Too dangerous, she texted back.

Remember the autistic boy and the cop?

Renata's reply didn't come as quickly. *On the video?*

Yes. Come listen.

Again, there was a delay.

"Is she going to come?" Judge Dee-Dee asked.

Gabriel raised his head and looked around. Goosebumps. He caught a glimpse of a figure in the shadowy restroom corridor, but it wasn't big enough to be a man. He waited for her to move, and when she did, saw that it was Renata, her Hispanic complexion paler than usual, cataloging the room. Judge Dee-Dee turned her head, spotted Renata, and turned back away.

Gabriel focused on Judge Dee-Dee's face, not wanting to make Renata uncomfortable. For a couple of minutes, they sat in uncomfortable silence. Then Renata slipped into the empty chair to Gabriel's right.

"Judge Dee-Dee was talking about cases where DFS sometimes jumps to conclusions," Gabriel said casually. "You know, how they sometimes think there is abuse or neglect going on when it's something else. A medical condition, or just circumstances."

"Sometimes an accident is just an accident," Renata contributed.

Judge Dee-Dee nodded.

"Even as a judge, there's little I can do to convince an investigator that they're going about a case wrong-headed, or that they may need to step back and take a look at it from another angle. They get so invested in one interpretation of the facts that they are blind to anything else."

Gabriel nodded. They'd seen it. She didn't need to tell them that.

"Substance abuse, for example," Judge Dee-Dee offered, "in a household where there is no evidence of alcohol or drugs at all. And yet… an investigator can still build a case for a mother who is addicted."

"That's just… bizarre," Gabriel said. "Can't the parents do anything about it? Offer some kind of proof?"

The waitress brought Judge Dee-Dee her chicken salad sandwich, and looked at Gabriel and Renata questioningly, waiting for them to say that they wanted to order.

"No, we're good," Gabriel told her.

"Water?" the waitress asked Renata.

"No."

Judge Dee-Dee took a dainty bite of her sandwich and dabbed at her lips with a napkin. "Maybe the parents could have some kind of drug testing?" she suggested.

Gabriel nodded. Maybe you couldn't prove a negative, but a clean drug test might at least give a social worker some measure of comfort.

"Such as hair strand testing?" Judge Dee-Dee went on.

Renata nearly exploded out of her seat. "Hair strand testing?" she demanded. "Junk science! The experts claim that they can tell how much of a drug you've had, and in what time period. There's no way they can determine that. Even just a positive or a negative can be completely wrong!"

Gabriel gripped the side of the table, glancing around to see that Renata was attracting some stares with her vehemence, even though her voice was barely above a whisper.

"Renata…"

Renata turned to look at him. "Do you know how many hundreds and thousands of families have been screwed over by hair strand tests administered by people who hold themselves out as experts? Any idea?"

Gabriel shook his head. "I had no idea there was any problem with it. I thought it was an established science, like blood or urine testing."

Renata's eyes were snapping. "Some of these places giving expert testing aren't even qualified to do forensic testing. They're giving testimony based on preliminary pre-screening! Not gas chromatograph, just a field test!"

"And that's not accurate," Gabriel deduced.

Renata rolled her eyes at him and looked at Judge Dee-Dee. "You let these guys testify in your court? Don't you know they're just snake oil salesmen?"

Judge Dee-Dee surveyed Renata with amusement. "I forget when I haven't seen you for a while just how smart you are. Your depth of knowledge really is extraordinary."

"Talk to me about fake science and conspiracy theories, and I'll keep the conversation going all day long," Renata agreed frankly.

"As it happens," Judge Dee-Dee put down her half-sandwich, "I will not accept preliminary screening tests as evidence in my courtroom. Unfortunately, I don't have any jurisdiction over what DFS uses internally and what kind of science they base their judgments on."

Gabriel brought the discussion back around full circle. "So the boy in the video, he was taken away from his family based on faulty hair-strand testing that DFS had performed?"

Judge Dee-Dee touched her lips with her napkin. "I can't share the specifics of any particular case with you."

"No. Of course not," Gabriel agreed. He glanced over at Renata and saw that he was right to have brought her into the conversation. She was already way ahead of him on the science involved in the boy's case. That put them one jump ahead of DFS.

"We'll look into things," Renata said. She put her hands on the table and started to rise.

"Renata…" Judge Dee-Dee made a motion for her to stay. "That's not why I wanted to talk to you."

Gabriel and Renata exchanged nervous looks. Renata was still poised to go. She didn't sit back down.

"What is it, then?" Renata challenged.

"I wanted to talk to you about your mother."

"*My* mother? Why?"

Judge Dee-Dee had been the one who had sent Renata's mother, Elena, to prison, before Gabriel had met her. Gabriel knew the basics. The police had shown up to perform a search and to remove Renata without the appropriate warrants and paperwork. Like any loving mother would have, Elena had physically blocked them and tried to fight them off to protect her progeny. And while Judge Dee-Dee had ruled that the police did not have the right to enter, she had also ruled that Elena had assaulted the police, which carried stiff penalties. Renata had been removed from her care after all and Elena had gone to prison.

"Your mother is being released."

Renata stared at her, frozen in place. "Why?"

"She's served half her sentence. Good behavior. Not someone we wanted to put into the prison system to begin with. So… she's being released."

"Why are you telling me?"

"Because she will be able to take custody of you. You can go back to live with her. Have a roof over your head." Judge Dee-Dee looked at Gabriel. "Maybe Gabriel too. You guys could get off the streets and have somewhere safe to live."

"And be sitting ducks if you decided to issue a warrant under some trumped-up kidnapping charge," Renata shot back. "That would suit you just fine, wouldn't it?"

"I think you know I wouldn't take any pleasure in having to issue a warrant for your arrest for anything. But I would be very happy if I knew that you were safe and being looked after by someone who knew how to properly take care of your physical needs."

Renata stared fiercely at Judge Dee-Dee. "My mother tried to kill me."

"There's no proof of that."

"You might need proof. I don't. I'm not going to hang around with her and pretend to be the happy mother and daughter when I know she was trying to kill me."

"You're being paranoid. I realize you can't help the way your brain works, but you're not being logical and reasonable. You are letting your imagination run away with you."

Judge Dee-Dee looked at Gabriel, encouraging him to weigh in. Gabriel shook his head.

"I don't know anything about it," he said. "I wasn't there and I don't know what happened."

"You know about Renata's paranoia."

"That doesn't mean I'm wrong," Renata retorted. "It's not illogical if I'm right! But the only way you're going to believe me is if you catch her red-handed, or she succeeds. Me, I'm not going to wait around."

Judge Dee-Dee sighed. She looked more tired and worn than usual. Gabriel felt sorry for her.

"What about a supervised visit? Wouldn't you like to see her, say hello, find out how she's doing? Reconnect with her, even if you don't trust her enough to live with her again?"

Renata hesitated for an instant, then shook her head. Gabriel reached out and took her hand to comfort her. He knew how lonely he was without his mother. He could only assume that deep down, Renata felt the same way, even if she did think Elena had been trying to harm her.

"I don't want to see her again," Renata said. "She's not part of my life anymore."

CHAPTER TEN

Usually, Uncle Kris came to Caleb's house, so he had only been at Uncle Kris's house a couple of times before. One time was when they had helped Uncle Kris to move there. Caleb remembered how empty the rooms had felt before they started moving Uncle Kris's boxes and furniture in. The air vibrated on his skin and their voices had bounced off the walls in a strange, disconcerting way. Caleb liked it better when the rooms had been filled with Uncle Kris's things and the air felt normal again.

Uncle Kris answered the door when Mr. Searle rang the bell. He smelled like cigarette smoke, and he seemed surprised to find them there, even though they must have been expected. He reached out and gave Caleb's hair a ruffle.

"Hey, buddy, how are you doing? Boy, you're getting tall, aren't you?"

Caleb nodded and entered the house. He remembered where the bedrooms were and which one had been set up as a guest room, so he headed there. Uncle Kris and Mr. Searle followed him.

"I see you know where everything is," Mr. Searle observed. He held the garbage bag out to Caleb.

Caleb snatched it away from him and upended the bag to dump every-thing onto the bed. "Not garbage," he insisted.

"No, it's not garbage."

Uncle Kris moved toward the chest of drawers against the wall. "I still have a lot of stuff in here. But I emptied out a drawer for you." He opened the top drawer. The little that Caleb had would fit in it, but he wondered where he would put everything else. He would need more clothes than they had given him at the group home. He would need somewhere to put his food and his collections. He turned slowly on the spot, looking around the room. There weren't very many shelves and there was little free closet space. At the group home, he'd had to share the room with three other boys, but there had been more room to store things.

"Look okay?" Uncle Kris asked, giving a short laugh. "I know it's going to take some adjusting to get used to a bachelor pad, but at least you have a room of your own."

"Okay," Caleb said.

They both looked at him, like they expected him to say more. People often gave him that look. Finding the right words wasn't easy for Caleb. He preferred silence over searching for the right words and phrases. If he didn't say anything, people often filled the silence with the words they wanted to hear anyway.

"You can get settled," Mr. Searle said eventually. "I need to talk to your uncle for a few minutes."

———

Caleb looked up at a movement in his doorway. Uncle Kris stood there looking at him. Uncle Kris smiled.

"What would you say to pizza?" he asked.

Caleb tried to parse the question. "I say… yay?"

Uncle Kris laughed. "Good man! Let's go."

Caleb followed Uncle Kris out of the room and went to the kitchen. But there was no pizza, nor any sign of an attempt to cook one. Caleb looked around, confused. Uncle Kris held Caleb's coat out to him.

"We're going out for pizza."

"Out?"

Uncle Kris jerked his head toward the door. "Out. For pizza."

"Oh." Caleb tossed his coat over a chair. "Don't need that."

"Put on your coat."

"Not cold."

"Put it on."

Caleb refused to pick it up. It was a familiar argument. He knew if he held firm, Uncle Kris would pick up the coat and take it with him so that if he did get cold, Caleb could put it on. But Caleb wouldn't get cold.

Uncle Kris raised an eyebrow. "Do you want to go out for pizza, or do you want to stay in your room with nothing to eat?"

"Pizza."

"Then put on your coat. I'm not about to get in trouble with DFS for not dressing you properly."

Caleb didn't move. Uncle Kris headed for the door. Caleb followed and caught the door before Uncle Kris could shut it. Uncle Kris grabbed his arm, pulled him back into the house, and marched him back to the guest room.

"You're staying home. I'm going out for pizza."

"No!" Caleb hit his forehead with his fist. "No! Caleb pizza!"

"If Caleb doesn't put on his coat, then Caleb doesn't go out for pizza," Uncle Kris said firmly. He stepped out into the hall and pulled Caleb's door shut.

Caleb shouted. He grabbed the door and wrenched it open before Uncle Kris could lock it.

"Are you going to put on your coat?"

Caleb hit his head again. Uncle Kris headed for the door. Caleb dashed into the kitchen and grabbed his coat. He followed Uncle Kris. Uncle Kris turned and looked at him.

"You have to be wearing the coat. You're not leaving the house until it's on."

Caleb threaded his arms through the sleeves. Uncle Kris gave a nod. "That's better. Don't try that nonsense with me."

———

The air in the car was so hot and dry, Caleb felt like he was smothering. He wanted to take his coat back off, but he was convinced by Uncle Kris's behavior that that would be a bad decision, so he suffered through it. They didn't have very far to go anyway, only a few blocks, and then they pulled in at a strip mall with a pizza restaurant. Caleb bounced excitedly. He never got to go out to a restaurant. He never got real pizza for supper. Sometimes he got it for the lunch program at school, but he never got restaurant pizza like on TV.

Uncle Kris led him in, smiled at the cheery waitress, and they were shown to a table. Uncle Kris took off his coat and hung it on a coat rack, so Caleb copied him, watching to make sure this was acceptable. Uncle Kris nodded and sat down. There were TVs around the restaurant, showing various different sports games. Uncle Kris liked football, and he was positioned so he could watch a football game. Caleb wasn't interested in football. He stared at the lights hanging from the ceiling, moving his eyes in and out of focus so that they blurred, starred, and danced as he watched them.

A waitress with a very short skirt came up to the table and spoke to Uncle Kris. He smiled at her and leaned closer to talk to her. The waitress turned toward Caleb and spoke to him, but the room was noisy with all of the people who were talking, and Caleb couldn't separate the sound of what she was saying from the background noise. He frowned and moved his head back and forth, trying to catch just her voice.

Uncle Kris reached across the table, shaking his head at Caleb and speaking to him. Caleb studied his face. Uncle Kris made a drinking motion with his hand, raising his brows as he voiced his question again.

Caleb nodded. "Drink. Yes."

Spread out hands. Still the questioning face. *What drink?*

"Coke?" Caleb suggested.

He expected Uncle Kris to tell him, "No. Water or orange juice," but he didn't. He just nodded his head at Caleb and the waitress. The waitress wrote it down and departed. Caleb grinned. Mom always said no to Coke.

Uncle Kris pushed a pizza menu in front of Caleb, leaning forward and tapping it with his finger. He spoke slowly, trying to give Caleb a chance to read his speech.

"What pizza do you like?"

Caleb looked down at the pictures of the thickly-loaded pizzas dripping with cheese. He smiled. "All of them."

Uncle Kris returned his smile. "Anything you *don't* like?"

Caleb shook his head. "Broccoli."

Uncle Kris laughed. "Okay. No broccoli. Do you like all-meat?" He tapped one of the pictures. Caleb looked at it. Pepperoni, bacon, sausage, all drowning in cheese. He nodded eagerly.

The waitress returned with their drinks, placing the Coke in front of

Caleb and a big glass of beer in front of Uncle Kris. Uncle Kris handed her the pizza menu, telling her they wanted the all-meat pizza. Caleb happily took a sip of his drink. After watching the waitress walk away, his eyes on her very short skirt, Uncle Kris leaned back and took a drink of his beer. Caleb watched him lick the froth from his lip.

"It's good?" he asked.

Uncle Kris nodded. "You never tasted beer?"

Caleb shook his head. Uncle Kris touched the glass, pushing it half an inch closer to Caleb.

"Go ahead."

Caleb looked at him, sure he'd misread Uncle Kris's face and gesture. Uncle Kris nodded again, and gave the glass another little nudge.

Caleb was almost afraid to try. He knew Mom would be very upset if she saw him drink beer. But she'd be upset about the Coke and the pizza too. He picked up the glass and took a big slurp.

He nearly choked. He'd thought it would be sweet and fizzy like root beer, but it was bitter and not at all like he'd expected. He couldn't understand why anyone would choose to drink something that tasted like that, much like he'd felt when he snuck one of his mother's chocolate-covered ginger candies and instead of a candied cherry, ended up with what felt like a mouthful of burning soap.

Caleb coughed and tried to swallow what was left in his mouth without spraying it all over the table. Uncle Kris darted forward with a couple of napkins and helped to dab Caleb's chin and mop up what had ended up on the table. He took his glass of beer back, laughing.

"You don't like it?" he asked.

"No!" Caleb grimaced, sticking out his tongue and trying to get the taste out of his mouth. "It's bad!"

Uncle Kris just laughed and turned his eyes back to the TV.

When the pizza came, Caleb studied it carefully and held it up to his nose to smell it. The waitress gave him a look that told him he was behaving strangely. Uncle Kris raised an eyebrow.

"You don't want it now?"

Caleb wanted to be sure he wasn't in for another nasty surprise like the taste of the beer. "It's good?"

"Of course it's good. What's wrong?"

Caleb nibbled the point of the slice tentatively. It was okay. It was hot, though, so he blew on it, waiting until he would be able to eat it without burning the roof of his mouth. Uncle Kris took a big bite of his and washed it down with a gulp of beer.

"If you don't like it, I'll eat yours."

"No." Caleb took another nibble. "It's good."

Uncle Kris watched the TV while he ate and didn't require Caleb to answer any questions about how he was or what he was doing. Uncle Kris had never been like the friends or relatives who drowned Caleb with questions. He'd been okay with Caleb just sitting around, being himself.

———

Caleb knew that he'd stuffed himself too full at the restaurant. Mom usually told him if he was eating too much, but Uncle Kris didn't. He just belched and watched the TV and waited for Caleb to finish. Caleb's stomach pressed tightly against the waistband of his pants, even though they were elastic, and acid kept backing up into his throat, making him think he was going to throw up.

"Had enough?" Uncle Kris asked. "Shall we take the rest home?"

Caleb nodded. He couldn't believe that two people had been able to eat most of the huge pizza. When Mom made pizza at home, everyone got their own little one, smaller than a dinner plate. The school lunch pizzas were a similar size, or else served only one slice at a time.

He walked out to the car hunched over slightly to protect his aching belly, and didn't put on his seatbelt when he got into the car. He noticed that Uncle Kris didn't either. When they got to the house, Uncle Kris didn't seem to notice that Caleb was sick. He hung up their coats.

"You have homework to get done?"

"Yes." Caleb held his hand over his stomach.

"You go ahead and get it done, then. When is your bedtime?"

"Ten o'clock."

"Lights out at ten, then. Mr. Searle said your bus gets here at seven-thirty. You can get yourself up?"

"Yes."

Uncle Kris nodded and went into his bedroom, where he turned the TV on and lay down on the bed to watch football. Caleb didn't know if it was the same game he had been watching at the restaurant or not. He stood there, looking at Uncle Kris's bedroom door, not sure what to do. Mom always knew when he was sick, and she helped him figure out what was wrong and what to do about it. Uncle Kris just told him to do his homework.

Caleb went into his room and did his best to work on his homework. He couldn't focus on the instructions. His heart was beating too hard and he was breathing too fast. His stomach kept jumping around. Caleb always waited until Mom said, "Do you need to throw up?" before going into the bathroom and hovering over the toilet to see if he had to. But she wasn't there, and Uncle Kris didn't ask him, or even come into his room to check on him.

Caleb went into the bathroom across the hall from his bedroom and sat on the edge of the tub, putting his hand over his stomach and waiting to see if he was going to be sick.

"Does it hurt?" Mom would ask. "Point to where it hurts the most."

Caleb couldn't point, and wasn't sure if it was pain or pressure that he felt, but he knew it wasn't right.

"Uncle Kris?" he called out.

There was no response. The TV was turned up too loud and Uncle Kris was too interested in it to hear him. A lot of times, Caleb got too interested in what he was doing to hear someone talking to him. Caleb hung over the toilet, waiting to see if he had to throw up.

CHAPTER ELEVEN

I found his mom's blog," Renata announced.

Gabriel shifted his chair closer to hers and looked at her computer screen. He glanced around, but the librarian was helping an older woman with her computer and looked like she would be occupied for some time. So she wouldn't be complaining that Gabriel and Renata were not allowed to share a computer, but needed to each use their own.

He looked at the banner heading of the page. Caleb's Miracle. A typical title for the blog of a mother about her special needs child. A scan of the titles of each of the recent blog entries showed an irregular diary of the various meetings and arguments with DFS. Gabriel shook his head. Riley was, if nothing else, tenacious.

"Parents don't realize they're just shooting themselves in the foot when they write a blog like this," Renata said, shaking her head. "They're just providing DFS with the ammunition they're looking for. And baiting hoax hunters."

"But in some cases, it is a hoax. How is anyone supposed to be able to tell the difference between someone who really has a special needs child and one who is just looking for sympathy or money?"

Renata didn't offer a magical formula. She scrolled down to the blog entry giving the details of DFS's decision they would not return Caleb to the home. Not until they could prove that the mother's drinking was under control, Gabriel noted. Judge Dee-Dee had said that there was no alcohol in the home. How exactly was Riley supposed to prove that she had stopped drinking? She couldn't have less than nothing.

"Yeah, look at this," Renata jabbed a finger at the screen.

Gabriel read Riley's heartbreaking account of how she had agreed to hair strand testing, certain that it would be clean and DFS would have to agree to return Caleb to them, only to have the DFS investigator come back and show them a lab test stating that she was a chronic and frequent alcohol abuser, with off-the-charts levels of alcohol found in her hair. Riley insisted that they must have mixed her hair up with someone else's and demanded a second hair strand test, with the same results.

"Baby Best." Renata pointed to the name of the lab that had done the testing. "They've had their results thrown out of court before. I can't believe DFS is still using them after it's been proven that their experts are totally unqualified laymen who have no idea how to do the tests or evaluate the results. Baby Best doesn't do gas chromatograph at all. They just rely on field tests, and field tests can't be relied on to give a proper positive or negative, let alone show how much a person is drinking or doping. They're only a pre-screen."

Gabriel had no idea how she could already know all of those details. He'd been following medical kidnap cases for a year, and he'd never even come across reports of fraudulent hair strand testing before. Yet Renata knew all of the details without any research.

"Look it up," Renata told him, reading his expression.

"I believe you."

"Look it up anyway. Verify and see if I've forgotten anything important. We have to get this right."

She didn't say that after the way things had gone with Seth, they had to be doubly careful, but Gabriel heard the warning anyway. They couldn't assume that Judge Dee-Dee's details were correct. They couldn't assume that Riley Hibbert was innocent. Sometimes parents did invent illnesses or make their children sick just for the attention. Alcoholic parents always denied they had a problem. Renata wasn't likely to get the details wrong, but they would double-check everything all along the way.

Gabriel turned back to his computer to type the search in. Out of the corner of his eye, he saw a librarian headed toward them had stopped when he turned back to his own computer. After watching him for a minute, she decided he was going to obey the rules and use his own computer terminal, and went back to patrolling for other offenders.

Renata had apparently caught the woman's movements as well, and swore under her breath. "Not going to be able to stay here much longer," she warned.

"I noticed." Gabriel scanned through the search results on the Baby Best lab. It was a clinic associated with a hospital that provided drug and alcohol testing for expectant mothers so that their babies could be properly treated when they were born. As Renata had mentioned when they were talking to Judge Dee-Dee, they were not experts qualified to give forensic evidence. Being prepared to treat a newborn for addiction was a far cry from being able to testify in court how much the mother was drinking. He narrowed the search to the type of testing they did, and saw that, as Renata had said, their results had been booted out of court previously for not using a confirmation method such as gas chromatography.

"On the money," he confirmed to Renata. "No gas chromatograph."

"These field tests can be triggered by things like alcohol in hair spray," Renata said. "You need proper confirmation."

"And that's all DFS based their decision on? This flawed testing?"

"Oh, no. We'll have to talk to Mom and Dad to find out what the other factors are. DFS had already decided they were guilty when they asked for the hair strand testing. They just wanted to tighten the noose."

"Anything in the blog?"

"Plenty. A DFS dream. Lots of drama over how much harder Caleb is getting to handle as a teenager. All of the doctor and therapy appointments. Hygiene issues. They'll say that it's all either to justify her abuse and cover for her alcoholism, or it's factitious disorder."

"Factitious…?"

"Munchausen by Proxy."

"Why didn't you just say that, then?"

"Because I'll bet you anything the social worker didn't call it Munchausen by Proxy. He would have called it factitious disorder. They have to keep changing up the terminology to make it sound like something new. Judges are more likely to rule in their favor if they don't know anything about the disease. They assume DFS is the authority and knows what they're talking about."

Gabriel shook his head.

"It's true," Renata asserted. She scrolled farther down in the blog. "We've got Caleb with broken bones more than once. She says the cop broke Caleb's ribs."

Which was entirely possible, when Gabriel mentally reviewed the video. "Could have."

"Could've," Renata agreed. Gabriel remembered how easily an orderly had broken Renata's rib restraining her at the hospital when they had first met. "Before that, we've got Caleb with a broken finger while helping dad out in the garage. And here's one," Renata brought up a photo, "of Caleb and mom with matching casts." Both the boy and his mother had casts on their forearms. "Caleb apparently fell out of a tree, and mom broke hers in a car accident." Renata fell silent as she read the details of their accidents. "There's another problem."

"What's that?"

"Mom's car accident. She refers back to a couple of others that she's had."

"Injury accidents?"

"She doesn't say. I'll have to see if she blogged about them at the time."

"What, then? You think she's covering for domestic abuse?"

"No. If DFS is already thinking she has a drinking problem, then having several car accidents looks pretty suspicious."

"Oh." That made perfect sense. But there had to be other explanations for her having had multiple accidents? Careless driver? Inattentive? Distracted by her son having a meltdown? Drunk driving was as good an explanation as any, and it was buttressed by the Baby Best hair strand test. A lock, as far as DFS was concerned.

"There's a ton of reading here," Renata said, still scrolling down. "I think she's been blogging since Caleb was born. I'm going to be here awhile. There's probably enough to fill several books. You want to see about getting some money and something to eat?"

Gabriel stretched. "Yeah, sure. You'll take a break to eat?"

Renata nodded without looking up.

"Renata."

"What?" She was still hyperfocusing on the screen, lost in the words. Gabriel nudged her shoulder. Renata flapped her hand to shoo him away. "Go make money. Eat food."

"I want to make sure you're going to eat."

She tore her eyes away from the blog. "What? Oh. Yeah. I said I would, yes."

"How are you fixed for formula? Do we need to get you more soon?"

"Not yet."

"You're not rationing, are you? You're eating as much as you're supposed to?"

She made an *X* over her heart. "Promise."

"Okay. Just making sure. You have to take care of yourself."

"You too, Gabriel Tate. Practice what you preach."

"I'm going now."

———

Caleb ignored the vibrating of his alarm when it went off in the morning. He was too sick to go to school. He'd spent half the night in the bathroom throwing up, and the other half worrying that he wasn't finished yet. It seemed like everything he had eaten had come back up again, and he felt shaky and weak when the sun started to peek in his window.

Uncle Kris didn't tell him to get up and get ready for school, or ask him if he was sick or if he was feeling better. He hadn't gone into the bathroom to comfort Caleb when he was throwing up, as Mom always would. Caleb had cried when he went to bed, wishing he could be back home in his own bed, with Mom and Dad there to tell him that everything would be okay and he would be feeling better in the morning.

Mid-morning, Caleb was starting to feel more like himself. He had slept and his stomach was making movements like it regretted having expelled everything the night before and it was time to eat some breakfast. Caleb got out of bed, rubbing his eyes. He put on his sound processor and wandered out to the kitchen, yawning, to see what he could find to eat.

Uncle Kris was sitting in the kitchen reading his tablet. Caleb wasn't sure what to say. He had expected Uncle Kris to be at work. Dad would have been at work.

Uncle Kris looked up. "What are you doing here?" he barked. "You're supposed to be at school!"

"I'm sick."

"What are you talking about? You ate like a pig yesterday!"

"Caleb sick. Threw up."

"You look just fine. Go get dressed. You're going to school."

"Need breakfast."

"Clothes first. You can eat in the car."

Mom always said no eating in the car.

Caleb went back to his room to get dressed.

When he returned to the kitchen, there were a couple of granola bars and a juice box on the kitchen table.

"That's breakfast," Uncle Kris said, nodding to them as he poured a drink from a glass bottle into a sports water bottle. It smelled sharp like vinegar.

Caleb picked up the granola bars and the juice box, and reached for the water bottle as Uncle Kris screwed on the top.

"Nope," Uncle Kris pulled it back from Caleb, "that's *my* breakfast. Go put on your coat."

Caleb obeyed and, in a few minutes, they were both in the car. Caleb fastened his seatbelt. Uncle Kris took a few big gulps from the water bottle. He sighed loudly and put it in one of the cupholders.

"You said you could get yourself up in the morning."

"I was sick."

"You wanted to sleep in. If you think you're sick enough to skip school, you'd better talk to me, and I'll decide. You can't just skip school."

Caleb watched Uncle Kris's face carefully. "Didn't skip."

"Don't talk back to me!"

Caleb was so startled by Uncle Kris's sharp retort that he fell silent, unable to formulate an answer. Uncle Kris started the engine and put the radio on. Caleb shook his head in irritation at all of the background noise. He opened his first granola bar and ate in silence. Uncle Kris drank from his water bottle.

When Uncle Kris pulled up in front of the school, Caleb unbuckled his seatbelt and opened his door to get out. Uncle Kris reached over and grabbed him by the front of the coat, preventing him from leaving. He leaned toward Caleb, his face red, and spoke to Caleb, his breath smelling strongly of his breakfast drink.

The radio and the engine were still on, making it hard for Caleb to hear Uncle Kris's words. Caleb shook his head and tapped his sound processor, his body coiled tight in anticipation of being struck. Mom and Dad didn't hit him, but other people did, and Caleb didn't want Uncle Kris to hit him.

"Can't hear!" he protested. "Caleb can't hear!"

Uncle Kris stabbed a finger at the radio to silence it.

"I'm doing you a favor," Uncle Kris said, his voice overwhelming Caleb after the removal of the radio noise. "I'm doing you a favor so you don't have to live in foster care where people will hurt you. Understand?"

Caleb nodded his head, the motion very small.

"I'm not your mom or your dad. They screwed things up. I'm not going to baby you. You're old enough to get yourself out of bed and off to school. I don't need DFS charging me because you are being lazy. You get up and you get to school on time. You understand?"

"Yes."

"I'm not your mom."

"Not my mom," Caleb echoed.

Uncle Kris looked at him for a minute, then let go of his coat. "Don't screw up again."

Caleb waited to see if there was anything else, then got out of the car and went into the school.

CHAPTER TWELVE

Gabriel and Renata had planned their interviews with the Hibberts and had decided that they didn't want to do them together. It was dangerous for them both to be in the same place for too long, and at a place like the Hibberts' house, where they couldn't lose themselves in a crowd but could easily be spotted and reported, they had to be doubly careful. If a social worker or policeman showed up, at least one of them would be safe. Gabriel stayed close by, keeping surveillance, watching for any suspicious vehicles, but he didn't go into the house with Renata.

She had agreed to take Riley, and Gabriel Wes, even though Renata was not particularly keen on interviewing Caleb's mother. Like DFS, she was suspicious of the amount of time Riley spent blogging about her difficulties with her son, putting their lives on display for anyone with an internet connection. Renata couldn't trust her own mother, she certainly couldn't trust anyone else's. Renata had not trusted Leva, Seth's mother, like Gabriel had. She'd never been sure that Leva wasn't playing for an audience. She had been right. So she was the best one to talk to Riley, even if she didn't want to do it.

They'd been able to warm Riley up before approaching her, so Renata didn't have to just show up on the woman's doorstep and try to talk herself in. They'd made contact by email, and then a phone call, and by then Riley was curious enough about what the Underground Railway did to agree to have Renata over for a talk.

Renata took one more long look up and down the street, but didn't see any unusual activity. There were lots of flower beds and too many bushes that blocked clear viewlines. Renata rang the doorbell. Riley was quick to answer it, as if she'd been waiting in the living room for Renata to show up.

She was medium height and build, with dark, shoulder-length hair. A little makeup, definitely a number of hair products in use, and a warm, uncertain smile.

"Come on in," she invited.

Renata slipped in the door. She looked around the living room and what she could see of the kitchen and hall from the front entryway.

"Can I look around before we talk?"

"Look around at what?"

Renata didn't answer directly. "I want to see what DFS saw," she said. "So I'll have a better idea of what they are thinking."

DFS had decided Riley was an alcoholic. But Judge Dee-Dee had said there were no drugs or alcohol in the house. That was the one thing in Riley's favor. That, and the fact that Baby Best was a scam and Riley's hair products had probably royally screwed up the results.

"Uh… I guess. I'm not sure what you're looking for, though."

Renata didn't bother trying to explain. She wanted to be in and out of there as quickly as she could, and that meant not spending needless time talking. She went into the hall and made a quick but thorough search of the master bedroom, guest room/study, and Caleb's overcrowded bedroom. It was obvious that the room had been cleaned in Caleb's absence, but a good scrubbing didn't hide the fact that Caleb was a hoarder, and Renata's brief search still turned up stashes of food that Riley hadn't come across in her clean-up. Tool marks on the doorknob suggested that it had recently been replaced or reinstalled. Just as she knew the DFS investigator would have done, Renata made a quick tour of the kitchen cupboards and fridge, and a trip down the stairs to have a look around at the unfinished basement. She returned to the living room and glanced around.

"You have pictures of Caleb?" she asked. "Journals or records from when he was born? I've looked through your blog, so I know his overall history. Just wondering what else you have."

"I have several binders of records," Riley agreed, and went back to the master bedroom to collect the four inch binders Renata had seen shelved there. Renata opened the first one and browsed through it while she considered what to ask Riley.

"He wets the bed?" she asked.

Riley blinked. "I don't see what—"

"I want to know what you're putting on your website and what you're not. You have more sets of sheets for his bed than for yours. The mattress has a plastic liner. So he wets the bed, right?"

Riley nodded. "Sometimes. Not often."

"But you kept that private. Didn't put it on your blog."

"I didn't think he'd appreciate having his friends know about it… if any of them ever read it…"

"If he had friends," Renata finished.

"He's a friendly boy. A nice boy. He should have friends. It's just… he doesn't ever bring them home."

"How did he break his arm?"

"Climbing a tree. He wasn't supposed to be climbing, but…" Riley gave a little shrug. "Kids!"

"He didn't get it in a car accident?"

"No. That's how I broke mine."

"What about domestic violence? You never get mad?"

"I get mad. Everyone gets mad. But I don't hit Caleb. I didn't break his arm. That was just an accident. Kids being kids."

"Kids," Renata picked up on the plural. "It wasn't just Caleb by himself?"

"No… he was at the park. There were other kids around. Challenging each other. Horsing around. Daring each other."

"You saw it happen?"

"I didn't see, exactly. I wasn't looking when it happened."

"But you were in the park. Trying to keep an eye on him."

"Yes. Trying to find the happy medium between hovering and giving him some independence."

Renata flipped through the first of the binders, a day-by-day journal of Caleb's first weeks in life. She studied the photos, reviewed the text for any keywords that might tell her what was wrong with him, and kept processing what she had seen in her walk through.

"What's his favorite subject in school?"

"His favorite…? I suppose… science?" Riley considered her own answer. "Yes. I think I'd have to say science."

"He likes to collect things."

"Oh, does he ever!" Riley shook her head in dismay. "When he was little, it was cute. You know, little kids collect everything, they have treasures that you just could never see the way they do. But as he got to be older, it seemed like he was getting worse instead of better. We were working with a psychologist who was treating him for OCD. But there's not a lot you can do. Trying out different medications, talking to him about letting go of things…"

"I'll bet that worked great," Renata said sarcastically.

Riley laughed. "No, you're right. He just got more and more insistent. His room now… I've gotten rid of stuff while he's been gone. I've been working on it, trying to make it more livable for when he comes back."

"I figured." Renata changed direction, "You said on your website he was getting more violent. He has an explosive temper."

Most mothers would have looked embarrassed over exposing that truth about a family member, even if it were true. But Riley didn't shy away from it. She nodded, seeming eager to talk about it.

"When you have little kids and they have tantrums, that's one thing. You are big enough to control them and make sure that things don't get out of hand. But when you have a child who is developmentally delayed, like Caleb, he's getting bigger and bigger, but he's not growing out of that toddler tantrum stage, and then you throw increased testosterone into the mix… We're doing the best we can to keep things under control, but I don't know how long we'll be able to manage before we have to start looking at alternatives." She stopped talking and took a couple of breaths. "I'm talking about residential facilities…"

"So maybe it's good he got taken away when he did. DFS can find a better placement for him and he won't blame you for it."

Riley drew her breath in quickly, shocked. She'd obviously been looking for sympathy, not pragmatism. "No. No, it wasn't time yet. We might have been able to find a way to turn him around before he got too violent. Kids develop in fits and starts. You never know when they're going to plateau, and then suddenly mature in unexpected ways. I'm always looking for new therapies, new ways to reach him and to help him to be… the best he can be."

Renata looked up from the pages of the binder. "When was he diagnosed as being deaf?"

"They do screening on all newborns. So… they knew he was impaired within a few days. He was still just a baby when we got the implant."

"When was he diagnosed with autism?"

Riley wound a lock of hair around her finger. "He was five. I know it's late for an autism diagnosis. They want to do all of the early intervention programs. But they thought that his language delays were because of his deafness or his seizures. Or maybe both. They didn't want to give him an autism diagnosis when he had other diagnoses that would explain his delays. I knew he was autistic before that. I just couldn't prove it. And we did get into early language intervention because of his deafness, so it didn't matter that he didn't have an autism diagnosis at that point."

"Did they ever find a reason for his Failure to Thrive?"

"That's… I really don't know why you need to know all of these things. I get that you help reunite kids who have been taken away from their parents, but how is this going to help?"

"If we can make DFS review the case and reverse their decision instead of having to… remove Caleb from his foster home… then that's the better option. Putting him through the Underground Railway has a lot of implications for you. You have to disappear. Leave your lives here behind. If DFS will return him, you can decide what you are going to do with your lives."

"But what is there that would make them change their minds?"

Renata leaned closer to Riley. "Baby Best is a scam. That alone should be enough for DFS to review the file. But it won't be. It's going to take more than that."

"What do you mean, they're a scam?"

"They couldn't perform a drug test if their lives depended on it. Your hair products…?" Renata nodded to Riley's carefully coiffed hair. "You use a hair spray with a 70% alcohol content. Then they field test your hair for alcohol. What do you think they're going to find?"

Riley stared at Renata, her eyes wide.

"The alcohol came from my hair spray? But don't they… I don't know… wash it first?"

"Maybe they do, maybe they don't. I wouldn't make any assumptions. But even if they do, how do you know how much alcohol your hair has absorbed that can't just be rinsed off?"

"Why didn't anyone tell me that? Why didn't... why didn't they ask me about hair products?"

"Because the point of the hair strand test wasn't to find the truth. It was to prove their hypothesis. Just about every test they send to Baby Best comes back positive. That's the whole idea."

Riley blinked. Her eyes were glazed, shocked by Renata's revelation. But that wasn't why Renata was there. She already knew about Baby Best. She already knew that whether Riley had alcohol-containing hair spray or not, the hair strand test was bogus. Renata didn't have time to dwell on it.

"Why did Caleb fail to thrive?"

"Can't we challenge the hair strand test? Can we prove through other methods that I'm not an alcoholic? There isn't a drop of alcohol in the house! I don't even like the stuff and I would never have it around Caleb."

"You'll challenge the hair strand test," Renata agreed. "We'll figure something out. But that isn't going to do it. They're still going to say you're a danger to Caleb, hair strand test or not."

"How can they? I'm not! I would never do anything to hurt him."

Renata didn't see any deception in Riley's eyes. But then, if Riley was a psychopath, she wouldn't. She might be perfectly comfortable with lying and not feel guilt over not telling the truth. DFS would follow the evidence and Renata had to do the same.

"Why are you avoiding my question?"

"What question?"

"Failure to Thrive. They're going to start every argument with FTT. You couldn't take care of him properly. You weren't feeding him properly. There was too much stress in the home. You didn't bond with him. They're going to use FTT to prove you were a bad mother from the start, whether you were an addict or not."

Riley sighed. "No. They never found an organic reason for his Failure to Thrive. He had to have a feeding tube because he wouldn't eat enough. He was starving to death and a tube was the only way to save him. I was so scared that once they put the tube in, we'd never get it back out. I fought it. And then... it was so easy. You wouldn't believe how much easier it was to just give him formula straight into his tube instead of fighting to get every ounce of food down his throat."

Renata pulled open one of the buttons on her shirt to show Riley her tube. "Trust me, I know."

Riley's eyes got wide. "I've never seen a teenager with a g-tube! Caleb got his out when he was about three. You still… you still use it? You never learned to eat?"

Renata buttoned her shirt again. "I can't. Anything I take by mouth, I get a reaction and my throat swells shut. The only thing I can tolerate is an amino acid formula, and it has to go straight into the tube."

"Wow. I've never heard of that."

"So Caleb got his tube out and they didn't have to put it back in? You managed to keep his weight up?"

"He's always been low weight, but we've been able to keep him around low-healthy rather than underweight. It's tough, because if it was up to him, all he'd eat is junk food. And that might help with his weight, but not with his nutritional needs. Or behavioral issues. He needs good, healthy food, but like a lot of kids with autism, all he wants is refined carbs and dairy."

Renata knew how that would go over with DFS. She had a child that she was struggling to get enough calories into, and she was limiting his calories based on their quality? Caleb was lucky they hadn't kept him on the tube, or his mother would still have him on straight formula to optimize his nutritional status. And Renata knew from experience that even the best formulas fell short.

Renata looked back down at the binder in her lap. "When he was born, were you taking anything? Drugs or alcohol? Legal or not?"

"No! I don't understand why you and DFS think that I've ever been on anything. I love Caleb. I would never expose my son to anything that might harm him."

"What about before you knew you were pregnant? Lots of women drink a little. Some wine to unwind at the end of the day. A beer after work or a margarita on girls' night out. It doesn't mean you were a drunk."

Renata forced her mind away from flashbacks to her own mother, Elena, and her glass of wine every night before bed. She insisted that it was good for her. Renata didn't imagine Elena had stopped the practice while she was pregnant. Renata couldn't point to it as the cause of any of her troubles, but there were studies examining damage to mitochondria in babies with Fetal Alcohol Spectrum Disorder.

"Caleb was planned. I didn't drink anything before he was born or during the pregnancy. I've never used any kind of recreational drugs."

Renata cocked her head, running the words through her mind. "But you were on prescription drugs?"

"Nothing that would have had any effect on Caleb. I asked at the time. The doctor said it was perfectly safe."

"What?"

Riley didn't answer right away. She looked down at the thick volume on Renata's knees.

"I started having issues with depression and anxiety."

"While you were pregnant?"

"Yes. But I asked. They said the meds couldn't have any effect on Caleb. They were perfectly safe."

"Why did you start having depression in the middle of the pregnancy?"

Riley frowned. She shook her head. "Why? No reason. A lot of people have depression or anxiety when they're pregnant."

"Did it stop when Caleb was born?"

"No. I still have some issues... but that doesn't have anything to do with Caleb being apprehended. They didn't do that because I'm on antidepressants. I've never done anything to hurt Caleb."

Renata closed her eyes, concentrating on the connections that she could feel, but couldn't quite verbalize yet.

"Did you tell DFS you had depression and anxiety?"

"Yes. They asked a lot of questions..."

"Did you get sick while you were pregnant?"

"Morning sickness, you mean? I had some, but never bad enough that I needed a prescription for that."

"No, I mean... colds, flu, any weird viruses...?"

"Well, sure. The flu. Tired, sore throat, muscle aches. Stuff goes around. But nothing concerning."

"What tests did Caleb have when he was born?"

"There are copies of his medical records and everything I could get my hands on, in there. I don't know for sure all of the tests they did. There are a lot of tests that are routine when a baby is born. Checks that every baby gets. And then there were tests that he had because he was sick. Low birth weight, jaundice, seizures, problems with feeding and putting on weight... they ran a lot of tests."

Across the street, a white van pulled in. No one got out. Renata shifted her position and could see the driver sitting in the front seat, his phone or a radio held to his mouth. She slid the book off her lap and put it on the couch. As much as she wanted to read and study it, she couldn't take it with her. The book was huge and heavy and would slow her down too much.

"I want you to write down for me all of the tests they did on Caleb, and the results. I want to know what was eliminated."

"All of the tests he had when he was born, or…?"

"Everything done when he was a baby. Cut it off at two years old. Or three, that's when his tube came out, right? All of the tests that were done before his tube came out."

"That's going to be a lot of work."

"Do you want him back, or not?" Renata snapped. A lot of work? Did Riley think it was going to be a walk in the park? That they were just going to be able to make a phone call and DFS would reverse their decision and send Caleb home?

"Yes. I'll do it. It's just that I don't see what bearing this has on anything."

The driver of the van was still talking on the phone. Renata got up. "Mind if I use the back door?"

"We're done? Are you leaving? I thought—"

"We'll be in touch. Get that information together. Someone will contact you."

Renata was careful not to cross in front of the living room window. She kept to the outside of the room in hopes that the van driver would not be able to see her shadow or any movements inside.

"What do we do about the hair strand testing?" Riley asked, following Renata. "You said we would do something about that."

Was she trying to delay Renata? Had she called the cops or someone else? Had Judge Dee-Dee put surveillance on the house, figuring that sooner or later, one of them would show up there?

Where was Gabriel? He hadn't sent her any warnings. Had he already been arrested?

"Renata? How can I prove the hair strand testing was wrong?" Riley persisted.

"SCRAM."

Riley stopped following Renata, frowning. Renata turned to face her for a moment, laughing in spite of her anxiety.

"Secure Continuous Remote Alcohol Monitor," she explained. "It's an ankle monitor. Look into it."

She cracked the back door open and listened for anything out of place. Footsteps, breathing, any sign someone was close by. Birds chirped, traffic swooshed in the distance. Renata slipped out the door. She made her way to the alley, but as she was about to open the gate, heard the crunch of footsteps on gravel. Slow and stealthy.

She waited. The footsteps got close, then they stopped. Someone was nearby, waiting for her. Renata jolted when her cell phone vibrated in her pocket. She slipped it out.

Time to get out.

No indication of any particular danger. Gabriel might just be worried about how long she was taking.

Watcher in back, Renata typed back.

Me.

Renata let out her breath. She opened the gate a crack and peered out. Gabriel. Alone. No cops. Renata exited, and they moved as quickly as they could without burning too much energy. They were a few blocks away before Renata looked at Gabriel for an explanation.

"Van in front," Gabriel said. "Did you see it too?"

"Yeah. Wouldn't be the first time I was scared off by the cable guy, but I didn't want to take any chances."

He nodded. "How did it go?"

"I can see why DFS is so concerned. I think we need to be careful. I don't want to do anything without being sure."

"Munchausen?"

"Maybe. Not to start with, though, I don't think. She might have decided she liked the spotlight after a while, but I don't think she's the reason he had so many problems when he was born. There's something else going on there."

They walked some more.

"She's very controlling," Renata said. "That can be a problem when you've got a kid with behavior problems. Battle of wills. Can lead to physical abuse."

Gabriel nodded soberly. He'd seen a lot in the time they'd been running the Underground Railway. He was so naive when she first met him, but he'd seen a lot since then. He'd learned what Renata already knew—that not every parent who claimed DFS had done them wrong was innocent. Not by a long shot.

CHAPTER THIRTEEN

After the scare with the van at the Hibberts' house, Gabriel didn't want to go anywhere near there for his interview with Wes. He didn't want to meet Wes at his office, either. Nowhere that he was on home ground. He arranged instead for a meeting on neutral ground, first suggesting a shopping mall, and then having Wes take the train to a park. Gabriel observed him from a distance to make sure that he wasn't with anyone or reporting the change in plans back to them on his phone. He watched for anyone who might be following Wes. Just because Wes followed the rules, that didn't mean someone else—Judge Dee-Dee or a cop or social worker who was involved—couldn't have Wes followed.

But Wes seemed to be clean. Gabriel waited a bit longer, and then approached. Wes looked through him at first, not expecting his contact to be a thin black teenager who looked like he was just a student who had strolled off the university grounds for a little fresh air.

"Uh—you're Gabriel?"

"And you're Wes Hibbert. Good to meet you."

"Oh. Well, you too. I'm sorry, I didn't realize that this… organization would be using people so young. Riley said that the woman she met with was very young, but I thought… it's just unexpected."

"That's the idea," Gabriel said, not bothering to tell Wes that the organization was actually run by teenagers. Adults had messed things up enough. Gabriel and his underage partners were easily overlooked. They could more easily navigate the technology and databases, having grown up with it, and it was easier for them to disappear and operate below the radar.

"Right. Of course. So…" Wes looked around, obviously still thinking that they were going to be joined by an adult who would take over, "… where do we start?"

"Let's sit down." Gabriel motioned to a park bench near the pond. It would be easier for him to conserve his energy if he didn't have to be wandering around while they talked.

"Do you guys really think you can help us? It seems sort of weird, after everyone else we talk to says we have to cooperate and not challenge the system. Lawyers, advocates, everyone we've talked to has said you can't fight the system. You have to do whatever they say, and just hope they'll bring Caleb back again."

"Sometimes DFS gives kids back when they realize they've made a mistake. But it can take a couple of years. During that time, a lot can go wrong. Autistic kids in the system… it's pretty hard on them. And if he has physical health problems too, it's that much worse."

"And you guys just whisk him away? We get new identities and avoid the law?"

"I don't know yet. We do our own investigating. We don't want to be wrong and put a kid back together with an abusive parent."

Wes's jaw clenched.

"It happens," Gabriel said. "Abusers can be tricky."

Wes's face relaxed. "Yes, they can. Kids stay stuck in abusive homes for years."

"Then you can understand why we don't want to take a kid who's escaped an abusive home just to put him right back in it."

"No. Of course not. We'll do whatever we can to show you that we're not going to hurt Caleb. Our home is the best place for him. We'll be open and transparent."

"Have you ever thought your wife might be abusive?"

Gabriel watched the shock chase across Wes's face. He opened his mouth with a sharp retort, then held back. When he answered, his voice was calm.

"I haven't ever seen her do anything abusive. You wonder sometimes, when you hear these horror stories. *Could that ever be us? Would we ever snap?* And when you hear about mothers who intentionally make their kids sick, you get that little chill, thinking, *What if that was your family? What if it was happening right under your nose?*"

Gabriel nodded and waited. Wes thought through his answer, shaking his head slightly.

"I don't believe that Riley is doing anything to hurt Caleb. I don't believe she ever could. I don't understand how it works, these women who pretend to love their children and make them so sick. Riley could never do that. It's not her."

"And what about you?"

"I wouldn't either. I might not have quite the same patience that Riley does, but I don't hit. I don't hurt my son."

Gabriel absorbed the emotion in Wes's words, and analyzed his previous comment about abused children being left in the home. He thought he sensed something deeper, behind what Wes had said.

"Is that what your father was like?"

Wes shook his head slowly. He studied Gabriel's face. "Did my wife say that? She told you…?"

"No. I'm just guessing."

"You're a pretty good guesser. It's not something I usually talk about."

"You said you would be open and transparent."

"Is this really part of that?"

"Yes."

Wes stared at the pond. Gabriel waited, knowing that he'd talk sooner or later. There was no sign of anyone watching or following them, so they could take their time.

"My father was an abusive drunk," Wes confessed. There was so much emotion behind the words that Gabriel was worried about what would happen when the dam burst. When Wes Hibbert let go, it was going to be an event.

Was this what the social worker had seen? A man on the edge of letting loose? Worried about what would happen if Caleb stood in the way of that fury? Just because Wes knew what it was like to be on the receiving end of violence, that didn't mean that he could never become an abuser himself. In fact, the opposite was true. Having been abused, he was far more likely to be an abuser. That was how he had been taught to handle life's difficulties.

"My brother and I… he'd say it was discipline. Punishing us for things we had done wrong. But it wasn't. It was just a big, drunk guy beating on someone smaller because he could. He told us we were bad kids. He had to discipline us, or we'd grow up to be bad men. Like him? I don't know if he thought he was a bad person, or if he really convinced himself that what he was doing was right. Maybe he didn't think anything at all. But he was a devil."

"That must have been awful for you. Nobody ever… tried to help?"

"People must have known what was going on. They must have at least suspected. But… we were alone. We stayed there until we were old enough to escape. Kris left when he was eighteen, old enough to get a job and his own place. I was younger. I left when I was sixteen. I just couldn't do it anymore. I figured living on the street or dying were both better options than staying."

Sixteen. Gabriel knew what it was like to be on the street at sixteen, trying to make his own way.

"I'm glad you got out. What about your mother? Did she live with you, or…?"

"She died after I left home."

Gabriel was afraid to ask for any details. Wes provided them anyway, without prompting.

"He killed her. He got manslaughter. Seven years."

"What happened after he got out? Have you been in contact?"

"No. I was notified when he got out, but I didn't go to meet him or call him to reconnect. I don't know where he is or what he's doing now, or if he's even still alive. In my fantasies, he killed himself in a drunk driving accident soon after he was released."

"Wow. That's awful."

"So you can understand why I say I would never, ever hit my son. You can ask Riley or anyone who knows me. I have never hit Caleb. I've yelled. I've slammed doors. I've walked away. I've never done anything to hurt him."

"With all of Caleb's issues, he couldn't have been easy to parent," Gabriel said. He knew that even with just his medical problems, it had been a difficult job for Keisha to raise him. For Elena, trying to raise a child like Renata, who had also suffered with paranoia and psychosis since she was a toddler, it was impossible. Caleb fell somewhere in between, with illness, hearing and communication difficulties, and all of the challenges that came with a child whose brain worked differently. With autism, OCD, and whatever other neurodiverse conditions Caleb had been diagnosed with, his parents had to be struggling.

"Easy is a word that I have never applied to Caleb," Wes agreed, letting out a sigh. "He needed constant care and attention as a baby. Just trying to keep him alive and knowing when he needed to be in the hospital... We constantly had doctors and nurses looking over our shoulders and criticizing us because of his weight or developmental delays. Like we weren't doing everything we could to help him. You look at the records Riley kept. Being able to raise Caleb to be a happy, confident teenager was a miracle. But just in case we were getting too cocky... this happens. Having him taken away from us because they think Riley is a closet drinker and that we are abusing him and starving him...? It's so bizarre to me. It's just the opposite of what our family is like."

"DFS doesn't need any proof. Just concerns. And in Caleb's case, there's lots of ammunition."

Wes grunted his acknowledgment.

Gabriel watched the various people out for an afternoon stroll. No one looked at him. No one saw anything out of place.

"Did you ever worry that your wife might be sharing too much?"

"Oh." Wes turned and looked at Gabriel. "Well... yes. The way I grew up... we never talked about our family business. We never told people what was going on. We didn't tell anyone anything. So living with someone like Riley who shares *everything*... it's been very uncomfortable. I try to just let her do her blogging and talk everything over with her friends, but there have been times when I've told her, 'Honey... everyone doesn't need to know about that.' She doesn't see any harm in sharing private information with *everyone*."

Gabriel nodded. "I looked over her blog. Not as closely as Renata, but yeah, I'd really be worried about the amount she is sharing with the world. Not just because it isn't any of their business, but because DFS is going to think she is attention-seeking. That she wants to be able to show off how bad Caleb's health and behavior is just to get attention."

"What does it matter if she gets attention for it? She puts all of her time and strength into raising Caleb. She should get the props."

"Unless she's making him sicker just to get the props."

Wes shook his head and looked Gabriel in the eye. "She doesn't have Munchausen by Proxy."

CHAPTER FOURTEEN

Renata usually woke up before Gabriel, but she was feeling off. She had slept longer than usual. As she shifted and rolled over, Gabriel looked at her, his face lit by the glow of his phone.

"Why do you have that on so early in the morning?" Renata complained.

He held down the power button to turn it off. "Just a quick check. Are you okay?"

Renata shrugged, irritated. It was a question she couldn't answer, and that bothered her. "We'd better get packed up before the cops come around."

She slid out of her sleeping bag into the chilly air. Her bones hurt. But they weren't going to get any better sitting around feeling sorry for herself. She started rolling up her sleeping bag and Gabriel did the same. The tent was tiny, but they were used to it, and in five minutes, everything was packed away into their backpacks.

"We're going to have to find somewhere else soon. It's getting too cold," Gabriel observed.

The previous winter had been hard on him. Not so bad for Renata, because she'd been stuck in the secure psych ward and had a warm bed every night. Gabriel had not fared so well outside. Soon they'd be in the same position again.

"Yeah," Renata agreed. She'd had short periods of homelessness when she'd run away before, but she hadn't had to tough it out all winter before. "We could move south for a few months."

"Maybe, yeah. Wouldn't have to go too far to get out of the valley and into warmer climes."

The valley was home, but Renata had to admit that warmer weather was a draw. It was going to be too cold to sleep on the ground much longer. Neither of them had any fat to keep them warm, and in spite of the fact that they had upgraded to polar sleeping bags, it was still cold and uncomfortable sleeping on the ground.

Renata struck off down the street, not sure what restaurant or coffee shop they would stop at. There were a few that were open twenty-four hours, but most of them didn't open until six for early-morning commuters.

"No messages this early?" Renata asked, nodding toward the pocket that held Gabriel's phone.

"Actually, there was one from Carmel."

Renata grimaced. She didn't want to know what Carmel had messaged Gabriel about. "I haven't heard from Ray in ages," she said. "We should reach out, make sure he's still okay."

"Carmel invited us over to her place. She knows that you have research to do, and said you may just as well do it on their computers. Save us racking up hours at the library where we might be noticed."

Renata snorted. She didn't need Carmel's help. There was nothing wrong with the library.

"She said we could sleep there the night. Have a hot meal."

"We can't stay overnight," Renata said automatically. Even if she hadn't cared about how close Gabriel was to Carmel, she wouldn't have agreed to stay there the night. It was too dangerous. The police hadn't given any indication that they knew about Carmel and her connection to the Underground Railway, but that didn't mean that they didn't. They might just be biding their time, watching the house, hoping that Gabriel or Renata would show up. "Going there for a few hours during the day isn't the same as sleeping over," she said. "The longer we stay somewhere, the better the chances are that we're going to get found out. What happens when the neighbors start noticing us hanging around there?"

"Then they figure someone came to visit. People do entertain overnight guests now and then. It's not something suspicious that you would call the police about."

They had stayed there for a few nights while recuperating after Seth's rescue, and no one had reported them or arrested them, but Renata wasn't going to agree to stay there more than a few hours. It was just too dangerous.

"Maybe we can go there to do some research," Renata said, "but we're not staying overnight."

Gabriel gave such a wide smile, his teeth bright white against the darkness of his skin, that Renata knew she'd made a mistake. Obviously, Gabriel and Carmel couldn't be trusted together. He was getting too close to her. It was going to lead to mistakes.

"I'll go," she offered. "You should stay away. Then if something happens, you'll still be safe."

Gabriel's grin disappeared. "No way. If you're going, I am too. I haven't seen Carmel in weeks."

He wouldn't see her in several more, if Renata had her way. She didn't say anything. Let Gabriel sweat it out.

Gabriel pointed to a coffee shop with its 'open' sign glowing in the window, and Renata nodded. The place was nearly empty. They found a back booth where Renata could have some privacy to hook up her tube and have her breakfast without people trying to kick them out. Gabriel went up to the counter to order himself a muffin. Renata was already dozing in her seat when he got back.

"Renata? You okay?"

Renata opened her eyes and blinked a few times. She moved sluggishly.

"I'm just tired… didn't sleep very well last night." She rubbed sore joints. Everything hurt. Renata rested her head against the wall, closing her eyes again.

"You need to get something to eat," Gabriel said. "Once you've got some sugar into your system, you'll feel better."

Renata didn't move. Gabriel could eat his breakfast. For the moment, all she wanted was to rest for a bit longer.

She was aware of Gabriel beside her, picking up her backpack and going through it. Renata cracked her eyelids and watched him pull out a premeasured bag of formula. Luckily, it was not cold enough outside for it to have frozen. Gabriel had seen her hook up her feeding tube enough times to know all of the steps. Renata closed her eyes again while he unfastened the one button on her shirt that he needed to get access. It wasn't long before Renata could feel the icy formula flowing into her stomach. She shuddered.

"It's cold."

Gabriel removed his coat and draped it over her, which both hid her tube from the other patrons and helped to warm up her outside, so her body would be able to regulate her internal temperature. He moved their backpacks aside and cuddled against her, sharing his body heat.

"Are you going to be okay?" he murmured into her hair.

Renata just breathed. Gabriel felt her cheek and forehead with the back of his hand. He put his hands under the coat and held the formula bag between his hands, warming it. Renata waited for her insides to stop shaking and for the calming feeling of her blood sugar stabilizing. She'd wake up properly and they'd be able to spend the day like they had planned.

She felt Gabriel disconnecting the bag and tidying up. "If you're not feeling any better, I'm going to take you to the hospital."

"I'm okay," Renata told him. "Just give me a few more minutes. Eat your muffin. Have a coffee."

As hard as she tried to keep her words crisp and clear, she knew they were coming out slurred. Gabriel took a couple of bites of his muffin. No matter how worried he was, he had to take care of his body or he wouldn't be able to help her. Renata stretched. She rubbed her arms and tried to convince herself that she was just fine. She was just short on sleep because of the cold night on the ground. But it hadn't been the first night she'd slept on the ground and she had slept longer than she normally would. There was more to it.

She rubbed her eyes and forced them open. "I'm fine," she told Gabriel, pushing his coat toward him. "Just a bug. Maybe the flu."

He put the coat back over her. "Make sure you're all warmed up before we have to go outside again. We can wait awhile."

She nodded. "Just don't call an ambulance. I'm okay."

Gabriel continued to eat, looking a little more relaxed.

He cleared his wrappers.

"We'll go to Carmel's. If you're feeling up to it, you can do research. If not, you can rest. You can't exactly sleep at the library."

Renata sighed. He was right. They needed to go somewhere safe where she could rest. Carmel had already invited them over, so it was the logical place to go.

———

Gabriel hated to wake Renata up, but he couldn't exactly carry her to Carmel's house like a sleeping child. He could help her, but he couldn't carry her.

"Renata. Hey. Wake up, Renata."

She stirred and blinked heavy lids at him. "Wha…?"

"This is our stop. Sorry."

She looked around, trying to orient herself. Finally, she nodded. "Yeah. Okay."

They both got up as the bus slowed and shuddered to a stop at the curb. Gabriel pulled his backpack on and took Renata's from her. He knew something was wrong when she didn't protest and say she could carry her own bag, thank you very much.

"It's not far." There was no reason for him to tell her, Renata knew where Carmel lived just as well as he did. She had brought him there the first time, in circumstances not so different, except that Gabriel had been the one who was crashing. "Just a little farther…"

Renata leaned on his arm, focused just on putting one foot in front of the other to get past the last few houses to Carmel's house.

Gabriel had texted Carmel from the bus and the pretty blond teen was coming down the sidewalk toward them, not sitting in her wheelchair, but pushing it in front of her. When she reached them, she set the brakes and Gabriel maneuvered Renata into the seat. The fact that Renata didn't at least make a token protest sent a chill of fear through him. He made sure she was stable, then released the brakes and took the handles from Carmel.

"I can do it," Carmel protested.

"I know, but… please let me."

Carmel stepped aside and let him take over. "What's wrong? You said she was sick, but…"

"I don't know. She said maybe it was the flu. She was fine yesterday, but last night…" Gabriel trailed off, deciding not to share the details. Renata wasn't exactly buddies with Carmel.

Carmel looked down at Renata, who had her eyes closed and her head canted to the side. "I hope that's all it is. You're sure we shouldn't call a doctor or get her to the hospital?"

"No… she said not to call an ambulance."

"What if she's having an allergic reaction or something serious?"

"She would have said if it was an allergy. She would have known that."

Gabriel reached Carmel's house and pushed the wheelchair up the ramp into the house. Carmel's mother met them. Blond, like Carmel, but not so thin, and her hair was shot with gray. She bent over Renata, worriedly asking questions.

"It's okay, Mrs. Oss," Gabriel said. "She thinks it's just a flu bug. We should just put her to bed. I'll keep an eye on her."

Used to taking care of her daughter, Mrs. Oss took Renata to the guest room Gabriel had previously occupied and efficiently transferred her to the bed and tucked her in.

"Thank you," Renata murmured, barely audible.

"What about food?" Mrs. Oss asked. "Could I get her ginger ale or toast…?"

Gabriel shook his head. It was amazing how quickly people could forget about the day-to-day challenges they faced. "She can't have anything by mouth. I gave her a feeding already."

Mrs. Oss pinked. "How could I forget! I knew that."

"I hope it's not a stomach bug," Gabriel said. "I don't know if I'm supposed to do anything about her tube if she throws up. Or if I should feed her again if she does… I don't want her sugar to tank."

"If she starts throwing up her formula, she'll need an IV," Mrs. Oss said. "We can't let her get dehydrated or hypoglycemic."

"So, the hospital?"

Mrs. Oss shook her head. "I have a friend who has given Carmel an IV before, here at the house. Going to the hospital, exposing her to all of the viruses and sources of infection that are rampant…"

"She would come and give a random guest an IV? Without a prescription?"

Mrs. Oss smiled. "I think we could convince her."

"Good. She didn't want to go to the hospital."

The woman nodded understandingly. "We'll avoid it if at all possible."

When Mrs. Oss left them alone, Carmel looked at Gabriel. "So what did you want to do? Did you want to work on research, or sit with her, or…?"

"Renata's better at the medical research then I am and I really don't want to leave her, in case things go south."

Carmel nodded understandingly. "I have a laptop, if you want to borrow it and work in here."

Gabriel wasn't sure whether he would be able to focus on it with Renata, but he nodded. "Yeah, that would be great. Thanks."

CHAPTER FIFTEEN

Caleb was having trouble settling into the routine at Uncle Kris's house. Mainly, because there didn't seem to be any routine or set rules. Sometimes Uncle Kris was home when Caleb got back from school, but sometimes he wasn't, and he had given Caleb a key to let himself in. Caleb had never gone home to an empty house before. Mom had always been there to meet him, no matter what else might be going on. Caleb wasn't sure what Uncle Kris's working hours were, or even what his job was. Uncle Kris didn't like it when he asked questions, which left Caleb feeling like he was out swimming in the middle of the ocean, surrounded by unknown dangers.

He found the door unlocked, which meant that Uncle Kris was home. Caleb didn't know if it was better or worse when Uncle Kris was home after school. Caleb thought he might like it better when he was alone.

Uncle Kris was in the kitchen getting a drink. He looked at Caleb with a sour expression, then looked at his watch.

"Is it that late already?" He swore. "I should have been out of here by now. Get yourself something to eat. A sandwich or leftovers from the fridge. Get your homework done. I won't be home until late."

Caleb frowned and tried to unwind Uncle Kris's rapid-fire instructions.

"Eight?" he repeated. "Back after eight?"

"No. *Late.*" Uncle Kris pointed to his mouth, drawing out the L sound.

"Pay attention!" He gave Caleb a little push on the shoulder. "I'll be home *late.*"

Caleb nodded, drawing back out of Uncle Kris's reach. "Late," he repeated. "Be late."

Uncle Kris muttered something as he turned away from Caleb. Caleb wasn't sure what it was, but decided not to ask more questions.

Uncle Kris put a bottle back in the cupboard and slammed the cupboard door shut. It bounced back open, and he slammed it again, keeping his hand on it to hold it shut. Caleb backed up. Uncle Kris glared at him.

"Don't look at me like that. Did I touch you?"

Caleb shook his head and took another step back. He wasn't sure how not to look like he did, but it was probably better if he were out of sight, then Uncle Kris couldn't complain about how he looked.

Uncle Kris took a couple of steps toward him. "You think it's so bad here? You've got no idea how bad things could be. Do you know what it was like when I was your age?"

Caleb retreated faster, fleeing to his room. But Uncle Kris followed him, and there was no lock on the door.

"Don't walk away from me when I'm talking to you!"

Caleb took off his backpack and pretended he had just been coming to the room to get his books out and organize his homework.

Uncle Kris towered over him. Caleb had never realized how tall he was before. As he had several times before, Uncle Kris grabbed Caleb by the front of his jacket and shirt and pulled him closer, lifting him up so that Caleb had to stand on his tiptoes.

"If I'm talking to you, you stay and listen! You're lucky, my daddy woulda beat the hell out of me for that kind of insubordinance."

Caleb tried to work through the word, replaying it on his lips and trying to match it up with a word he had heard or read before.

Uncle Kris slapped him across the face. Caleb stiffened with shock.

"I—"

"Don't act like a moron! You think I don't know what kind of grades you get at school? You're not stupid. So don't play that game with me."

Caleb fluttered his hand beside his face. He didn't understand why Uncle Kris was angry. The man's foul breath was hot on Caleb's face, spittle spraying when he talked.

"Don't—"

Uncle Kris hit him again, slapping him across the opposite ear. The sound processor flew off Caleb's head on the other side. Caleb tried to catch it and to keep it properly connected, but failed, and it fell to the floor somewhere. Caleb brought his hands up to cover both ears.

"Don't hit Caleb!"

Uncle Kris shoved him, and Caleb was thrown back onto the bed, which seemed a much better place to fall than the floor. Caleb screwed his eyes shut, which meant he couldn't see the subsequent blows coming. His stomach, his chest, his side. Caleb curled up in a ball, trying to protect himself. The blows stopped, and Caleb squinted through his eyelids, cracked just a tiny bit open. Uncle Kris was still shouting, but Caleb couldn't make out what he was saying. Uncle Kris turned on his heel and marched back out of the bedroom.

Caleb stayed on the bed and waited to see if Uncle Kris was going to come back. He reached out and touched the wall, feeling for the vibrations as Uncle Kris stomped around the house, and then as the front door slammed.

He stayed there for a long time, feeling for any more vibrations, any sign that Uncle Kris was still in the house and might come back. But the walls were silent and still.

The places where Uncle Kris's blows had fallen ached. Caleb rubbed them, feeling his heartbeat pulsing in each one. He slid out of the bed and crawled across the floor to where his sound processor had fallen. He reconnected it and wrapped it around his ear. He put his head down on the carpet and closed his eyes.

CHAPTER SIXTEEN

Renata stirred and turned over. Gabriel watched her, waiting to see if she were going to wake up, making sure that she didn't tangle up her line. He looked at the clock, wondering if it was time to try for another feeding.

"No!" Renata protested.

"Sh," Gabriel soothed. "It's okay."

Her hand explored the IV on her opposite arm, eyes still closed. "No. No hospitals. I told you…"

"No hospitals. You're not in a hospital."

Her eyes opened and she turned her head to look at him. "Gabriel?"

"Yeah. It's okay. You're alright."

She lay staring straight up at the ceiling. Gabriel waited for her eyes to droop and for her to drop off to sleep again. She had woken several times, but each time she fell back asleep within the minute.

"Where are we?"

"Carmel's."

"Still?"

"Yeah."

Renata felt the IV in her arm, frowning. She eventually raised her head to look down at her arm, and up at the IV bag hanging from one of the posts of the bed. She looked around the rest of the room.

"I have an IV."

"It's just dextrose."

Renata rubbed her eyes, looking at it.

"I could react—"

"D5W," Gabriel assure her. "That's all."

"No Ringer's?"

"No."

She let out a breath. "Good. Who put it in?"

"Friend of Carmel's mother." Gabriel raised a hand to silence any protests. "She doesn't know anything. You're just a friend of Carmel's who got a bad case of the flu while sleeping over. No point in extreme measures for a bit of dehydration. She didn't see your tube. Doesn't know anything about us."

"Did she see you?"

"No."

Renata closed her eyes again. Gabriel waited for her breathing to lengthen. Renata rubbed her forehead.

"Feeling better."

"Yeah? Good. Just a twenty-four hour bug."

She nodded.

In a few hours, Renata was up, disconnected from her IV, prowling the house restlessly. The IV had apparently made her mitochondria happy, and she had more than her usual energy. But Gabriel was worried that the extra burst of energy had brought with it a higher level of vigilance.

"Carmel is in communication with Judge Dee-Dee," Renata pointed out to Gabriel when Carmel left the room to talk to her mother. "How do you know she's not calling her right now to tell her where we are? She's always been jealous of me. She wants me out of the way so she has you to herself."

Gabriel laughed. "Carmel's just a friend. She's not jealous of you, and you don't need to be… *worried* about her." Gabriel carefully avoided using the word *paranoid*. "If she wanted to turn us in to Judge Dee-Dee before, she could have. But she didn't. Judge Dee-Dee doesn't want to have to have us arrested anyway. She wants us out here, where we can do good work. She's the one who suggested we look at Caleb, why would she stop us now?"

"Carmel didn't invite you here just as a friendly gesture. She wants something. She wants you."

"Then calling the police wouldn't get her what she wanted, would it? She can't have me arrested and have me around."

Renata went to the doorway and looked out, listening and watching to see what Carmel and her mother were doing.

"They put an IV into me. They could have given me something. Something to make me sick, or to track me, or nanobots to do something else."

"I was here the whole time. It was just D5W."

"It was labeled D5W, that doesn't mean that's what it really was."

"She didn't put anything in your IV," Gabriel assured her. "She just made sure your blood sugar didn't crash because you got sick."

"I don't trust her," Renata muttered. "My mom tried to poison me. Why would I expect Carmel's mother to be any different?"

"I watched the whole time. You're not feeling sick or in pain, are you? If it was poison, you'd be feeling worse, not better."

Renata paced across the room, then back to the door.

"Jumping out of my skin. We need to get out of here."

Normally, Gabriel would go with Renata's instinct when she said it was time to move on. But he didn't want to end up stranded with her somewhere if her energy flagged again.

"You need to stay here until you've had a good night's sleep and I know you're stable. You don't want to end up in hospital, right?"

"No."

Gabriel cast his mind around for something to take her thoughts off of Carmel and escaping.

"Do you want the laptop? You wanted to do some medical research."

Renata looked at him like he was crazy. "I can't do research at a time like this."

"A time like what?"

"When we're—when I'm—"

"When you're sick? You can lay down again if you need to sleep."

"No... give me the laptop, then."

Gabriel picked it up from the floor beside the chair where he had left it.

"Do you want to sit on the bed?"

She nodded, and after a few more moments peering out the bedroom door, she returned to the bed and sat down. Gabriel handed the computer to her.

"Sure you're up to it?"

"Of course I am! No stupid bug is going to keep me down for long."

Gabriel smiled in satisfaction as she opened the computer lid and got to work.

Carmel rolled up to the doorway in her wheelchair. "Hey, supper is on, Gabe."

Gabriel looked at Renata. "Do you mind if I…"

"Yeah, go ahead."

"I can bring it back in here. Do you want me to sit with you?"

"I'm busy and I don't want to smell your nauseating food. Go enjoy it in the company of your lady friend."

Gabriel looked at her. "There's nothing going on between Carmel and me. We're just that—friends."

"Go." Renata flapped her hand at him, shooing him out.

Gabriel obeyed and followed Carmel out of the room.

"Is she okay?"

Gabriel nodded. "Sorry. She's a little… anxious right now. Hopefully, she'll get into her research and she'll forget to be paranoid about everybody else."

"It's fine. I'm just worried about her."

"She's sort of… stuck on you being interested in me. Like the two of you are rivals." Gabriel shook his head.

Carmel gave him a puzzled look.

Gabriel raised his hands in a shrug. "It's just part of her illness."

"Sure."

Gabriel inhaled the scent of the cooking food as he walked into the kitchen. "That smells great, Mrs. Oss. I'm drooling already!"

She gave him a big smile. "No need to flatter me. Sit down, sit down. Did Renata want to come out and sit with us and visit? She doesn't need to stay in the bedroom just because she isn't eating."

"No. She's going to do some work on the computer." Gabriel exchanged looks with Carmel and didn't explain in any greater detail.

"The computer will still be there later…"

"It's okay. Really. She needs some time to herself."

Mrs. Oss nodded and motioned again for them to sit down.

———

After dinner, feeling full and happy, Gabriel went back to the bedroom to see how Renata was getting along. Having taken care of his own physical needs, he was a little calmer and more patient with regard to Renata's suspicions. It wasn't like she could help what she thought, and it wasn't really anything to do with Gabriel. He couldn't do anything about it, so there really wasn't any point in getting wrapped up in her anxieties and trying to talk her out of them.

Renata didn't even look up when he walked into the room. So much for her jealousy toward Carmel. As soon as she started working on medical research, everything else took a back burner.

Gabriel looked over the books in the bookcase beside the bed and picked out a mystery that looked interesting. He did his best to immerse himself in the story, but he couldn't keep focused on it, and kept reading the same page over and over again.

"I know you haven't had enough time," he said to Renata, "I'm just wondering if you've got any leads."

Renata nodded without looking up from the glow of her LCD screen. "Yeah. A few."

"So maybe there is a medical explanation for what Caleb went through, and it wasn't a problem with bonding or neglect or Munchausen?"

"It's thirteen years ago, so it's not like we can be sure, unless it's something that stays in his system or produces antibodies that are still there now. We can speculate, but whether we can actually find something that can be proven… that's another story. But there are some real possibilities."

"It will help. It doesn't prove that they're not abusive, but each thing in their report that we can disprove… eventually, they'll have to admit that it isn't a case of abuse, just undiagnosed medical issues."

"Maybe."

"Maybe?"

"You're working on the assumption that there is no abuse."

"Well, yes. We have to start somewhere."

"I'm not willing to start there. Maybe there isn't abuse, but I'm not going to assume."

"We know she's not an alcoholic—"

"You assume she's not an alcoholic."

"There was no alcohol in the house. With an unexpected DFS visit. There was no way for them to know that they were going to get a home visit that day. No way for them to know that they should clear out any bottles."

"Riley Hibbert was at home when she got word that Caleb was at the police station, and that he wouldn't be released to her. She knew the jig was up at that point. She could have disposed of the evidence, knowing that they were going to want to inspect the home sooner or later."

Gabriel frowned, thinking it through. "Yeah. I guess you're right."

"Your problem is that you don't think like a criminal. You assume that everyone is innocent."

"Isn't that what we're supposed to do? Innocent until proven guilty?"

"Not with DFS."

"No," Gabriel sighed. "Never with DFS."

"If your goal is to take kids out of the home, you start with the presumption of guilt."

Gabriel looked back down at his paperback and started reading again. They couldn't rush things. Caleb was, hopefully, in a safe foster home. He would be okay until they managed to figure out how to get him back home, assuming his parents were, in fact, innocent. He didn't get the same vibe off of Mr. Hibbert as he had gotten off of Leva, but it had taken more than one meeting with Leva for him to realize there was something wrong with her. He hadn't twigged to it immediately.

The evening drew on, and Gabriel's eyelids were getting heavy. He hadn't slept during the day like Renata had. They always went to sleep as early as they could when they were sleeping rough, knowing that they would get rousted in the early morning hours before dawn.

Renata took a deep breath in, and looked up from her screen. "Okay."

"Okay? What have you got?"

"More than one option, actually. But the one that floats to the top of my list is Cytomegalovirus."

"Cytomega…"

"Cytomegalovirus. CMV. We might be looking at a case of congenital CMV infection."

"What would the symptoms of CMV infection be?"

"Low birth weight or prematurity. Hearing loss. Seizures. Delayed milestones. Liver problems could show up as jaundice."

Gabriel sat up. "You're kidding. So why didn't they diagnose him?"

"Like I said, there are a few things that could cause it. They should have been looking for a cause. With all of the problems he had as a newborn, they should have known it wasn't just a random collection of symptoms. But in looking at Riley's records, it seems like they were just treating each symptom as a separate, discrete problem, rather than as one syndrome with a recognizable constellation of symptoms."

"And CMV isn't something they tested for?"

"I don't know. I asked her to pull together a list of all of the tests that had been done on him, but I don't have anything yet. Maybe she doesn't want to help as much as she would like us to think she does."

"It's pretty uncommon? The doctors wouldn't have recognized it?"

"It's actually really common, but most babies don't have any symptoms. It's just dormant. But some babies get really sick, like Caleb did."

"So if we could prove..." Gabriel trailed off. They had already discussed that. They couldn't prove what he'd had thirteen years prior. Not unless there were tests done at the time that showed he did have CMV. "I mean... if we could show that this is a possibility..."

"I don't know that it would make DFS reconsider the case," Renata said. "But it's something. It's a start."

———

Caleb awoke with a start at the presence of someone in his room. He blinked his eyes blearily in the dark, looking around. When he lived at home, sometimes Mom or Dad came into his room at night, especially when he was sick. Maybe Uncle Kris had heard him throwing up earlier and had come in to see if he were feeling better. Caleb rolled over to face Uncle Kris as the silhouette approached the side of his bed.

He couldn't see Uncle Kris's face well enough to see what he was saying. He could smell the drink coming off of his skin and in his foul breath. He thought that Uncle Kris might be sick too, he could smell the putrid smell of stomach acid as well as the drink.

Uncle Kris sat on the edge of the bed beside Caleb, still talking and breathing in his face. Caleb pulled back slightly, nauseated. Uncle Kris's movements were slow and loose, not the tight, fast movements like when he was angry. When they went out to eat together, Uncle Kris was usually calm and pleasant. Any other time of day, Caleb had to be on the alert, not sure what to expect.

Uncle Kris reached over and ruffled Caleb's hair like he used to do all the time when he came to visit when Caleb still lived with Mom and Dad. Caleb still couldn't make his lips out in the darkness, but he thought he could see Uncle Kris calling him 'buddy,' like he did so often when he rubbed Caleb's head and was in a good mood.

His hand was warm and gentle, comforting Caleb. He imagined Uncle Kris saying, "I'm sorry you're so sick, buddy. Just relax and I'll sit with you for a few minutes until you fall back asleep. You'll feel better in the morning."

Caleb closed his eyes, nestling into his cozy nest of blankets, pretending that it was Dad sitting with him instead of Uncle Kris. Uncle Kris stroked his hair. Caleb rolled over onto his stomach and Uncle Kris rubbed his back, his hand soothing the knots and aches. Caleb let out a contented sigh. He could almost imagine that he was back home again, that he was safe, and that everything was going to be okay.

Uncle Kris lifted the edge of the blankets and slid his legs in underneath, followed by the rest of his body.

Caleb stiffened in surprise. Was Uncle Kris feeling too sick to make it back to his own room? He had probably been telling Caleb what he was doing, but without his sound processor, Caleb hadn't been able to hear him, or to see what he said in the darkness of the room. Caleb moved over to make space for Uncle Kris.

Sometimes, when he was very sick, Mom let Caleb lie down with her on her bed, and she would rub his back and cuddle with him and try to help him to sleep. Uncle Kris started to rub Caleb's back again. After a few minutes, he lifted and pushed back Caleb's shoulder, turning Caleb's body toward him so they were face-to-face. Uncle Kris kissed him on the forehead and then on the cheek.

He pressed his warm body against Caleb's, cuddling close.

CHAPTER SEVENTEEN

Caleb slid into his seat slowly, trying not to disturb the class, but his desk slid sideways a little, making a loud scraping noise that made everyone look up or turn around.

Mrs. Bradshaw looked at Caleb. "Everybody back to work," she instructed the students. She walked over to Caleb's desk. "Would you come with me for a moment, Caleb?"

Caleb looked at her, uncertain what to do.

"Come," Mrs. Bradshaw said, making a motion toward the door of the classroom. "Please."

Caleb didn't want to get back up again, but she didn't change her mind, waiting for him to do as he was asked. Caleb gave a deep sigh, and leaned forward to get up. His body didn't want to move. Parts of his body throbbed. Caleb just wanted to sit down in his desk and rest.

Mrs. Bradshaw took him out into the hallway, and closed the door behind her so that the class couldn't hear what they were saying.

"Why are you late again today?"

Caleb swallowed and looked down at the floor. "Caleb's alarm," he said. "Didn't wake up. Missed the bus."

"Why didn't your alarm wake you up?"

Caleb snapped his fingers beside his face.

"Caleb." Mrs. Bradshaw touched Caleb's arm, trying to get him to stop stimming and lower his hand.

Caleb raised his other hand, covering his eye and smoothing his eyebrow. "Didn't wake up. Caleb didn't wake up."

"Maybe you need to set a louder alarm. Or set it to go off earlier. Maybe put it across the room so you have to get up to shut it off."

Caleb shook his head quickly. "On my bed. Can't hear it."

"Then you need to turn it up or put it somewhere you can hear it."

"No." Caleb touched his sound processor and mimed taking it off. "Can't hear at night. Alarm…" He touched her hand lightly and vibrated his hand against it.

Mrs. Bradshaw's expression cleared. "You have a vibrating alarm on your bed. Because you have to take your hearing aid out at night."

Caleb nodded.

"Can you adjust it? Make it vibrate harder? Put it closer to you?"

Caleb gave a helpless shrug. Even though he had sometimes ignored his alarm and gone back to sleep when he was living with Mom and Dad, he'd always felt it go off in the morning. The problem wasn't with the alarm.

"Maybe your mom—maybe you uncle could help you to wake up on time? Could you ask him to check in on you to make sure that you get up?"

Caleb shook his head. He never knew what time Uncle Kris was going to be up. Sometimes he was up before Caleb was in the morning, sometimes he was still asleep when Caleb headed to school. Sometimes he wasn't there at all and Caleb didn't know whether he had left early in the morning, or not gotten home in the night. He wasn't going to ask Uncle Kris to wake him up. Even when Uncle Kris was in a good mood, he didn't like Caleb asking him for things. He told him to take care of himself. Uncle Kris wasn't his mother and hadn't asked for Caleb to come stay with him. He'd never planned on being the parent of a thirteen-year-old boy.

"You can't keep being late. Your marks are going down, and I think part of the reason for that is that you're not getting here for all of your morning lessons. You need to be here to learn. I can't give you a separate, individual lesson. There are a lot of students who need extra help, not just you. And they are here in the morning when they're supposed to be."

Caleb nodded, looking down at his shoes. He noticed that his toe was starting to push its way through the top of his shoe. Mom would have taken him out to shop for new shoes and made him throw the old ones away.

Sometimes, Caleb pretended to throw something away, but then he hid it in his room so he didn't have to get rid of it. He didn't like parting with his possessions.

Mrs. Bradshaw looked down at Caleb's shoe and gave a little smile. "Boys your age grow out of their clothes so fast! Sometimes it seems like they grow three inches in a month." She looked at his face and frowned a little. "You're growing up so fast."

Caleb stood there, waiting. Eventually, Mrs. Bradshaw opened the classroom door again. There was a burst of noise, giving away the antics that had been going on while the students were unsupervised, and then sudden silence as they pretended they had been working hard the whole time.

Caleb walked back to his desk and looked around to see what books everyone else had out. He sat down and waited for Mrs. Bradshaw to show him what to do.

———

Renata hadn't wanted to meet with Riley Hibbert at her home again. She had wanted to set up their meeting to be somewhere they were less likely to be followed or surveilled. The van that had pulled across the street during the previous visit sent her paranoia buzzing out of control, and she didn't want to be trapped in there again.

But the big binders full of medical records were too heavy and unwieldy to take to an apparently casual meeting at the mall or the park. Even taking them to the library would be difficult to explain; they were just too large. Renata needed to review them. Not just the infant years; she might have questions about Caleb's symptoms at other ages and couldn't predict whether she would need all of the books or just one or two.

So she agreed to meet there again, but she and Gabriel took a hard look around before she would go into the house. They checked every car and van on the street, looking for anyone who shouldn't be sitting there or for any unexplained mirrors, antennas, or other equipment. It took an hour just to check all of the vehicles, houses, and vantage points on the Hibberts' street. That still left the back alley for Gabriel to patrol looking for anything else that might be suspicious while Renata was inside.

Finally, Renata decided it was safe to go in.

She knocked on the back door, and it took Riley a few minutes to get there and open it. She was confused by Renata going to the back door instead of the front, and not using the doorbell.

"Hi. Uh, come in. Is everything okay?"

"I don't like meeting here," Renata told her bluntly. "If we didn't need the books, I wouldn't have come here. We should find somewhere less obvious."

"Oh. I'm sorry, then. But no one knows you're here. Only Wes and me."

And Gabriel. And Carmel, if Gabriel had updated her. And Judge Dee-Dee, if Carmel had told her. And maybe everyone on the police force, if Judge Dee-Dee had decided it was time to shut the Underground Railway down. Renata drummed her fingers anxiously on the side of her leg.

"Let's get at it, then," Riley said. "I don't want to keep you here any longer than you are comfortable."

Too late.

Renata followed Riley to the kitchen table, which Riley had picked as the best place to spread out the books and be able to access everything at once. Renata glanced over everything.

"Did you make me a list?" she demanded. If Riley hadn't completed the assignment Renata had given her, Renata wasn't going to believe a word she said about wanting her son back. If she wanted Caleb back, she would do whatever Renata asked her to, even if it were difficult and time-consuming.

"A list? Oh, of all of the tests that Caleb had. I put it…" Riley moved the binders around, and pulled out a printed page. "Here it is."

Renata took it from her hand and sat down at the table. About a third of the way down the first page was an entry that she hadn't expected.

CMV: negative

Renata looked up from the page at Riley. Negative? "They tested for CMV?" she asked.

Riley moved to where she could look over Renata's shoulder at the list. Renata pointed to the test.

"Yes."

"And it was negative?"

"That's what I put. So it must have been."

"Check it again. Maybe you were looking at two different things and filled it in wrong."

"I don't think so." But Riley went to the earliest binder, and started moving through the sections. It only took a minute for her to focus in on the photocopied lab sheet. "Here it is."

Renata looked at the test to confirm that it was the CMV test. Then that it was negative. She looked at the top to see whether it was really Caleb's test, or whether they had given Riley someone else's test by mistake. Caleb's name was at the top.

Of course, the lab could have made a mistake. They could have mixed up samples. They could have entered the wrong finding or entered it on the wrong record. There were a dozen ways the results could have been recorded wrong.

Riley was watching Renata's face. "Is that it, then? That was the only possibility?"

Renata rallied. "No. I think it was a congenital infection, but it might have been a different virus, like rubella, or it could have been bacterial. Or even parasitic. There's plenty more to check. That was just at the top of my list."

Riley gave her a tight smile. "Well, at least they thought to test for that. At least they did something right."

Renata nodded. "Sure. Okay. Let's take a look at these other tests. Did you include the tests that you had while you were pregnant?"

"No… those would be in a different book. I didn't think about that. I can go through them while you look at that one."

Renata nodded, her eyes fixed on the page. "Yeah. That would be good."

———

Renata finished going through the various tests Caleb had been put through, flipping through the binders to look at the detailed results for some of them. She shook her head as she looked through the hospital records and Riley's notes and blog posts.

"Find something?" Riley asked.

Renata looked up from the book. "DFS sees Failure to Thrive, and they automatically think addiction, abuse, or neglect. But in cases like this, where you've got so many other things going on with his health, it should be obvious there's a medical problem, even if the doctors weren't able to come up with a proper diagnosis."

"Exactly. We were right there working with the doctors and the hospital staff all the way through this. I wasn't some absentee parent, disappearing for hours or days at a time to go drink. There were never any concerns expressed by the doctors that I smelled like booze or wasn't as attentive as I should be. I didn't even go home at night. I slept there beside him so I'd know if he had a seizure or threw up or had breathing problems. The staff weren't negligent, but they had so many patients to take care of. I could only be sure he was okay if I was there with him."

"So then they assume you're intentionally making him sick."

"We never had any doctors accuse us of that. Not until DFS decided that I was attention-seeking. Did I make him deaf? Did I make him autistic? Or allegedly deaf and allegedly autistic, if you want to use the language in their reports."

"Allegedly deaf," Renata repeated. "How can he be allegedly deaf? He's got a cochlear!"

Riley gave a dramatic shrug and roll of her eyes. She passed Renata a paper. "My prenatal tests."

Renata looked through them thoughtfully. She put her finger under one of the antibody tests. "You didn't have any immunity to toxoplasmosis."

"No. I don't remember that very well. The doctor said it was a really common infection, about half the world's population has it, but it wasn't something they could immunize against. That's the one where you're supposed to avoid kitty litter, undercooked meats, and soft cheeses, right?"

Renata was impressed. "That's the one," she agreed.

"It's some kind of worm?"

"It's a parasite. But not a worm. It's a single-cell organism. So it can get right inside your cells, right into the neurons themselves."

"And it could infect Caleb if I got it while I was pregnant."

"Yeah. That's why they tested you. They should have kept monitoring it through your pregnancy. They only did the test once?"

"Yes… they told me what things to watch out for. They didn't say I needed to be retested."

"They should have."

"How could I have gotten infected? I did everything they said. I didn't eat anything they said not to. We didn't have a cat. We've never had a cat."

Renata didn't answer immediately. She looked away for a few minutes, then back at Riley.

"Have you always been a gardener?" she asked, thinking of the gardens surrounding the house.

Riley sighed, looking out the window. "I don't have nearly the time I used to to work on it. I used to do so much more."

"So, digging around in flower beds, you could still come into contact with toxoplasmosis. It can survive in the soil for a year or more. You can't see it. Even if you were aware of it and used gloves, there wasn't any time that you walked out to the car and pulled out a weed in a flower bed you were walking past?"

"Yes. Of course I have. It could be that easy? I could pull a weed and have that cause all of Caleb's problems? That seems…" she searched for a word. "It's just… unfair. How can you avoid this bug?"

"You really can't. There are parts of the world where ninety percent of the population has been infected. You can do all of the right things, trying to keep your hands clean and not eating the things that normally carry toxo, and still get it."

"But I wasn't sick."

"You don't have to be. A high percentage of cases are asymptomatic. And the most common symptoms are just like flu. Swollen lymph nodes, achiness, not even a fever."

Riley looked at the list of tests she had given Renata earlier. "And they never tested Caleb for it?"

Renata picked it back up again, studying it closely. She felt a strange excitement building inside of her. A growing certainty that she was right. She had found the answer.

"No. He was never tested. There are some countries that test all newborns, but most of them don't. Costs too much money."

"Is there any way for us to know if he did have it? I mean, even if we were able to have him tested for antibodies now and he was positive, that would just mean that he's had it at some time. It wouldn't necessarily mean he had it when he was born."

"No. You'd have to be able to test his blood when he was born. Did you bank his cord blood? I thought in one of your blogs…" Renata reached for the binder to check, but Riley was already nodding.

"Yes. There was a lot of talk about how it might be used for blood transfusions or autoimmune treatments someday, and we thought, 'why would you not?' Why just dump something that could be so potentially helpful down the line?"

Renata's heart was thumping hard. Not only did they have a potential diagnosis, but they had a way to test whether Caleb had toxoplasmosis when he was born.

"You've got to get ahold of the company that banked it, then. Get a sample of his blood sent to a lab for testing. If we can prove that he had toxo when he was born, then there's an explanation for all of the problems he had. We can prove that it wasn't just Failure to Thrive because of neglect or because you were doing something to make him sicker."

"And do you think that will make a difference? Is DFS even going to care at this point? They already took Caleb away from us. What are the chances they're going to change their minds?"

"Not good," Renata admitted. "Even when they are proven wrong, they tend to say he's in danger if he's in your care anyway, even if there's no reason for it. They're stubborn."

CHAPTER EIGHTEEN

Caleb paced back and forth anxiously. It was the first chance that he'd had to see his parents since he had been taken away from them, and he was impatient to get started.

"Are you ready to go?" Uncle Kris asked.

Caleb nodded. "Ready. Let's go."

"You got your coat?"

Caleb held it up.

"You need to put it on."

Caleb didn't argue, but pushed his arms into the sleeves. "Ready. Ready to go."

"Okay." Uncle Kris patted him on the back. "Let's go see your mom and dad, then."

In the car, Caleb wanted Uncle Kris to drive faster, even though he knew it was against the law. He didn't want to be in an accident. He'd been in an accident before, while Mom was driving, and it was scary. He didn't want to go through that again. But he wanted to get there faster. He wanted to get home and to be able to go to his room and see his things and to see Mom and Dad again.

"Where are we going?" Looking out the window, Caleb could see they had missed the turnoff to go home. Uncle Kris was going the wrong way.

Uncle Kris looked over at him, eyebrows up. Then he shook his head.

"Did you think we were going to the house? No, we have to go some-where else for the meeting. DFS wouldn't let us do it at your house."

"Home is where Caleb's things are."

"It doesn't matter. They're not going to let you go there. It was to be a supervised visit on neutral ground."

"Why?"

"Who knows? It isn't like they won't be able to get you away again if you go back to your house. Maybe they're worried about firearms. That Wes and Riley could try to take you back by force or threaten to hurt you."

Caleb shook his head. "They wouldn't!"

"No. Of course not. But DFS has lots of rules. They don't make sense in every case, but they have to follow the rules all the time just in case."

"I want to go home."

"Of course you do. I'd take you there if I could, but then they would take you away from me and put you in some foster home or group home where you didn't know anybody. You want to stay with me, don't you? Better to stay with Uncle Kris than to be sent to some home where you didn't have any idea what it was going to be like."

Caleb thought about that and didn't answer. Would it be better to have to go to a different home instead of staying with Uncle Kris? When he had stayed at the group home before he had been sent to Uncle Kris's house, he hadn't liked it. He didn't like other people touching his things or making fun of him. And they had forced him to follow new rules there, too. The other boys had told him he'd be punished if he didn't follow the rules. That was the way it worked at a group home. Was that any better than living with Uncle Kris? At least at Uncle Kris's, he had his own bedroom and Uncle Kris usually left him alone and didn't tell him what he had to do.

"You okay?"

Caleb looked at Uncle Kris and saw he was looking at Caleb with a frown. Caleb nodded his head up and down, not really wanting to answer.

"Why are you looking so serious all of the sudden? Don't you want to see your mom and dad?"

"I do."

Uncle Kris drove for a few minutes without saying anything. Then he spoke. "You don't want your parents to be worried about you. So you need to be careful of what you say to them. They'll want to know that you're happy and doing okay living with me. Understand?"

Caleb nodded, but he wasn't sure he did understand exactly what Uncle Kris meant. Maybe if Mom and Dad knew about how Uncle Kris got mad sometimes, they wouldn't want him to stay there. Maybe they'd tell him it was better to live in a group home.

"You tell them you're happy and having a good time," Uncle Kris ordered. "You don't want them to be worried about you."

"Okay."

"There are some pretty nasty foster homes out there. You don't want to end up in the type of home I lived in when I was growing up."

Caleb was pretty sure that Uncle Kris had grown up in the same place as Dad had, but Dad had never said what it was like there. Caleb knew that Dad's mom and dad were dead. But he didn't know what they were like when they were alive.

"What are you going to tell them?" Uncle Kris drilled.

"I like it and we're having a good time."

"Try putting a smile on your face when you say it."

Caleb looked out the window, wondering how long it was going to take before they got there.

———

"Mom!" Caleb launched himself at Mom, arms out, running straight into her and giving her a tight squeeze so she would give him one back. She turned her body as he tackled her, so that he ran into her side instead of her front, and she staggered back a step or two. Then she was hugging him back, squeezing tight and giving him a kiss on the top of his head, his forehead, and both of his cheeks, until Caleb withdrew, protesting.

"No kissing, Mom!"

She laughed. "You say you don't want kisses, but I know better! Oh, give me another squeeze."

Caleb wrapped his arms around her and tightened his arms like a boa constrictor.

"Whoa, too tight." Mom loosened his arms. "No squashing me to death."

"You like it," he teased her.

More hugging and kissing, then Caleb squirmed away again. He went to Dad and hugged him, but not as vigorously as he had Riley. Dad ruffled his hair and kissed him on top of the head. "How have you been, buddy? It's so good to see you again."

Caleb snuggled into Dad's body. "Missed you too."

Dad pulled back after a minute, but Caleb clung to him. "Come on, Caleb. Let's sit down."

He extricated himself from Caleb's hold and the three of them sat down on a tattered loveseat, with Caleb squished between Mom and Dad, sitting on both of their laps and putting his arms around both of them. Riley laughed and snuggled with him.

"So, how has it been at Uncle Kris's?" Dad asked.

"Good. It's good and we have fun," Caleb said.

Dad looked over at Uncle Kris, who had stayed in the visiting room and was sitting in a stained armchair.

"I'll bet Uncle Kris lets you get away with all kinds of things that Mom wouldn't."

Caleb pressed his cheek against Mom's. "I miss Mom."

"Of course you do. We both miss you too. We're doing everything we can to get you back, but it takes time to get anything done."

Mr. Searle, sitting outside of their circle and pretending to be reading through a report, spoke up. "No discussion of Caleb returning home."

They were all quiet for a few minutes.

"Having fun with Uncle Kris," Caleb echoed.

"That's good. You've always liked Uncle Kris, haven't you?"

Caleb tried to think of how to answer the question. He did not always like Uncle Kris, but Uncle Kris had told him not to say that he was unhappy there, or he would be moved somewhere worse.

"It's good and fun."

"How is school?" Mom asked. "Are you keeping up?"

Caleb thought about Mrs. Bradshaw. "Mrs. Bradshaw says Caleb's getting tall."

"You are!" Mom agreed. "Next time I see you, you're going to be taller than I am!"

Caleb stuck out his foot. "Caleb needs new shoes."

"You're growing right through the ends of those! Kris, do you think you could take him out and get some new shoes? I'll give you the money. Just don't let him tell you he needs the most expensive ones. He's growing so fast, he'll bleed us dry."

Uncle Kris's face was red. "I can afford to buy him shoes," he growled. "I just didn't notice that he needed them."

"I'm not criticizing you. He probably needed new ones before he even came to stay with you."

Uncle Kris still looked angry. Caleb hid his face against Mom's shoulder. Mom rubbed his shoulder. "It's okay, Caleb. We're not fighting. We're just having a discussion. Nobody is mad."

"You buy Caleb shoes."

"I can't take you out shopping. Uncle Kris will have to take you so that you get something that fits you properly. If I just guess, they won't fit you."

"No. You."

"Uncle Kris will do just fine. And when you get new shoes, what happens to these?"

Caleb kicked his feet and didn't answer.

"Caleb. When you get new shoes, these ones go in the garbage," Mom instructed.

Caleb knew there wasn't any point arguing about it. Uncle Kris didn't like him keeping things, and would throw them out even if Caleb wanted to keep them.

"In the garbage," he echoed.

"That's right. So school is good?"

Caleb nodded.

"There has been a noticeable dip in his marks," Mr. Searle contributed, looking up from his report again. "But that's pretty normal with the disruption in his circumstances. Kids get distracted by being moved to a new home and have trouble focusing. It's good that he's been able to stay in the same class so that he hasn't missed anything."

Mom nodded understandingly and rubbed Caleb's head. "You make sure you ask for help when you need it."

Caleb looked over at Uncle Kris.

"Yes, you can ask Uncle Kris when you need help too," Mom said.

But that wasn't what Caleb had been thinking.

"He's still racking up tardies," Mr. Searle contributed.

"You need to get up on time," Mom told Caleb. "You can't sleep in and loll around all morning. You know you need to be a big boy and get yourself up in time to catch the bus."

"I do," Caleb protested. He tried to always get up when his alarm went.

He tried to get himself ready for school, but lots of times he failed, and usually that meant he had to walk to school, which took time.

Uncle Kris was scowling.

"It's his executive function," Mom said. "Getting organized and to school is a lot of little steps to keep track of. Autism makes that hard to do."

"He's old enough to get himself ready for school," Uncle Kris said.

Mr. Searle nodded agreement.

"He may be old enough," Mom said, "but you have to accommodate his disabilities. He can't take care of himself any more than he can hear without his cochlear implant. If you expect him to do something that is beyond his ability, you're just setting him up for failure. You need to help him to be more independent, giving him the right supports, not taking them away."

"Nobody is taking any supports away," Mr. Searle disagreed. "He still has all the same services he had at home."

"But it's not just services."

"You're not parenting him right now. You need to let Kris determine the right course of action."

Mom's voice rose, making Caleb shrink back from her. "How can you expect someone who has no parenting experience or training to take care of a teenager with disabilities? I have thirteen years' worth of experience taking care of Caleb. I've done all of the training, all of the classes. I'm the one who has been by his side since he was born. I know how to take care of him better than anyone else."

Mr. Searle showed his teeth in a shark-like smile. "I'm glad you brought up training and classes. DFS has received your multiple complaints about the way this case has been handled and the challenges you have made to the evidence. A determination has been made that this information will not be reviewed until you have both taken parenting classes."

"He's thirteen! Why would we need parenting classes? We've already learned all of that."

"There are new advancements. New suggestions as to how to handle things. If it's been a while since you took classes, things may have changed significantly since then. There has been a lot more information published the last few years about managing autism and the various issues Caleb has."

"Do you think we're not up on all of the latest research? Have you even looked at my website?"

Mr. Searle's expression did not change, but his voice was colder than ever.

"If you want to have Caleb's case reviewed, you need to do your part. We need to see that you're taking this seriously and would be ready to provide the best possible experience for Caleb if he was returned to your custody."

"Mom," Caleb touched Mom's cheek. "Want to go home."

"I know you do. And I want you to come home." She sighed and looked at Searle, shaking her head. "We'll take whatever classes you want us to. But you and I both know that we don't need them."

Mr. Searle didn't smile and agree.

———

The visit was too short. When Mr. Searle said it was time for Caleb to go home, he had at first been happy. He wanted to go home. But when it became clear that Mr. Searle didn't mean it was time to go home with Mom and Dad, but with Uncle Kris, Caleb's anger welled up from his belly and came out in a screaming, molten flow of fury.

Caleb tore at his hair, hit his face, and scratched long, bloody scratches down his arms. When Mom tried to hold him, Mr. Searle made her and Dad leave the room, shouting at her not to interfere. In a few minutes, Mom and Dad had been replaced by a couple of large men who each grabbed one of Caleb's arms to force him to be still. Caleb screamed and thrashed, trying to escape them.

"Go home!" he yelled at Mr. Searle. "Caleb go home!"

His voice was too loud inside his own head, and when Mr. Searle tried to talk to him, Caleb tore the sound processor off of his ear and threw it at him, silencing all of the voices. He could scream and rage as much as he liked without having to suffer the pain of the noise.

The men tried to force him to the ground. As soon as his feet left the floor, Caleb started kicking, still furious, still intent on making sure that no one could stop him from going home. No one could make him go with Uncle Kris. He had to go home. As Mom sometimes said, he wasn't going to take any more of their nonsense.

They managed to get him down on the floor and turn him over, tying his wrists together with a plastic strap. One sat on his legs and also tied his ankles. Caleb thrashed to escape. They picked him up between them and took Caleb to another room, one that was completely empty. They put him in the middle of it and left, pulling the door shut behind them.

Caleb closed his eyes and screamed as loud as he could, giving voice to his rage. No one came back in. After a few minutes, he stopped screaming. No one was coming to get him. No one cared that he was screaming. He couldn't do anything to vent the rage and get it out of his body. He regretted having taken his sound processor out. As he lay there, still, no longer screaming, he was in total silence. He couldn't hear whether anyone was talking to him or calling him through the door. The air was still. The only sound vibrations he could feel through the floor were the low rumble of the heating system.

Caleb lay there for a long time, waiting for someone to come back and get him. His arms hurt the way they were pulled behind his back. After a while, he squirmed and inched his way from the middle of the room over to the wall and pushed himself with his feet to get up into a sitting position. He waited for someone to come in, and still no one came.

Caleb thumped his head back against the wall. It was soft and rubbery, padded like a gym mat, but it still caused a sharp burst of sensation when he banged his head back against it.

He started banging it harder, ignoring the starbursts popping into his vision. He banged harder. He got so dizzy he had to stop for a minute, but then he kept going, losing himself in the swirling darkness and the nausea.

CHAPTER NINETEEN

Searle met with the doctor, not happy about having had to wait for so long to get any answers.

"How is he?"

"He'll be okay," the doctor said, "though he'll probably have a pretty good headache. There is swelling, but it's not to the level that we're going to have to do surgery to relieve the pressure. We sometimes see this kind of injury in kids on the spectrum. You don't know what set him off?"

Searle grunted. "I certainly do. Has he done this before? Been hospitalized for an incident like this?"

The doctor flipped through the pages on his clipboard. "We pulled up what we could of his previous admittance records. I don't see anything like this before. Is he on any medication? If he's stopped taking his meds, that could have triggered something like this..."

"No. He's not on anything right now."

"Might be a good idea to consider it. I can make some recommendations, but you should bring his regular doctor into the loop. Does he have a neurologist or psychologist?"

"I have a list of doctors he has seen before."

"If you don't have anyone who specializes in autism spectrum disorder, I can give you some names. You really should be dealing with someone with expertise."

Searle nodded. "I'll see who is on our approved list. I'm sure we have someone."

The doctor scratched the side of his nose, pushing his glasses up. "I am a little concerned if this is new behavior. In a child with autism, it could indicate that he is sick or in pain. We should dig down deeper to find the cause."

"I don't think there is anything to be concerned about. He's in a different home. Before, his mother would have tried to quiet him down. Maybe she would have succeeded. But he's getting too big for her to handle. He needs to be able to control himself, or to be put somewhere they can look after him properly."

"They've turned him over because they can't handle him anymore?"

Searle hesitated. It would have been easy just to agree and leave it at that. It wouldn't make any difference to the doctor whether it were the truth or not. Then he shook his head.

"No. He was apprehended."

"From a home where they've previously been able to control his self-harming behavior?"

"There's no guarantee that his parents would have been able to head this off either. It was a pretty bad tantrum."

"This isn't a tantrum."

"That's what it looked like. Maybe that's not politically correct, but he was like a two-year-old who had something taken away from him."

"A two-year-old would not have done this to himself. Unless he had autism. You need to lose the idea that this is willful behavior. We need to figure out what we can do to help him. I think medication would be the first step. Then we'll have to see what else we can do for him."

"Can I check in with him now?"

"You can have a look, but he is sedated. You won't be able to talk with him.

Searle took a breath and let it out slowly. "There really isn't any point, then, I suppose." He dug into his pocket and pulled out Caleb's hearing aid. "He threw this while he was having his... fit. I don't think it's broken. He'll need it when he wakes up."

"That he will." The doctor slid it into one of the large pockets of his lab coat. "I hope he hasn't done anything to damage his implant. If he has, he'll need to have surgery to put it back in place."

"When will he be able to go home?"

"If he's calm when he wakes up, he can go home tomorrow. If there still appear to be problems, we might need to keep him here until we can resolve them."

"Alright. I'll let his uncle know."

———

Caleb was in bed for a long time, dozing and feeling fuzzy-headed. He thought that he must be sick, and hoped that Uncle Kris wouldn't be upset with him for missing school. Mr. Searle had also said that Caleb needed to get to school on time, and he'd be mad too.

He realized as the dopiness started to pass away that he wasn't in his bed in Uncle Kris's room, but in a hospital. He'd been in enough hospitals to immediately recognize his surroundings. But it wasn't the Sick Kids hospital, where his mother usually took him. She said that even though he wasn't a little kid anymore, they were still the best hospital to take care of him.

He started to move around restlessly, but his hands were in soft cuffs affixed to the bed, so he couldn't get up or change his position other than to squirm around a little bit.

A doctor came to see him after a while, smiling and pulling the curtain back and talking to Caleb. Caleb shook his head. The doctor put down his clipboard and made hand gestures at Caleb, but Caleb shook his head again, still not understanding. He and Mom had some gestures that they used between them when he didn't have his sound processor on, but they were just things like 'have a drink?' or 'go to sleep.' He had never learned ASL. Caleb looked around for his sound processor. If his Mom had been there, she would have left it all charged up and ready to go for him when he woke up.

The sound processor was on the little shelf beside the bed. Caleb nodded to it. "Need that."

The doctor fetched it for him. Caleb lay still while the doctor figured out how to connect it up, and wrapped it around Caleb's ear. It wasn't sitting properly, so it wasn't comfortable, but at least it was turned on.

"Is that better?"

Caleb nodded. "Better."

"How are you feeling today?"

Caleb wanted to rub his eyes. He was still feeling muzzy and disoriented. "What happened?"

"You had a meltdown. You were hitting your head. You hurt yourself."

Caleb turned his head back and forth, feeling the place on the back of his head that rested on his pillow. It was bandaged and swollen. His head was uncomfortable and he had shimmery edges around his vision that weren't usually there. He thought back to why he would have hurt himself, and gradually the memory of the visit with Mom and Dad and his meltdown when Searle said it was time to go home seeped back into his brain.

"Yeah. Caleb remember."

The doctor sat down on the edge of Caleb's bed, like they were family or friends having a visit. "Do you want to tell me what you were so upset about?"

"Wanted to go home. With Mom."

The doctor nodded slowly. "But you're not living with them anymore."

"Live with Uncle Kris."

"And that's not the same, is it? Even if he is good to you, you still miss your mom."

Caleb nodded. "Miss Mom and Dad."

"Well, we want to see if we can help you to not have a meltdown like that again. We don't want you to hurt yourself. You don't want to hurt yourself, do you?"

"Want Mom."

"We can prescribe you some pills that will help you to be calmer and not get upset so fast. How does that sound?"

Caleb shook his head.

"You want to feel better, don't you?" the doctor prompted.

Caleb couldn't think of a way to argue with that. "Yes."

"We want to help you."

"Don't want pills. Don't need them."

"There's nothing wrong with taking something to help even you out. No one wants to have a meltdown and hurt themselves like that."

Caleb pulled on the wrist restraints. "Take these off?"

"Are you calm? You're not going to hurt yourself again?"

Caleb shook his head, not sure how to answer both questions at once. The doctor leaned over and removed one restraint, and then the other. Caleb pulled his wrists free and held them close to his body, rubbing them.

The doctor watched him, not getting up to go. "You have other bruises on your body too. We couldn't help noticing when we changed you."

Caleb looked down at his hospital gown, his face getting hot. He didn't like thinking about the doctor and nurses taking his clothes off. He flapped his fingers in front of his eye, trying to dissipate the anxiety. The doctor didn't make him stop.

"Can you tell me how you got the other bruises?"

Caleb shook his head. "Caleb is clumsy. Runs into things. Falls down."

The doctor nodded slowly. "I see. I wondered if maybe you were being bothered by kids at school…?"

Caleb had been pushed around and hit by the other boys at school before. He wasn't like them and they didn't like people who were different.

"Some kids hit," he agreed.

"Yes, they do. Can you talk to your teacher or a counselor at school about the kids who hit?"

"No. They'll hit more."

He'd been through that before. He didn't need to have them targeting him again.

"We don't want you getting hurt. Some of those bruises look like they really hurt."

"No."

"They don't hurt?"

Caleb shook his head.

"Who do you live with? Do you live with other kids?"

"No. Just Caleb."

"Who takes care of you?"

"Uncle Kris."

"Does Uncle Kris hit you?"

Caleb's head was bothering him, making him feel like the room was rising and falling, like a boat on the water. He concentrated on the right answer.

"Caleb likes Uncle Kris. We have fun."

"Are you sure?"

The doctor stared at him hard, trying to hold his gaze. Caleb turned his head to the side, avoiding the searchlight gaze. "Are you sure?" he echoed, uncertain how to answer the query. He didn't have any doubt about whether Uncle Kris hit him, or what the right answer was to the question.

"Your Uncle Kris never hits you? Or hurts you in other ways?"

"We have fun. Caleb likes it. Don't want to move."

"Okay… if you change your mind, you need to tell your social worker, okay? Do you understand that? You can tell him anytime. Or tell your teacher at school or another adult that you trust. If Uncle Kris or someone else is hurting you, you need to tell someone. And if kids at school are bullying you, you need to tell that, or it's not going to stop."

Caleb pressed his fingertips to his temples. "You fix my head?"

"Are you in a lot of pain? I can increase the painkillers."

The circling darkness was not far away. Caleb's body was restless and uncomfortable. The pressure in his head made it feel like his ears were going to pop.

If Mom were there, she'd be able to tell him whether he had a headache or if he was sick. She always figured it out first and told the doctors what to do.

"Want Mom."

"I'll increase your painkillers a little. We'll see if that helps."

CHAPTER TWENTY

abriel and Renata had separated for the day, with Renata making phone calls and looking into possible living arrangements for the winter and Gabriel panhandling and making a visit to the hospital to see how Caleb was doing.

Gabriel was thrown back to his own time in the hospital. He'd had a lot of hospital visits over the years, but the last time he had woken up in hospital, it had been without his mother at his side and his life had changed forever. He couldn't help but see the similarities between himself and Caleb, alone and scared and trying to figure out why everything was happening to them. Caleb was, at least, not locked in psych, but he easily could have been, with his self-harming behavior. Instead, he was in a children's ward, and when Gabriel looked in on him, the restraint straps drooped empty and Caleb was able to move around in his bed, if not in the ward.

"Who are you?" Caleb asked Gabriel, looking him over with wide eyes. Gabriel was obviously not a doctor or nurse, and he wasn't anyone that Caleb knew from before.

"My name is Gabriel. I'm a friend. I just came to see how you are doing."

Caleb stared at Gabriel blankly, and Gabriel wondered for a moment whether he had understood what Gabriel said, or whether his cochlear implant was acting up or he was feeling the effects of whatever drugs they had him on.

"Want to go home," Caleb said finally, his voice breaking.

"I know, Caleb. It's never any fun being in hospital, is it?"

Caleb rubbed his stomach, looking anxious and uncomfortable. "Miss Mom."

"Yeah, I'll bet you do. She misses you too and wants you to know that she loves you."

"You talk to her?"

"Not today, but I have talked to her. She feels bad that you're so unhappy. It really scared her when you had that… meltdown, and she couldn't help you."

"Caleb…" The boy trailed off and couldn't seem to find his train of thought. There were tears in his eyes. He rubbed his stomach again.

Gabriel realized seconds before it happened that Caleb was going to be sick. He looked around quickly, grabbing a bedpan and thrusting it into Caleb's lap an instant before Caleb let out a cough and then acrid vomit gushed from his mouth. Miraculously, he managed to hit the bullseye and get it into the bedpan. Gabriel looked away and backed up, trying not to trigger his own gag reflex.

When Caleb finished throwing up, he started to cry. He coughed and spat and thrust the bedpan toward Gabriel. Gabriel took it gingerly to dump and rinse out. He hit the call button beside the bed before going into the bathroom. When he returned, Caleb was wiping and blowing his nose with copious amounts of tissue from the bedside shelf and a nurse came in to see what was wrong.

"He's throwing up," Gabriel told her.

The nurse startled, not expecting someone else to be in the room.

"Sorry," Gabriel apologized, putting his hands up. He handed the bedpan back to Caleb. "What's wrong? Does he have the flu?"

"He won't keep anything down," she said in irritation. "I don't know what to do with him. It doesn't seem to be a virus. He says he's hungry and wants to eat, but then he just squirms and cries until he throws up again."

She talked about Caleb like he wasn't even there. She took his wrist and checked his pulse. She shook her head.

"What's he been eating?" Gabriel asked.

"We've been trying to keep it bland. Toast, crackers, oatmeal. Liquids.

But it just won't stay down, will it, Caleb?"

Caleb nodded, tears running down his cheeks. Gabriel felt bad for him. He rubbed Caleb's head.

"You know he's celiac, right?"

The nurse stared at Gabriel. She looked over at Caleb, then back at Gabriel again. "You've got to be kidding me."

Gabriel gave an apologetic shrug. "Somebody should have told you. Toast and crackers are just going to make it worse."

"I'll say. Caleb, why didn't you tell me you couldn't eat those things?"

"Caleb can eat toast," Caleb said sullenly.

"But your mom buys special bread for you, doesn't she?" Gabriel asked. Caleb nodded.

"You need to make sure people know that," the nurse said, shaking her head again. "Why didn't the social worker or his uncle tell us?"

Gabriel looked over at Caleb. "Did you tell Uncle Kris you had to have special bread?"

"No."

"You've just been eating normal bread at Uncle Kris's?"

Caleb nodded.

"Well, it's no wonder he's so malnourished." The nurse picked up his chart and made a notation on it. "We'll get Special Diets up here to do up a new meal plan. Have you been throwing up at home too, Caleb? Or had diarrhea?"

"Sick lots," Caleb agreed. He put his hand over his stomach.

"Are you going to get sick again?" Gabriel asked worriedly.

"Again?" Caleb echoed. "Get sick again?"

"He doesn't seem to have any idea when he's going to throw up, poor boy," the nurse said. "We have to keep changing him." She straightened Caleb's sheets and checked his pulse again. "You try going back to sleep," she suggested. "Being sick takes a lot out of you." She walked briskly out, leaving Caleb and Gabriel alone together.

Gabriel stroked Caleb's head, trying to comfort him. "Once they get you back on your special diet, you should feel a lot better."

"Then go home."

"Back to Uncle Kris."

Caleb's face crumpled. "Caleb go home."

"Don't you like it at Uncle Kris's?"

"Home." Caleb seemed to be at the end of his tether. "Just go home."

"We're going to help you to get home as soon as we can. Until then, Uncle Kris's is probably the best place for you. He takes good care of you, doesn't he?"

Caleb picked at his sheets, making a low moaning noise in his throat.

"Uncle Kris feeds you and helps you get ready for school?" Gabriel prompted. "Takes you to the doctor?"

Caleb shook his head. Gabriel frowned.

"What do you and Uncle Kris like to do together?"

Caleb considered seriously, his finger tracing the hem of the sheet. "Go eat. Pizza. Wings."

"Gluten-free pizza. You need to get gluten-free."

"Uncle Kris's is better."

"I'll bet it is. But we need to tell him to get you gluten-free."

Caleb shook his head. "Uncle Kris get mad."

"What does Uncle Kris do when he gets mad?"

Caleb bit his lip and didn't look at Gabriel. Gabriel pulled a chair over so he could sit down to talk to Caleb.

"Does he shout?"

Caleb gave an infinitesimal nod and a grimace.

"Yeah? I'm sorry he yells at you. He shouldn't do that, should he?"

Caleb nodded more definitely. Gabriel considered how to approach the subject further without putting ideas into Caleb's head.

"Does Uncle Kris do anything else when he yells? Maybe when he gets mad, he thinks you can't hear him." Gabriel motioned to the cochlear implant. "Or… some people are just really loud."

Caleb looked at Gabriel sideways and didn't answer.

"What does Uncle Kris get mad about?"

"Don't know," Caleb said forcefully, his frustration obvious. "Looking wrong. Insub…" he struggled to form the word properly. "Insub-or-nance."

Gabriel studied him. "Insubordination?"

Caleb frowned, not sure. "What's it mean?"

"Not doing what you're told… disobeying an order."

"Yes. That."

"But you're trying, aren't you? You're trying to do what he says, not to be disobedient."

Caleb sniffled, several more tears running down his face. "I try," he agreed, "but Uncle Kris gets mad. Lots."

"You don't like being yelled at."

Caleb wiped his nose with the back of his hand. "Or hit!"

Gabriel swore in his head, but was careful not to change his expression. He didn't want Caleb to reconsider what he had said and stop talking.

"No," he agreed. "No one likes to be hit. You shouldn't have to stay somewhere you're getting hit."

"Should go back home."

"What about your dad, though. Doesn't your dad hit you?"

Caleb's shock at the question was undoubtedly genuine. His eyes widened and his mouth dropped open. "No! Dad doesn't hit!"

"Never? Not even when he's really mad?"

"No. He yells… he goes away… never hits!"

Gabriel could remember his discussion with Wes on the subject. He decided to push it just a little further. He didn't want to have another case like Seth's, where they had reunited a boy with his abuser instead of keeping him safe. Social Services had been right and Gabriel had been wrong, letting personal opinion cloud his objectivity.

"But your dad grew up in a home where they hit him. That's why Uncle Kris hits. So your dad must hit too."

"No!" Caleb started snapping his fingers in front of his face. "Dad never!"

"Okay. Okay, I believe you. I'm sorry. I just had to make sure."

"Dad never," Caleb repeated softly.

"Just Uncle Kris."

Caleb nodded solemnly.

———

It was with a heavy heart that Gabriel went back to meet up with Renata. He had hoped that Caleb would be in a safe place, so that they could work with the Hibberts within the law, helping them to successfully challenge DFS and have Caleb returned to them. As exciting as it was to spirit away a child to reunite him with his parents, Gabriel wanted to be able to change things within DFS too. Renata didn't believe that they could ever be changed. Foster care and medical experimentation brought too much money into the organization for them to want to change anything.

He found Renata at the library, in an animated discussion with Ray, one of their original team of four. Nick had died, and for a while they thought they had lost Ray too, but he had made an unexpected reappearance and sometimes helped them out a bit before disappearing again. Gabriel and Renata were the ones running the Underground Railway, Ray only helping occasionally. Dark-haired and handsome, Ray usually wore a dark hoodie to hide his face and stay anonymous. The hood was down and he looked comfortable and relaxed.

"Hey, Gabe!" Ray greeted heartily. "Long time, no see!"

"Well… you keep disappearing, so how are we supposed to keep track of you?"

"You're not." Ray made no apology for his absences. "But I'm here now, and I was just getting caught up with Renny."

Gabriel nodded. He tried to signal to Renata with his eyes that he wanted a few minutes alone with her, but she was hyped up by whatever she and Ray had been discussing and wasn't ready to leave.

"I just got back from seeing Caleb," Gabriel said.

"Yeah. How's he doing?"

"Not great. Apparently no one knew he was celiac, so he's been sick."

"At the hospital?"

"At home with Kris too. Either Kris didn't know, or he didn't think there was any need to follow a special diet. Been taking Caleb out for pizza and junk."

"And he hasn't been having symptoms? Some celiacs really don't, you know…"

"He has. He's throwing up all over the place."

Renata turned suddenly serious, the fun she'd been having with Ray disappearing.

"Kris has been taking him out for pizza, and Caleb has been throwing up all the time, and Kris didn't notice? Didn't care?"

Gabriel gave a shrug. "How could he not know the poor kid was so sick? He's underweight, the nurse said he was malnourished. He wasn't before he left Riley and Wes."

Renata swore. She sat down, thinking about it. Recognizing that they were talking serious business, Ray sat down as well, the joviality leaving his manner.

"We have to get him back to his parents. DFS is still sitting on the brakes. Riley's been wearing the alcohol monitor, so they know she's not an alcoholic. They're getting the cord blood tested, and then they'll be able to show why Caleb had Failure to Thrive and so many medical problems over the years. But you know how long they take to get kids back to their parents…"

Ray leaned in. "So… is it time to take him?"

"I don't know," Renata said. "If they're going to give him back, it's best to stay out of the way until they get it sorted out. Then they don't have to go into hiding… though they'll probably want to at least move out of state afterward."

They were quiet. Renata looked at Gabriel, and he knew that she could read him better than anyone else. They had grown so close that the communication between them was almost telepathic at times.

"You haven't told me everything."

Gabriel shook his head. "No."

"You have to tell me, Gabe. We both have to know everything."

"You remember I told you that Wes's father was abusive?"

"Yeah, of course."

"And sometimes, kids who grow up being abused, they can become abusers."

"Wes? No. You told me no! If he's abusive, then we can't take Caleb back there. Even if Riley and Wes split up, we can't be sure that they won't get back together again right after we were out of the picture. Then Caleb would be right back where he started." Renata's voice was rising. Gabriel looked around, making sure they weren't attracting the attention of the librarians or other library patrons.

"No. Not Wes."

"But you just said—"

"Wes's father is also Kris's father."

Renata swore again, getting it this time. "So DFS does what they do best, they take him out of his perfectly fine, loving, non-abusive home, and put him into the home of an abuser. Isn't that just brilliant!"

There were shushing noises from the other patrons as Renata's voice rose above what they could tolerate. Gabriel didn't tell her to pipe down. There was no point. Either she would listen to the shushing or she wouldn't. If he censured her, she'd target him, and he didn't need to be in Renata's crosshairs. Ray met Gabriel's eyes, and he decided to follow Gabriel's example and keep quiet.

"We can't leave Caleb there," Renata said in a lower tone.

Gabriel nodded his agreement.

Ray was eager to get in on the action. "Let's make a plan, then. Let's figure this out."

Gabriel held up both hands. "We can't move too fast. We don't want to attract attention. We don't want to rush into things."

"I didn't say 'let's go get him now'," Ray said, rolling his eyes. "I said let's make a plan. So let's do it. Let's plan."

Gabriel looked at Ray for a moment, then at Renata. Ray had helped them out sporadically, but he didn't know how Renata felt about him being privy to all of the details. They liked to spread an operation out so that no one person had the whole plan. Then if something went sideways and they were questioned, they couldn't spill everything. And they couldn't work both sides, passing information on to the police, DFS, or the courts. Could Ray be trusted? He'd never stayed with them for long.

"Maybe Renata and I should talk things through first…"

Ray sat back, folding his arms across his chest. "Thanks a bunch, Gabriel. You don't want me involved? You don't trust me?"

Gabriel didn't answer right away. He looked at Renata, waiting for her answer. If Renata trusted him, Gabriel wouldn't go against her. Renata was more likely to be paranoid than not careful enough.

Renata hesitated. It wasn't an easy decision for her, either. "This is just preliminary," she said finally. "We aren't putting anything into action right now. Just discussing possibilities."

"So it's okay?"

"He can stay."

"Okay." Gabriel shrugged at Ray. "Sorry. We just have to be careful, you know?"

"Oh, trust me, I know," Ray agreed. "I've had Dr. Death on my tail, too. That's why I can't believe you would suspect me. But whatever. You have to be careful. Or you wouldn't still be walking around free."

Gabriel and Renata nodded at the same time. Under the library table, Renata took Gabriel's hand. Whether to reassure him or herself, he didn't know. They were stronger together.

"So do you want to take Caleb from the hospital?" Ray suggested.

"Before his evil uncle can get his hands on him again?"

Gabriel grimaced. "It's getting harder and harder to take kids from the hospital. They increase security every time another story gets out. Besides, we know he's safe at the hospital. Now that they know about his diet, they can work on feeding him properly and getting him healthy again. Taking a kid who is already frail and going on the run… he wouldn't be able to survive on the streets or a lot of the places we would normally want to take him."

"The hospital won't let his uncle hurt him," Renata agreed. "Especially not if they get a hint that Kris could be trouble. But they won't keep him for long. Once he's not throwing up anymore, they'll be talking about releasing him."

"He's got the head injury too."

Ray watched them discuss it back and forth.

"Yeah, but they won't keep him for more than a day or two for that, not unless it gets worse," Renata said with certainty.

"Why don't we call in a report to DFS," Ray suggested. "Tell them that Uncle Kris is abusive. Then they'll move him."

"We don't know where they'd move him," Renata said. "It could be to somewhere a lot worse."

"What's worse than being beaten up by your own uncle?"

They all looked at each other. They had all been in foster care. They knew things could always be worse. The prime directive in foster care was not to complain because things could always get worse. Get identified as a troublemaker, and you might easily get put into some hole you could never crawl out of.

"Do you have any idea about the statistics of kids in foster care?" Renata demanded.

"Abuse and death statistics. I know. More likely to be abused. More likely to be killed in foster care. I've heard it before."

"What about sexual abuse? You have any idea how many kids with autism are sexually abused?"

Ray shifted uncomfortably and pulled his hood up over his head. "Do I need to?"

"More than eighty percent of autistic women have been sexually abused. And most of them, it's not just one time. It's repeated. Ten times or more. If Caleb gets moved to some random foster family or group home, you think he's going to be able to protect himself against that kind of abuse any more than he is against Kris smacking him around? We can't tell them to move him."

"Okay, okay." Ray held up both hands to stop her. "Okay, Renny. So you don't want to take him from the hospital and you don't want him sent to another foster family. Then we wait until he is sent back to Kris." He looked back and forth between Gabriel and Renata. "Right? Is there some other option I'm missing?"

Gabriel nodded. "Yeah. I think that's the best. We get in there once he's sent back home. Take him when he's going to or from school. No security to worry about. Just one kid on his way to school."

"He takes the bus," Renata pointed out.

"Not every day."

Renata looked like she was going to challenge him, then shrugged. "Okay. Not every day. He misses the bus some days. His mom said he had trouble getting up and getting moving in time. I doubt if Kris has been able to do any better. Especially not if Caleb has been sick. It's a lot harder to keep your head straight and get to school on time when you're feeling rotten."

They all nodded. Plenty of experience in that area.

"So we do what we can to keep him in hospital," Gabriel said. "As long as we can, so he's strong enough to move. Then when he gets home, we get him out as quickly as we can. Before Kris has a chance to start hurting him again."

Renata nodded slowly, her eyes far away.

"Renata?"

"Yeah. That sounds good. See if we can nudge the hospital to teach him about his diet. Make sure that he's not self-harming any further. Keep Uncle Kris away. Whatever we can do. In the meantime..."

"Yeah?"

"Does he trust you?"

"I don't know about that. He just met me today. But he trusted me enough to tell me about Kris."

"You need to get his trust. You're going to need to convince him to come with us voluntarily. A runaway, not a kidnapping."

"Yeah. Okay. I'll do my best."

"You have to. We can't pull him out of there against his will."

CHAPTER TWENTY-ONE

When Renata excused herself to use the facilities, Ray inched his chair closer to Gabriel to address him in a low voice.

"Listen. Did you know Renata's mom is getting out of prison?"

Gabriel nodded. "Yeah. I heard. How did you hear? Did she tell you that?"

"Renny? No, never. She would never tell me that. I was talking to Carmel."

"Who told Carmel? Judge Dee-Dee?"

Ray hesitated. "I don't know. She didn't tell me how she found out. Just told me Renata's mom was getting out."

"Renata doesn't want to meet with her."

"If you had the chance, wouldn't you go see your mom? I know I'd love the chance to visit with my family again."

"Yeah, I would. But I don't think my mother tried to kill me. Renata does. She thinks Elena tried to poison her."

"Crazy chick. Doesn't she realize how unlikely that is?"

"I don't know her mom, do you? You can't judge that without even meeting her."

"If she had tried to kill Renata, they would have found some kind of evidence. They would have charged her."

"Yeah," Gabriel said. "Because we haven't had any experience with conspiracies or an attempted murder that was never prosecuted."

Ray cocked his head to the side and gave a shrug. "Okay. You got me there."

"Renata knows her mom. If she doesn't trust her… maybe there's a reason for it. I know she goes over the top… I know she goes off on tangents… believes wildly unbelievable conspiracy theories. But she's protected herself and us, too. If it wasn't for her paranoia, none of us would be here today."

———

Gabriel stopped at the nurse's desk at the center of the ward before going in to see Caleb.

"How is Caleb doing? Is he doing any better on a gluten-free diet?"

Nurse Cathy, according to the badge on her uniform, finished what she was writing before looking up. She looked at Gabriel for a moment as if evaluating whether he was somebody she should talk to or not. Then she smiled, relaxing.

"Yes, his stomach seems to have settled down, finally. It's pretty hard to heal properly when you can't get any nutrition. We've put him on a liquid supplement as well, to boost his calorie intake and his nutrition. Get as many vitamins and minerals into him as we can. Who knows what kind of damage has been done to his digestive tract by eating so much gluten lately. It causes all kinds of malabsorption issues."

Gabriel nodded. He didn't have to eat gluten-free, but he knew what it was like to have to deal with allergies and getting enough nutrition for his body.

"I'm sure he's happy not be throwing up all the time. Poor guy."

Nurse Cathy nodded. "And believe me, we're glad not to have to be cleaning up after him several times a day. He'll be getting out of here before too long. His guardian will have to be instructed in how to take care of him properly, how to check ingredients for sources of gluten at the very least, meal planning… Caleb isn't old enough to take care of himself, yet. We like kids to be in charge of their own health as much as possible and to learn to advocate for themselves, but with Caleb's developmental disorder… I don't think he's ready for that yet."

"He seemed to be pretty happy with eating gluten pizzas with Uncle Kris. I'm not sure he's ready to be in charge of his own diet."

Nurse Cathy gave a little smile of agreement. Gabriel moved forward to lean on the counter. He tried to give the impression of a casual, chatty teenager, rather than someone on a mission. He did not want her cluing in to the fact that he was one of the leaders of the Underground Railway, if she had ever heard about it or happened to be talking to a friend about the encounter.

"You know that Caleb's not with his parents right now…"

"Yes. We understand that. They have been obeying DFS and haven't come here to visit with him."

"They're trying to get him back, so they're trying to do everything they say. When he was born, they had his cord blood preserved, in case it was ever needed for a blood transfusion, stem cells, or some other procedure."

Nurse Cathy's curiosity showed, but she didn't ask him what that had to do with anything.

"They just had a lab test done to see if Caleb had any infections when he was born. They thought from Caleb's medical issues when he was born that maybe he had CMV or another congenital infection."

"Did they find anything?"

Gabriel nodded. "They just got back a positive toxoplasmosis test."

"Toxoplasmosis."

"Do you know anything about it? I'm not sure if it's something you'd see very often in this ward…"

"I'd have to do a little refresher. I know it can cause eye infections or lung problems. It's very common, but often asymptomatic."

"Right. But a congenital infection can cause pretty serious problems. Blindness or deafness, low birth weight, jaundice, Failure to Thrive…"

"Is that why Caleb is deaf?"

"It would certainly explain it. It also increases the chances of autism, celiac disease, and other problems."

Nurse Cathy raised her eyebrows. "And you're telling me this because…"

"Because it doesn't go away. It can be reactivated at any time by stress, viruses, immune deficits…"

"So it could be active now."

"I don't imagine you deal with a lot of toxoplasmosis infections."

"No. I can bring it to the doctor's attention, and we can run a few tests, maybe get him on an anti-parasite protocol to kill off any active infection before it starts to compromise his health."

Gabriel nodded, smiling. "That would be great. You might have to keep him here a little longer just to be sure. And maybe you could explain to DFS that this is something he has had since birth and that caused many of his medical problems at birth and since then."

Nurse Cathy smiled. "I'm your gopher now, am I?"

"Do you think they're going to listen if I tell them that? Or if Caleb's parents try to explain it?"

"You would probably not get very far," she admitted.

"Yeah. But if it comes from the medical professionals... maybe they'll reconsider the conclusions they've already made that his mother caused his medical issues intentionally."

"And is there anything else you think we should be aware of?"

Gabriel looked around, thinking and taking his time, as if he didn't have a list of planned topics. "Has his uncle come to visit him very often?"

"No, we haven't seen very much of him."

"Mmm. Maybe that's a good thing."

There was a pause. Nurse Cathy looked down at her paperwork. She looked back up at Gabriel. "You seem to know a lot about Caleb and his family."

"I'm just a friend. I want him to feel better. I don't want him to be... sick or hurt."

"What exactly do you know about his uncle?"

"Just from what Caleb said... I think he might be... abusive."

"That's quite the accusation. Have you talked to DFS about it?"

"I'm not making any accusations. Just saying, it might be a good idea to keep an eye on things. I don't have any proof, certainly nothing to make a report... but I thought if you could keep an eye on him while he's here... make sure he's ready to go home before you release him."

"That's not up to me."

"No... but I don't think his uncle is prepared to take care of any acute medical needs. If you were releasing him to his mother, he could be released sooner. But Uncle Kris... I think you need to make sure Caleb is really well before he leaves."

CHAPTER TWENTY-TWO

Gabriel had received a message about a potential case that he needed to make contact on. He was always wary about first contact. It could be someone who was desperate to get their child back, but it could also be someone who just wanted to use the Underground Railway for their own purposes. Parents who were abusive didn't just give up when DFS apprehended their children. For some reason, in spite of violence or neglect that they showed toward their children, they still wanted them back. They didn't just shrug and go on with their lives when their children were taken. Or it could be someone who wanted Gabriel and his organization stopped. DFS, the police, complicit doctors and judges did not like to be made fools of by a bunch of rag-tag children. They had their empire set up, and they didn't want anyone getting in the way.

Initial meetings always took place in a public place. A busy public place. Gabriel favored malls, and especially food courts. That helped to prevent any physical attacks and gave him the opportunity to disappear into a crowd. He wasn't fast but, after being on the run for as long as he had been, he could make himself disappear pretty quickly.

Gabriel looked around for the woman he was supposed to be meeting. He'd gotten there early to scope out the food court to make sure there were no police or other suspicious characters hanging around. He knew the mall pretty well, including the unmarked passageways that were only supposed to be used by the staff, so he was comfortable with his escape routes. Even the police often didn't think about any doors other than those that were public, marked with big red *exit* signs.

The woman had been described as middle-aged, Hispanic, with an average height and slim build. He could usually spot someone looking for him pretty quickly. Standing around awkwardly, scanning the faces of the crowd for the black teen they knew they were supposed to be looking for. Even in a population that was predominantly white, Gabriel still had ways of blending in until he was ready to be seen.

She arrived early as well. Not as early as Gabriel; he was already there, watching for her. She looked outward from the food court, watching for his arrival from the two main routes into the eating area. Gabriel watched her nervous anticipation for a little while. She didn't appear to be communicating with anyone. If she had an earwig transmitter, she didn't appear to be using it. She hadn't brought a friend to help keep a lookout.

Eventually, Gabriel approached her from behind and slipped into the seat beside her, sliding a cup of coffee in front of her as if they were friends who had been planning to meet up. Or, since she was so much older than he was, maybe she could be his tutor or boss. "Sophia?"

She startled and looked at him. "Oh! Yes; I guess you must be Gabriel!" She was flustered, not having expected him to come from behind her.

"I was just getting a coffee," Gabriel told her, as if he'd only arrived a few moments earlier. He looked around at the crowds. "Have some."

"Actually… I don't drink coffee."

"Then pretend to take a sip. Or put both hands around it. It's a prop, so we don't look out of place."

"Of course." She didn't look natural in the way she picked up the cup, Like she was embarrassed to be seen with it. He should have gotten her cookie or a side of fries instead. But coffee was cheap and Gabriel didn't want to throw money around when the woman might not even be a legitimate lead. Now that money was wasted. Gabriel lifted his own coffee to his lips. Not something that Keisha, his mother, would have wanted him drinking. She had always been very strict with his diet, insisting on only the highest-quality food to help boost his cellular energy. She had read everything and done all that she could to give him every advantage. But Gabriel liked a hot coffee to keep him going. Just a mild stimulant. He didn't have many.

Not like some people who had five cups a day and always had a cup in their hands.

"So, Sophia, what can I do for you?"

There was something familiar about her. Gabriel searched his mental catalog to try to identify her. Had they met before? Was she a TV news reporter? Had he seen her before under some other guise? Gabriel didn't like to be at a disadvantage. He was already thinking about escape routes.

"I think you know my daughter," Sophia said tentatively.

So she wasn't there to get her child back from the system. Not unless the daughter was someone they'd already had contact with, either moving her or rejecting her as a candidate. Gabriel studied the woman's familiar features, trying to connect them with someone he had already met.

Gabriel closed his eyes when it fell into place. "Your name isn't Sophia."

"It's my middle name. I didn't think you would meet with me if I said…"

"Your name is Elena."

She nodded. "I'm sorry. But I had to meet you."

"Renata has already said she doesn't want to see you. Can't you respect that?"

"I do. I'm not here meeting with her, am I? I could have used the same story to come here and meet her instead of you. But I didn't."

"Yeah… that's true. But why are you making contact at all when she said no?"

"If you know my daughter as well as they say you do, then you know about her illness and about her psychiatric problems. I didn't cause those. I didn't do something to her that caused her mito or her mental illness. Those are just things she was born with. Something that went wrong when she was developing."

"I know that. I have mito too."

"I know she doesn't want to meet with me, but that's because of her mental problems. It's not actually her choice."

"She didn't choose the paranoia," Gabriel said slowly, "but she did decide not to meet you. I can't go against that."

"I'm not asking you to. I just want… I thought that by contacting you, you could tell me how she's doing. If she's getting on okay. Maybe when you think the time is right, you could tell her that we met, and that… I wasn't such an awful person. I'm not the monster she thinks I am."

"It must be really hard to have her turn against you like that." Gabriel took a sip of his coffee, letting his eyes roam around, checking for someone else Elena might have brought with her. She had broken their trust already by giving a false name and reason for meeting him. She wasn't trustworthy and could have exposed them in some way. "I've seen her turn against other people, people who were only trying to help her. I'm always afraid that one day she's going to wake up, and I'll be the enemy instead of a friend."

Elena nodded, her eyes shining with unshed tears. "Yes. Exactly. I cared for her and nurtured her and protected her. I would never do anything to hurt her or put her in danger. But I was the main person in her life, and it was only a matter of time until she decided that I was trying to harm her." Elena shook her head. "It was the worst feeling. Seeing her slide away from me like that. Not just to lose her physically, like I had so many times before when she had to have special care I couldn't provide, but to have her slip away from me mentally, to turn against me. You can't imagine what that was like."

Gabriel could. Like he had told her, he'd seen it happen with Renata. Gabriel was the person who was with Renata the most. Sooner or later, she was likely to decide he couldn't be trusted. She would think that he was trying to poison her or harm her in some other way, and he would never get her trust back again.

"I'm sorry," he said, "really sorry for what happened to you. But I can't help. If I do, she'll turn against me that much faster."

Elena stared off into the distance. Gabriel wondered if she were remembering Renata as a little girl, before she had started to hate her mother. But Renata had told him that even as a toddler, she'd had mental illness. She'd been in the psych ward for evaluation when she was just two. Elena had really never known her daughter without the dark specters of paranoia and psychosis.

"She's okay?" Elena asked. "I still worry about her, you know. No matter how long we are apart, I'll always worry about her and wonder how she is. She's still my daughter, no matter what."

"She's pretty good right now. She's been stable for a few months, out of hospital and managing on her own. Our own. I try to look after her too, but she's so smart, she's usually a few steps ahead of me."

"Are you two… a couple?"

"Uh… no. It's not romantic. We're friends. Partners. But we've never added that… complication."

Elena laughed. "I've never heard it called that before. But it is. Very complicated. Don't jump into anything before you're ready. With Renata's illness… I don't know if she'll ever be ready. Be careful."

"I am. We're very close. Maybe someday, but… I don't know. We're young. We shouldn't have to worry about that yet."

Elena nodded her agreement. "I'm glad that the two of you are taking care of each other. I'm glad to know that someone is looking after my baby. Trust me… I know that it isn't easy."

"It must have been hard, trying to raise her while she was so sick."

"It was. I'm a single mom, so I couldn't be with her all the time. I needed to find care for her, and sometimes, there just wasn't anyone who could do it. I'd have to quit my job, try to live on social assistance, while taking care of this child who was… unmanageable. And even if it wasn't for her mental state, there was still her feeding tube and her allergies and trying to manage her mito. She'd rage, and use up all of her energy, crash and be completely comatose. It was terrifying."

Gabriel had seen it happen himself and had to agree. It was terrifying. Renata was so quick to anger, even though she had to know what it would do to her when she let it fly. It was just out of her control. She didn't decide to crash, just like she didn't decide to be paranoid.

"I admit that I'm not the perfect mom. I've lost my temper with her. I've lost hope. A parent should never give up on their child, but there were so many times that I just felt helpless to do anything for Renata."

"Some kids with mito don't even survive, and it isn't like Renata only had a mild case. With her not even being able to eat… it's a wonder you managed to even keep her alive. Don't sell yourself short. That takes a lot of strength."

"Renata is the one who is strong. She fought through so many illnesses that the doctors said she'd never survive. She was my miracle baby in so many ways. But she was also my burden. One that I couldn't carry by myself."

"I don't think anyone could have." Gabriel found it strange to be trying to comfort the woman that Renata regarded as her enemy. He hadn't seen how Elena had raised Renata first hand. How often she had been there and how often she had left Renata's care to the hospital or the foster system.

Gabriel knew that his own illness had been a burden on his mother, trying to raise him alone with his father overseas. She had at least had an income source so she could be with Gabriel instead of at work. He felt guilty for all she had had to suffer through in raising him, and she hadn't had to battle the demons of psychosis.

"I love Renata," Elena declared. "Maybe I failed her, but I still love her. I hope she knows that, deep down."

Gabriel couldn't comment on that. He hadn't seen any sign that Renata had any tender feelings left for her mother. Deep down? Deep, deep down?

"I fought for her. She knows I fought for her," Elena said insistently, waiting for Gabriel to reassure her of Renata's enduring love.

Gabriel nodded. "She knows that," he agreed. "It's just that... she also thinks you tried to kill her."

"I didn't. I wouldn't do that."

Gabriel sighed. "You can't change what she thinks and neither can I."

"But you believe me, don't you? *You* don't think that I tried to kill my little girl?"

Gabriel looked into her distraught face and wished that he could give her the reassurance she so desperately wanted. But he couldn't do it. He hadn't believed that Leva would do anything to hurt her son, but she had poisoned him, starved him, and pushed him over the upper-level railing in the mall. He didn't know if he would ever be able to look at a parent again without wondering if what he saw was just a mask.

Renata said that her mother had tried to poison her. With some theories, she could be 'talked down' and admit that they might just be paranoia, but this wasn't one of them. Elena admitted to being overwhelmed and losing all hope. Parents *did* kill their disabled children. Such stories were in the news frequently, with public mourners sympathizing with the killers. *Yes, we understand, it was too much. No one could judge unless they were in the same circumstances. Sometimes, such a child was better off not having to endure a lifetime of disability.*

"I didn't," Elena said, still trying to get him to agree that she hadn't tried to kill her daughter. "In spite of all that I went through, I would never have harmed Renata or tried to take her life."

Her words made Gabriel shift uncomfortably. In spite of all of what *Elena* had gone through, not what Renata had gone through. 'Never would have' instead of 'didn't,' as if they were discussing a hypothetical instead of what had really happened.

"I wasn't there," Gabriel said. "I don't know what did or didn't happen. I'm not getting between the two of you. I'm not going to tell you about Renata, and I'm not going to carry messages to her or act as her proxy. I wouldn't have come here if I had known it was you I was meeting. You knew that, or you wouldn't have tried to hide your identity."

He held Elena's gaze. He felt like he was being rude, but he held it anyway, until Elena looked away.

"You're being a good friend to her," Elena said. "But if you buy into her paranoid theories, that doesn't help her. It just makes it worse."

Gabriel stood up. He picked up his coffee. "I'm going to go now."

He took a quick scan around the food court, trying to pick out anyone who might be watching them. Anyone who might try to follow him back to Renata. He didn't see anyone, but that didn't mean they weren't there. He took a sip of his coffee and walked away.

———

Renata looked at the time again, starting to get angry. Where was Gabriel? They had agreed to meet to discuss Caleb's arrangements.

Relying on public transportation meant that sometimes there were delays. Buses didn't show up, or they ran late or broke down. Stuff happened. But Renata had started to worry about whether something had happened to Gabriel. It could be something simple, like falling asleep on the bus and missing his stop.

But it could also be something serious. A blood sugar crisis. Getting mugged for his panhandling money. Being picked up by the police and held on kidnapping warrants. Dr. De Klerk might have decided that enough time had passed for him to make another attempt on their lives, now that they were no longer in the limelight. And he was right. Who would notice another John or Jane Doe in the morgue, a homeless teen who had apparently gotten on the wrong side of a gang or other nastiness?

Worrying about Gabriel led to Renata being angry at him for making her worry. He had better have a darn good reason for standing her up. Missing the bus wasn't going to cut it. He'd better be bleeding.

Finally, she powered on her phone to check for any messages. Though neither of them liked to advertise their locations by using cell phones, they were a necessary evil, and each of them checked for messages at least a couple of times a day. They only kept their phones turned on when they were expecting an important call. They always purchased pre-filled phones, never refilled them after the minutes expired, and only shared their numbers with a few people within the organization. If there were any chance a phone had been compromised, they destroyed it immediately.

It was a couple of minutes before the splash screen disappeared and Renata could input her security code to unlock the phone. There was a text message waiting for her. Renata took a deep breath, trying to calm herself before reading it. Adrenaline would make her burn through her cellular energy reserves too fast, which she couldn't afford. Renata tapped the text icon.

Gabriel had sent only one character. The number nine. Their code for an emergency. Call right away.

Renata swore. He had sent it two hours before.

She called him back, waiting impatiently for the number to connect and start ringing. She was afraid that he wouldn't answer.

Two hours before.

He could be in a shallow grave at the side of some country road or rotting in a jail cell. Why hadn't she checked earlier? The phone might ring forever or be answered by an unknown voice, some policeman or jail guard.

"Renata." Gabriel's voice was in her ear.

"What is it? What's wrong?" she demanded.

"It was a set-up," Gabriel said.

It took a split second for Renata to remember he was supposed to be meeting with a new contact. A set-up? Who had set them up?"

"There was no Sophia. Sophia is your mother's middle name."

How could any self-respecting paranoid person have missed that clue? Renata couldn't believe she hadn't made the connection.

"It was Elena? She wanted to meet with you?"

"Yeah. I'm sorry. I never realized or I wouldn't have gone. I should have figured it out."

"It's okay. She can be tricky. What did she have to say?"

"We can talk about it later. I don't want to be on the phone long. I'm going to ditch it. I'm worried about whether she might have had a partner or anyone helping her. I didn't see anyone follow me, but…"

"You're going to go dark?"

"I can't take the chance of leading them to you or anyone else. Give it at least a couple of days. Until we're both satisfied that no one could have followed me."

"But you can't leave now. Not when we're about to get Caleb." Renata's heart started to beat too fast.

"You'll have to go ahead without me. We can't put it off. Can't chance him getting hurt while we stand by."

"But you're his contact. You're the one he trusts."

"You're good at making friends. You'll have him eating out of your hand in no time."

"I can't do it on my own!" She was trying to keep panic at bay, not sure she was succeeding.

"You'll have to get someone else to help you. Not Carmel. Not anyone who has had connection with Judge Dee-Dee. I'll pick up a new phone in a couple of days to get an update."

Renata was making rapid connections, looking for threats from multiple perspectives.

"I'm going to get a clean phone too," she decided.

"How about using Katt as our contact person?"

"Katt?" Renata considered. She still had Katt's number written in her notebook. It had been too long since they had last talked to remember it. "Yeah, I think I still have it. What if it's been disconnected?"

"Then Nelson."

"Okay. I'll call Katt in two days to get your new number. Failing her, Nelson."

"Okay." Gabriel betrayed his emotions with a shaky breath. "We'll talk in a couple days, then. Bye."

They both disconnected. Renata stood there, frozen, trying to ease the tightness in her throat.

CHAPTER TWENTY-THREE

Renata took a look around the park, watching for anyone or anything out of place before looking back at Alexander and Ray.

Renata knew that she'd been snapping at them, but she was really stressing out over Gabriel having to back out in the middle of an operation. They always knew it could happen. They'd talked about procedures and safety measures a hundred times before. But she hadn't expected to lose him right as they were about to push the button.

Of course, Gabriel had continued to run things when she had been in hospital for months, so she would just have to suck it up and manage for a couple of days without him.

"We have to make sure everything runs smoothly," she told Alexander briskly. "I want the route he walks to and from school and the route the bus takes. I want to know all of the bus schedules for the buses that are along the way. What time school starts and if there are any anomalies. Any special events? Professional days? After school tutoring? We want to know every snag ahead of time."

"How am I supposed to get all of that?"

"The school has a website. So does the transit. His mom is probably still getting notices of all of the school events in her email. She can give you the password or forward them to you. She probably knows or can figure out what time the bus gets to Kris's house. It's the same bus he used to take to get to Riley's."

"Okay. Okay, I'm on it."

Alexander was a good guy. He had helped them a little while back to get his younger brother away from an abusive foster home and back to his parents. Alexander had been worried by Gregory's behavior during a supervised visit, and he'd been right to be. Gregory had been living in horrific conditions and had shown unmistakable PTSD symptoms. Months later, the boy still couldn't sleep with the lights off. Yet even with his history, Alexander didn't seem like he had his full focus on the operation. Not like he had when it had been Gregory they were helping.

"You remember what this feels like?" Renata asked. "You remember what it was like for Gregory? How important it was to get him out of there as soon as we could? That's the kind of effort you've got to put into this. Imagine it's Gregory we're trying to help again."

Alexander's lips flattened into a thin line. He nodded. "Okay. Yeah. I know this kid is someone's family."

Renata nodded.

"Ray? How about you? We got the time he's being released? We want eyes on him as much as we can. Maybe we can't watch him in the house, but any time he's out, we want someone reporting on his movements."

"I've got it, Renny. Don't worry about me. He's supposed to be released from the hospital tomorrow morning. We all know that being released in the morning means that if we're lucky, he'll be out at noon. But we'll be ready just in case. We'll make sure that he's going back to Kris's house and that the rest of his routine is back to normal. He won't be back at school tomorrow, but hopefully the day after that. We'll have to decide whether morning or afternoon is the optimal time to take him."

"Probably morning," Renata said, "but I want to look at the bus schedules first. When Alexander's got that pulled together.

Alexander gave a nod and a little salute to show that he was still listening, while he tapped information into his laptop computer.

"Where are we going to keep him?" Ray asked, "and how long? We can't wait for too long."

"The timing is dicey. DFS is making noises like they could approve Caleb to go back to his mom and dad in a few days. But we all know how unlikely that is. With DFS, 'soon' means 'maybe next year.' Or maybe even the year after that. They like to draw it out as long as possible. They'll say that it's in the works, or they didn't get approval yet, or their supervisor decided to add one more requirement, and it means the parents are going to have to take another class or do counseling for six months before they'll consider it."

"Have we got a safe house?"

"We've got a basement suite in a friendly's house," Renata agreed. "But we have to stay out of sight. If this blows up in the media, Caleb can't be seen by anyone. Neither can any of us—anyone whose face gets on the TV is going to have to stay hidden."

"At least we're not talking about sleeping rough or some rat trap motel."

"We talked about it, but if we follow the same procedure too many times, we become predictable. And… I don't think Caleb is strong enough to sleep rough. He'd end up back in hospital again and we wouldn't have gotten anywhere. In a motel, any odd behavior might attract attention."

Ray nodded. Renata scowled, not liking his expression. It was that same expression all of the guys got when they figured they needed to take care of Renata. She wasn't any fragile snowflake. She was strong, and she was the one who was in charge, not him.

"That's what we're doing," she snapped. "Any other questions?"

"No," he said calmly. "I'm good."

"Good. We've all got our jobs to do. Everybody can't know all of the moving parts. We have to keep it compartmentalized so that nobody knows the whole plan."

———

Renata sat at the bus stop, watching for Caleb. He had, not unexpectedly, slept late or not been able to get himself ready in time, and had missed the school bus. From what Riley had said, that wasn't unusual even when he was at home. Now that he was living with someone who couldn't even be bothered to get his diet right, it was pretty much a given that he was going to miss the bus more often than not.

A city bus slowed as it approached the bus stop, and Renata shook her head to indicate she wasn't getting on. The bus sped up and blew past her, showering her with a fine spray of grit and exhaust. Renata shaded her eyes until it was past, then looked around again for Caleb.

She hadn't expected him to take so long. Ten minutes after the bus was gone, maybe, but not a whole hour. And apparently, still longer. She took a look around to make sure she was alone and would not be overheard, then pulled out her walkie-talkie.

"Any sign of him yet?"

"Not yet," Ray informed her. "What do you want me to do?"

"He could be sick or hurt. Do you think we should check on him?"

"We should wait a bit. We don't want the neighbors seeing us going up to the house, lurking around, looking in windows, or ringing the doorbell. They'll know that we don't belong there."

"Okay. Waiting. Let me know if you see some sign of him."

Renata slid the walkie-talkie back away, and leaned her head back, closing her eyes and letting her body relax. She didn't usually nap during the day, but a lot of her body's energy had been going into planning and worrying, so it wanted to recharge.

She wasn't sure how long she had been dozing when the walkie-talkie squelch made her jump. Renata looked around before answering.

"Yeah?"

"I can see movement in the house. I think he's up."

"About time! He's slept half the day away!"

"Just because you're used to getting up before dawn…"

"Well… yeah, that does make a difference."

"The rest of the world likes to sleep a little later. Take their time…"

"Get off the radio," Renata snapped. "It's for official communications only, not philosophical discussion."

"None of this is *official*," Ray argued.

But he didn't say anything else. Renata put her radio away and sat up straighter. If Caleb was up, then Renata needed to start watching for him. Ray should let her know when he was on his way, but if he weren't able to talk safely, he'd keep radio silence and Caleb could make an unexpected appearance. Renata wasn't sure how long it would take him to get ready. Riley said that he was pretty slow without someone to light a fire under him.

She stood up to make sure she didn't doze off again, and watched for Caleb to start walking down the street.

"He's leaving the house," Ray advised.

Renata took out her walkie-talkie. "Roger. Turning off now. I won't turn it back on until we're getting close to the safe house."

"Good luck."

It was a couple of minutes, and then Renata saw Caleb walking down the street. He moved slowly, more of a wander than a purposeful walk. Not excited about going to school. Not worried about being late. Just going because that's what he was supposed to be doing.

"Hey, Caleb."

He didn't see her at first. Renata called his name again and he swiveled, looking for who had called him. His eyes rested on Renata, and he cocked his head slightly, thinking back and trying to place her.

"It's Renata," she reminded him. "We met at the hospital."

Caleb nodded vigorously. "Yeah, I remember! You live here?" He made a gesture to indicate the neighborhood. Renata didn't bother to answer.

"I was wondering… do you really want to go to school today? You and I could hang out together instead."

Caleb grinned widely. "Yeah!"

He certainly didn't need much convincing.

"Maybe you could come stay with me until you can go back to your parents again."

Caleb's eyes got wide at this suggestion. He looked at her, eyes popping. "You have a house? Your own?"

"I have a place, a basement suite, and you could come stay there until DFS gets things sorted out with your parents."

He didn't seem to be at all suspicious of her. She'd prepared the ground the best she could when she'd gone to see him a couple of times at the hospital. But she hadn't been sure how he would react when she suggested that he leave Uncle Kris's house permanently.

"Caleb come live with you?" He was used to repeating things he wasn't sure of. It was possible he'd misheard her and he obviously didn't want to risk misunderstanding that.

"Yes." Renata nodded to confirm visually. "You can stay with me instead of Uncle Kris."

Caleb turned his head back and forth, scanning the streets for his uncle. Renata did a quick reconnaissance, but didn't see anyone suspicious.

"Caleb like." He nodded. "And no school?"

"No. If you go to school, they'll just take you back to Uncle Kris's house. We want to leave without anyone knowing where you are."

Caleb nodded his agreement. He looked in the direction of the school, then back at her.

"Where we go?"

Renata smiled. Easy peasy. "This way." She touched his arm lightly to guide him and he walked beside her without any hesitation. Renata scanned the horizon for any looming trouble.

It was almost too easy.

CHAPTER TWENTY-FOUR

She was right.

They had only gotten a block or two when a black sedan pulled over so fast that its tires squealed. Caleb looked around, startled by the sound and looking for its source. When he saw the car, he grabbed at Renata's arm.

"Uncle Kris!"

Renata swore. She turned to face the tall, angry man getting out of the vehicle.

"Caleb! What the hell are you doing? You're supposed to be at school!"

Caleb's face was white. His mouth moved, searching for a response. He patted Renata's arm.

"My friend…"

"Who are you?" Kris demanded, glaring at Renata. His face was red and furious. Renata could understand why Caleb would fear him, even if he hadn't been hurt before. Kris was big, and he was terrifying.

"I'm just a friend," Renata said. "We're walking to school. Caleb was late, so I thought I'd walk with him."

"You're going the wrong way to go to school."

"There's a shortcut this way," Renata bluffed. "You can cut through the park."

She had no idea whether there was a park close by or not. Kris's eyes showed confusion, but he wasn't sure enough to challenge the statement.

"So this is why your marks have been dropping," he growled at Caleb. "You're being distracted by a girl!"

Caleb's eyes were on Kris's face, doing his best to read him and figure out what to do or say.

"My friend," he said, patting her arm.

"Well, I don't want you to have anything else to do with her. You can just stay away from her," Kris rounded on Renata. "Or do you want to be charged for interfering with Caleb? Do you know what it's called when you mess around a kid like him, who doesn't have the judgment to know any better?"

Renata's anger rose at the accusation. Her heart was pounding hard, and she tried to control her reaction. He wasn't going to hit her right there in the street—was he? The worst he could do was take Caleb to school. Not a problem. Alexander was stationed closer to the school just in case Caleb chose a different route and got there without Renata being able to intercept him. Alexander would keep eyes on Caleb until they had another opportunity to make contact.

"I haven't done anything to Caleb." Renata made a show of looking at her watch. "Are you going to drive us to school? It's getting late."

"Drive you?" She had judged him well; as soon as she suggested he drive them, he rebelled against the idea of driving either one of them "You think you can just do whatever you want and there will be no consequences? I'm not giving either one of you a ride! You can get there under your own power. But you…" He advanced toward Renata. "You are going to stay away from him."

Renata put a little more space between herself and Caleb, hoping that would satisfy Kris. He would see that she was obeying and just walk away. But Kris's face was flushed and he didn't back off. When he got closer, Renata could smell alcohol seeping from his pores. He hadn't been at the house; he'd been out drinking and was just getting home halfway through the morning.

"There's nothing to be upset about." Renata put up her hands in a surrendering gesture. "I'm not going to do anything to hurt Caleb. If you don't want me near him, that's fine."

Her words had no effect on him. He might as well have been the one who was deaf. He gave Renata a shove. Not just a little nudge, but a hard push that made her take a couple of steps backward in order to keep her feet.

Caleb gave a bellow like a bull elephant and rushed his uncle. He might have been helpless to protect himself, but his impotence didn't extend to others. His sense of justice was well-developed and he wasn't going to let Kris hurt Renata.

Kris was even more surprised by this than Renata and he was not prepared when Caleb hit him. He didn't have his hands or arms up to stop the rush. He didn't have his feet properly planted to stabilize himself. Caleb hit him, and with the extra weight of the books in his backpack, they both went crashing to the ground.

"Caleb!" Renata tried to stop him. "Caleb, come on. Come with me."

But Caleb was incensed. Whatever had been going on at Uncle Kris's house fueled his attack. His inexpert blows rained down on Kris, who kept turning his face to the side trying to avoid them, making incoherent noises of protest.

"Caleb." Renata tried to pull him back by his backpack. "Caleb, stop. Leave him alone now."

It took all of her strength to pull him off. Skinny little Caleb was a lot stronger than he looked.

Kris lay on the sidewalk, groaning. Renata's brain worked madly, trying to sort out the best plan of action. If the whole operation was blown, they might not get a second chance to rescue Caleb.

"Get his phone," she told Caleb. "Does he have a phone?"

Caleb nodded, staring at her and not sure what he should do.

"Get it." Renata repeated.

She walked toward the car. Kris had pulled it over and stopped it at the side of the road, but he'd left it running. The key was still in the ignition.

Caleb took a moment, and then followed her. His hands flapped wildly beside his face; stimming was the only thing keeping him from melting down.

"Renata!" he called, trying to catch up.

"You got his phone?"

Caleb handed it to her.

"Get in the car."

"But…" Caleb looked back toward Kris.

"Just do it," Renata snapped. "You have to listen to me. You have to do what you're told, if you want to get out of here safely."

Caleb's gait was awkward. He got into the car and pulled his door shut. Renata got into the driver's seat. She moved the seat forward and checked the positions of her mirrors.

"Renata going to drive?" Caleb asked.

"Yes."

He rocked in his seat, still flapping his hands wildly, moaning.

"Renata knows how?"

Renata didn't answer. She tried to move the gear shift, but it was locked in place. Renata tried again. She checked the key, turned the ignition off and on again and tried to move the gear shift. It will wouldn't move. Renata tried to slow her breathing and concentrate on the problem. Was the car broken? Had Kris done something to lock it, so that it couldn't be taken without his permission? It wasn't a new car. It didn't seem to have any special features or add-ons. Renata tried to force the gear.

"Brake," Caleb said.

"What?"

"You have to push the brake."

Renata first depressed the gas pedal, making the engine roar, and then the brake pedal. With the pedal down, she tried the gear shift again, and it worked.

"Sheesh," she muttered. "Maybe I should learn this stuff."

Caleb's eyes were wide, showing the whites around his iris. Renata's ignorance had confirmed his suspicion that she had never driven a car before.

"Going to Renata's house?" Caleb asked.

"No. We're going back to Caleb's house. Uncle Kris's house."

He stared at her, baffled. Renata drove the car, creeping down the street at a snail's pace, back to Kris's house, only a few blocks away. She kept checking her mirrors for any sign of Kris, sure he was going to get up and come running after them. Caleb had punched Kris several times, but he hadn't killed him. Hadn't even knocked him out. Just surprised him more than anything.

"Not Caleb's house." Caleb insisted. "Not Uncle Kris's house!"

"We're not staying there. We're just going to drive Uncle Kris's car home for him. He can't drive it right now, so we're going to do that for him."

The speed of Caleb's flapping slowed to a slightly less frantic pace. "Where we go then?"

"Just wait. We'll catch the bus. It will be okay."

In a few minutes, they were in front of the house.

"Do you need anything here?" Renata asked Caleb. "If we're not going to be coming back here, is there anything you need to take with you?"

Caleb opened his door.

"No collections," Renata warned. "You have to be able to fit it into your backpack. You can leave your schoolbooks here. Whatever you take with you has to fit in your backpack. You've got two minutes, so you have to move."

Caleb headed toward the house. Renata pulled out her walkie-talkie and switched it on.

"Ray, are you still close?"

There was only silence in response. Renata swore. She opened the car door and locked the electric locks. She watched the house, waiting for Caleb to get his things together. She kept watch for any sign of Kris.

There were no sirens. No one had found him yet. No one had called for police or ambulance. Or if they had, the emergency responders were busy or too far away.

The walkie-talkie squawked to life, making her jump. "Ray here."

"Ray! Thank goodness, I thought you were gone."

"There were too many people around to talk. What's going on? What's wrong?"

"Kris showed up."

Ray swore. "Did he get Caleb?"

"No… Caleb got him. He's hurt. Not bad. A few blocks away. I've got his car and phone. We're back at the house."

"I can't get back there for a while. What do you need me to do?"

"Caleb is getting whatever he needs, then we're going to run." Renata looked at her watch. "The next bus should be here in ten minutes."

"So we're still on?"

"Yeah. We're still on. If you could make your way back here and keep an eye on what happens. Then report back to me later this afternoon. We might have to change things up."

"Okay. I'll get back as quickly as I can."

Renata looked at the house, impatient for Caleb to get back out.

"Come on, Caleb," she murmured. "We gotta get moving."

There was still no sign of Uncle Kris, but he could be on them any minute. Someone could find him, he could get his hands on a phone. He could put the police onto them.

Finally, she saw Caleb coming out of the house. He walked up to the car, shouldering his backpack.

"We go?"

He went around the car to get back in the passenger seat and Renata shook her head. "We're going to catch the bus."

Caleb frowned. "Why?" He gestured to the car.

"The car is staying here."

Ignoring Caleb's frown and confusion, Renata raised Kris's phone and tapped the screen. She dialed emergency. She ignored the dispatcher's questions.

"Somebody's been hurt," she said. "A man. He needs medical attention." She described Kris's location the best she could, then disconnected the call. She wiped the phone with her shirt and tossed it into the car. She shut the door, locking the phone and keys inside. "Okay. Let's go."

———

They were sitting on a bench at the bus stop when they heard the sirens. Renata had known that she wouldn't be able to get away on the bus before the police or ambulance showed up to deal with Kris, but she was counting on the fact that the police weren't going to be looking for kids sitting at bus stops. They would be looking first for the car, then for kids on the run. It would take a while for them to get a coherent description out of Kris and then to get those descriptions out over the air. By the time they got everything organized to make a real search for the two of them, they would be long gone, probably already at the safe house.

But Caleb didn't know any of Renata's inner thoughts and plans, and he started to panic the moment he heard sirens.

"No, no! Police!"

"It's okay. They're not going to come after you. They're just going to make sure Uncle Kris is okay."

"Uncle Kris will tell them! Find Caleb!"

"No, they won't. Because they don't know where we're going. Only one person knows where you're going."

A slight exaggeration, but it worked for her purposes.

"Who?" Caleb demanded. Then looking into her face, he guessed, "Renata?"

"Renata," she agreed. "Renata is the only one who knows where you're going. Uncle Kris doesn't know. The police don't know. Your school teachers don't know. Your parents don't know. Renata is the only one. You will be safe."

He considered this, but the sirens were getting louder and louder, making him frantic. "They're coming! They find us!"

"No. They don't even know who to look for. We're just a couple of kids waiting for a bus. They don't know what happened. And even if they did, they wouldn't be coming after us, because we didn't do anything wrong, did we?"

Caleb pounded his fist against his forehead. "Hit Uncle Kris. Pushed him down and hit him. Not good! That was bad, Caleb!"

"Kris hit you, didn't he? Did he get in trouble for that?"

Caleb paused in beating his forehead and looked at her. "No."

"No. They didn't come after him when he hurt you, and they're not going to come after you either. It's that simple."

He subsided to just stimming by snapping his fingers beside his face. "Where Renata live?"

"The place we're going to is a basement, the downstairs of a house. It's set up as a separate apartment, so we won't have to worry about anyone else seeing us. We'll just hang out there for a while."

Until when? Until DFS decided that Caleb could go home? Even without the latest developments, that might never happen. There was no guarantee they would ever allow him to return to his parents. Renata would have to decide which way the wind was blowing, and if Caleb wasn't ever going to be released to his parents, then they would have to disappear. Renata would have to take Caleb to meet them at some distant place unrelated to any of them.

She didn't want to tell him that it would only be a few days and get his hopes up. And she didn't want to tell him that it might be weeks, or even longer.

They liked to do things quickly with the Underground Railway. They had to make sure that they weren't followed and discovered, but once they had done what they could to shake any tails, they moved along again and reunited parents with their child within a few days. The thought of Caleb having to live in an isolated basement suite for days or weeks while they sorted things out did not make her happy.

The sirens moved past where they were sitting and stopped somewhere nearby.

Uncle Kris would be taken care of. He wasn't going to lie there bleeding out or his brain swelling. He would be taken care of.

Caleb sighed with relief when the sirens stopped. In spite of her own reassurances, Renata looked around, watching for any problems. No policemen appeared. No scent dogs.

The bus pulled up to the stop and Renata got up, relieved.

"You see? No problem. We're going to be long gone by the time anyone actually starts looking for us."

Caleb nodded. He followed her into the bus, watched her pay the fare, and then sat down on the seat she pointed him towards, rocking slightly but not obviously stimming anymore. They hopefully didn't look quite odd enough for people to notice and remember them later.

Luckily, the bus didn't go past either Kris's house, or the spot where he had attacked them. The meandering trip to the safe house took a long time, but was uneventful. Almost.

———

Renata had to force herself to stay awake on the last leg of the bus trip. The encounter with Kris had exhausted her reserves, and she still had to stay alert and on top of things for the rest of the journey or Caleb would be stranded with no idea what to do with her, where to go, or how to manage on his own. She called ahead to Alexander, who had headed to the safe house ahead of them, taking a less circuitous route so that he would get there ahead of them and could warn them off if there were any issues.

"Hey," Alexander greeted, "you just about here?"

"Getting close," Renata said. "Look, I know we said you were to wait there for us, but there's been a change of plans."

"Uh—okay. What do you want me to do?"

"Come meet the bus. Make sure me and Caleb get off safe."

Alexander made an indecisive noise. "Are you okay? What's wrong?"

"I'm crashing. I don't know if I can stay awake and get Caleb off the bus in the right place."

Caleb had been watching out the window of the bus, but at Renata's words, he turned and looked at her in concern.

"Crashing?" he repeated.

"Okay, I'll be there," Alexander agreed. "I'm leaving now. Give the phone to Caleb and put him on."

Renata handed the phone to Caleb and put her head back, closing her eyes. The exhaustion washed over her, so strong that she felt immersed in it. Caleb talked with Alexander on the phone, relaying information on where they were and what Renata was doing. Renata just drifted, relieved that someone else was in charge. It seemed like all too soon before Caleb was shaking her hard by the arm.

"Have to get off, Renata. Get off here."

He stood up and was shaking her arm hard, trying to pull her to her feet.

"Don't go," he told the bus driver. "Renata is tired."

There was a dry chuckle in reply. Renata held on to him, pulling herself to her feet. Her body protested, every cell feeling empty and exhausted. Caleb pulled her backpack out of her grip and helped support her on her feet. Renata shuffled with him to the door and, holding on to the railings, attempted to navigate her way down the three steps to the exit. Hands reached up to her and Alexander pulled her out of the bus, keeping her from falling. Caleb got out of the bus behind her, then the bus pulled away from the curb, leaving them behind.

"That wasn't exactly an unobtrusive exit," Alexander grumbled. "Are you okay to walk for a bit, Caleb?"

"Caleb can walk," Caleb answered cheerfully.

"And you can carry both backpacks?"

"Caleb is strong."

"Good man. Tell me if they get too heavy and I'll take one of them. But for now…" Alexander was bending Renata over, and she thought he was going to put her down on the ground. He could at least have the courtesy to walk her to the door. But he didn't put her on the ground. He folded her into a small, tent-like cave. Used to the tiny pup-tent she and Gabriel shared when they were sleeping rough, Renata promptly curled up and went to sleep.

CHAPTER TWENTY-FIVE

For a while before Renata woke up, she was aware of a TV playing and people's voices fading in and out. She could smell food. It didn't feel like a hospital. But it didn't feel like anywhere familiar, either.

Renata opened her eyes. She was in a bed in a small, dark bedroom. She could still smell cooking aromas and hear the TV.

"I'm just going to see if she's up," a male voice said. The bedroom door opened, spilling lamplight into the room that made Renata squint. She raised her hand to her eyes to shield them. "She's awake!"

"Let me!" another voice insisted. "Caleb wants to see."

Caleb pushed in beside the larger silhouette. Renata squinted to identify everyone. "Ray?"

"And Caleb!" Caleb chimed in excitedly.

Renata smiled. "And Caleb." She blinked and tried to let her eyes adjust to the dimness of the room. "I guess that must mean we got to the safe house."

"Caleb helped!"

"You did." Renata sat up slowly and gingerly leaned back against the wall behind her. "Why don't you tell me what you did?"

Caleb pushed by Ray to get into the room. He sat on the side of the bed.

"You crashed," he told her.

"Yes. Too much excitement." Renata touched her feeding tube. "I guess someone fed me lunch." She wouldn't have woken up if they hadn't gotten some sugar into her system.

"That would have been Alexander," Ray said. "I didn't get here until an hour or two ago."

"Alexander," Caleb made a motion to indicate Alexander somewhere in the next room or another part of the suite. "He looked up Renata's tube."

"Looked up my tube?" Renata repeated, trying to visualize what Caleb described. Why would he be looking inside her tube?

"On internet."

"Oh." The light went on. "He looked it up on the internet to figure out how to use it."

Caleb nodded proudly, as if he himself had accomplished the feat.

"You guys were both really smart." Renata tested out her arms and legs, flexing her muscles. Everything seemed to be in working order, though she was still tired and sore. "I'm going to get up. We can talk better out there."

Caleb stood by and solicitously offered his hand to help her up and then his arm to lean on as Renata shuffled to the door. She blinked in the brighter light of the TV room and made her way to the couch. Caleb cuddled up to her on the couch. Renata looked at Ray and Alexander for their reports.

"Do we need to move?" she asked. "They're going to know which bus stop we got off at, since I ended up making such a scene."

"I had Caleb get you off early," Alexander said. "I didn't have a car, so I couldn't make it any farther away, but we're at least a couple of miles from where you got off."

"A couple miles?" Renata repeated. She couldn't imagine how Alexander could have transported her that far without a car. "How did you manage that?"

Alexander grinned. "You know those trailers you can pull behind your bike if you want to go out for a ride with your toddler or your dog?"

Renata laughed. "Are you serious? Those are so small!"

"Luckily, you're not a big girl. You didn't seem to mind."

Renata remembered the safe, cocooned feeling that all was well. She chuckled again, shaking her head. "You're very inventive. I never would have thought of it!"

"It was my mom's, and she used it long after we were toddlers. I knew you could fit a small adult in one if you put your mind to it."

"So you biked, and Caleb carried the bags, and I slept. I know who got the best end of that deal!"

"Caleb is strong," Caleb said proudly, tapping his chest.

"Yes, you are."

Renata thought about the distance from the bus stop to the safe house. "So they have a better idea of where we went than we would like. But we're probably okay for a few days. They're going to search the immediate area first. Especially since I was practically comatose. They're not going to think I could get more than a block away. Or to the hospital. They'll probably be able to identify me now, if they couldn't based on Kris's description." She looked at Ray for his report on Uncle Kris.

"I kept an eye on things for as long I could, keeping under cover," Ray said. "Kris got immediate medical attention from the cops and paramedics. Didn't go to hospital. He hitched a ride home with the cops, and discovered his car and other items where you left them."

Renata nodded. "Good. I didn't want any warrants for grand theft."

"I couldn't figure out why you just didn't take it to escape, but I guess I get that."

"So how much got into the media? Anything?"

Ray nodded. He pulled out a tablet computer and tapped through a few screens, then started a video and put it on Renata's knees so she could watch. Renata listened to the perky woman reporter discuss the unusual disappearance of Caleb Hibbert, a thirteen-year-old boy with autism. She went through the apparent assault on Uncle Kris, a later sighting on the bus, and the current request the police had out for more information from anyone who had any knowledge of the events.

"Mom!" Caleb said excitedly, tapping the tablet screen and pausing the video play. And he was right, Riley and Wes were in the background, talking with the police. Renata didn't see Mr. Searle anywhere. Where was the snake?

"Don't touch the screen," she told Caleb, and started it playing again, this time keeping her eyes on the background figures. Riley and Wes and the police. No Mr. Searle. Renata turned to Caleb. "What's your mom saying? Can you tell?"

Caleb dragged the time indicator backward and then watched it play again. He stared at his mother's lips, the person he was most used to reading.

"*Where... Caleb,*" Caleb reported, "*Why... not looking for Caleb?*" Caleb turned to Renata. "Call Mom! Tell her where Caleb is!"

"She can't know where you are. Until DFS is ready for you to go home, she can't know where you are. She has to tell the truth when she talks to the police."

"She wants to know!"

"It's a secret, Caleb. She can't know yet."

He put his hands over his face, rigid.

"Caleb, you wouldn't want to have to go back to Uncle Kris, would you?" Renata coaxed.

"No!"

"Or to another foster home or group home?"

"No."

"Then you need to stay here, and keep it a secret, until we can get you back to your mom and dad. We can't tell her, but she knows we have you somewhere safe."

"Want to go home." He bit the side of his hand.

"I don't know when you'll be able to go home. But it won't be long before you see your mom and dad. Just a few days."

"Today!"

"No. If you want to see them today, you watch them on the video," Renata pointed to the tablet. "Okay? You can see them. And soon, you'll be able to be with them again."

Caleb picked up the tablet and chucked it across the room. Renata looked at him, giving him a glare that would have made any mother proud. "Well, it looks like someone is ready for bed."

Caleb's jaw dropped in shock. "No!"

"If you're going to act like a two-year-old, you're going to go have a nap like a two-year-old."

Caleb stood up off of the couch and retrieved the tablet. He deposited it meekly in Renata's lap. "Sorry."

"I don't know. I think you still might need to go to bed."

"No. Caleb be good."

He sat on the floor and stared fixedly at the TV. Renata glanced over at

Alexander and Ray. Alexander made a fingernail-polishing motion on his chest.

"Nicely done."

Ray held up his hands. "I'm being good," he told her. "Please don't send me to bed either!"

———

Renata soon headed back to bed herself. Ray and Alexander promised to stick around for the night to supervise Caleb while Renata got her energy back, so she had her evening meal and tucked herself into bed. She could hear the boys watching TV and occasionally talking to each other, but the sound on the TV and their voices were low so that the upstairs neighbors wouldn't be able to eavesdrop on them.

She had been asleep for several hours when Caleb's voice woke her up. He was weeping and calling out. Renata waited for one of the guys to take care of it, but Caleb kept crying, so Renata got up. She went to the door and looked out into the family room. Caleb was sleeping on the floor, thrashing around. Ray was snoring away, oblivious. Alexander sat up, rubbing his eyes.

"Caleb. Caleb! Wake up. You're just having a dream, buddy."

There was no answer from Caleb. He continued to cry.

"He probably took his sound processor out to sleep," Renata said. "He won't be able to hear anything you say."

Alexander startled, his face turning quickly toward Renata. "Sheesh, you scared the daylights out of me!" He crawled across to where Caleb was sleeping and, in spite of Renata's words, he still spoke soothingly as he reached out to rub Caleb's back or to shake him awake. "Wake up, buddy."

He gave Caleb's shoulder a nudge. "Wake up. Come on, it's just a bad dream."

Renata's heart gave a little throb. She wondered how many times Alexander had done this with Gregory, waking him out of nightmares of his time with his foster family. Calming and reassuring him.

Alexander shook Caleb's shoulder harder, and Renata could tell by the way Caleb's body language suddenly changed that he had woken up. But he didn't stop crying.

"It's okay, Caleb," Alexander soothed. He rubbed Caleb's back. "It's just a dream."

"No," Caleb moaned. "Don't. Don't touch Caleb." He pulled away from Alexander, trying to put space between them.

"It's okay. No one is going to hurt you."

"Don't touch Caleb." Caleb rolled into a ball, hugging his arms around his knees.

"Is he afraid I'm going to hit him?" Alexander asked Renata. He tried to rub Caleb's shoulder again to reassure him he was safe. But his attempt only made Caleb cry out again, sobbing into his knees.

"No… I don't know if that's it," Renata said. She tiptoed into the room and turned on one of the lamps. The light was too bright at first, hurting their eyes even though it was only on the lowest setting. Renata blinked, her eyes tearing up. Then she moved over to where Caleb was and crouched in front of him.

"Caleb. You're okay, Caleb, you're safe."

He blinked at her several times before he seemed to become aware of his surroundings.

"Wake up," Renata repeated. "It's just a bad dream."

Caleb looked around the dim room. "Uncle Kris?"

"He's not here." Renata shook her head.

"Where?"

"He's at his house. Far away."

Caleb pushed himself up to a sitting position and looked slowly around him. He saw Alexander, and moved closer to Renata, looking over his shoulder at Alexander.

"No one is going to hurt you," Renata told him.

He reached over and hugged her. Renata put her arms around him and tried to comfort him, murmuring to him and hoping that just the feeling of her throat vibrating against him would reassure him.

"Don't touch," Caleb said. "No touch."

She waited until he pulled back from her a little and could see her face.

"Who touched you?" she asked. "Uncle Kris?"

Caleb started to snap his fingers.

"Does Uncle Kris come into your room when you're sleeping?"

Caleb rubbed his eyes, whining. Alexander sat behind him, his eyes dark hollows, mouth turning down. "Poor kid."

Renata wanted to stroke Caleb's hair, but was worried about any action that might trigger a worse reaction.

"Uncle Kris can't come here," she told him when he looked at her again. "He doesn't know where you are. He's not going to touch you again."

Caleb sobbed and sniffled, nodding. "No more."

"No more. And we'll tell your mom and dad, so they know not to let Uncle Kris come visit when you go back home."

"Go home."

"Yeah. Soon. We'll make sure it's safe."

Caleb rested his head on Renata's shoulder and closed his eyes. But it was a long time before he lay down and went back to sleep.

CHAPTER TWENTY-SIX

Because Renata and Caleb had been spotted, Gabriel waited longer than the agreed-upon two days before contacting her to ensure that she hadn't been discovered and the police weren't just waiting to see if Gabriel would show up so they could nab them all together.

Gabriel got Renata's new number from Katt. He dialed the phone. He didn't expect to actually get through. Renata didn't like to leave her phone on, and being in a safe house, she wouldn't want anything to lead the police to them. But they were both using new phones and they hadn't contacted anyone but Katt, so they were as safe as they were ever going to be.

Renata picked up. "Gabe?"

"Renata. Hey, how are you? Are you okay?"

"Yeah, I'm fine." She sounded momentarily confused by his question, then understood. "Oh, you saw the TV coverage? Yeah. I bonked. Confronting Kris during the escape was not part of the plan and I didn't have the reserves to keep going. But I'm fine. All recovered. A bit of rest and a meal, and I was fine."

"Good. I was worried. But they didn't say that they had found you, and I knew the first place they would have looked was in the hospital. You obviously weren't there, so I hoped that meant you were okay."

"Alexander was a genius and got me off the bus a few stops early so that they wouldn't know where we were. We've been keeping under cover, so no one has seen either of us since we got here."

Gabriel could hear Caleb trying to talk to Renata.

"And how is he?"

"No, it's not your mom," Renata told Caleb impatiently. She answered Gabriel, "He's… perseverating."

"Ah. Do you want me there? Is it safe for me to come, do you think?"

"Yeah, shouldn't be any problem. We've been careful not to have a lot of people coming and going and attracting attention. And of course, Caleb and I can't go out or we'll be seen. I haven't seen your picture in the media coverage at all, so it should be fine."

"Okay. I'll be there sometime today. How are you set for food? Is there something Caleb would particularly like?"

Renata covered up the phone microphone to talk to Caleb, who was hovering over her, insisting she needed to call Riley. "Caleb—"

"Is it Mom? Want to talk to Mom."

"I told you it's not your mom. It's Gabriel. You remember Gabriel from when you were at the hospital?"

Caleb considered for a moment. "Uh-huh."

"He's going to come see us today. He wants to know what you want to eat?"

"Pizza!"

Renata spoke again into the phone. "Sorry… any chance you could manage a gluten-free pizza?"

"Sure. I'm sure you're probably both getting cabin fever by now. Food will help."

"Sounds good. I'll see you when you get here."

———

Renata ended the call as Gabriel said goodbye. Caleb bounced around.

"You call her now? Call Mom."

"No. Not yet. It won't be much longer now, Caleb."

Caleb smacked his hand on the wall, making a report like a gun. "You said before! It's been long!"

"I know it's been a long time. It's been long for me too."

Renata had never known that two days could be so long. She'd spent plenty of time waiting for doctors or procedures, or for a social worker to pick her up to take her to another home, but the time had never drawn out as long as it did with Caleb asking every two minutes when they were going to call Riley. He was so stuck on calling Riley that Renata wasn't at all sure they'd be able to interrupt the constant pestering with food, even pizza.

He was like an endlessly looped video, repeating over and over again. Putting him to bed the night before had been a huge ordeal, trying first to get him into bed, and then to stay there and go to sleep. He had some meds that the hospital had sent home with him, but Renata had eventually had to resort to a sleep remedy Riley had recommended, then shut his door and refused to answer any further pleas for attention.

Of course, he hadn't stayed shut in the room and she couldn't lock him in. She couldn't go to sleep until after he did, because he could just let himself out of the basement apartment and either wander off or find his way home. She wasn't sure what time it was when he had eventually passed out on the couch, and Renata had finally been able to close her own eyes and get a few minutes of rest in.

He'd slept in, but Renata's body was used to having to be up before dawn, so she hadn't been able to sleep past six no matter how hard she'd tried.

<hr>

Gabriel could see when he arrived at the safe house that Renata was exhausted. She had dark circles under her eyes and was at the end of her rope with Caleb, snapping at him when he spoke to her.

Caleb too was frustrated. He wasn't used to being cooped up in a dark basement. He'd seen his parents on the TV and he wanted to see them. He couldn't understand why they would stop him from going home. They had been nice to him and told him that he'd be able to see them again, and then they hadn't let him.

"Why don't you take the bedroom and sleep for a while?" Gabriel suggested to Renata. "I'll take over with Caleb."

She didn't even bother a token protest. She gave Gabriel a hug. "He's all yours," she advised, and retreated to the other room.

"I brought pizza," Gabriel showed Caleb the boxes. "I need you to help me make them. You tell me which one you want for dinner and we'll put it in the oven."

Caleb trailed him into the kitchen. "Want to see Mom," he told Gabriel. He too sounded exhausted. Gabriel wasn't even sure he was aware what he was asking anymore, he'd been stuck in the same track for so long.

"Which one? I thought this one looked really good," Gabriel selected one of the boxes at random.

"Don't want that one," Caleb dismissed. He took the boxes from Gabriel and studied each one carefully. Eventually, he picked one of them out. "That one."

"Okay. Let's get it into the oven, then."

Caleb watched him remove the pizza from its box and plastic wrapping.

"Uncle Kris eats good pizza."

"That's what I hear. But it's not gluten-free, and that's not good for your tummy, is it?"

"Good for my mouth."

"I hear you! I wish I could eat everything that I liked. But when something makes you sick, you have to stop eating it, don't you?"

"Want pizza."

"And you're getting it. This pizza is all safe. So you can eat it and not get sick, as long as you don't gobble it down too fast or eat too much."

"Hurts my tummy."

"When you eat it too fast or have too much? Yeah, it does. So we'll have to make sure you eat slowly, right?"

Caleb watched Gabriel put the pizza in the oven and set the temperature. They turned on the interior light of the oven and stared in the little window.

"Not ready yet."

"Nope. We just put it in. It's going to take a while. Do you want to watch TV while we wait?" Gabriel wasn't above using whatever bribes worked. Riley and Wes would have to deal with any bad habits Gabriel let Caleb develop. But that would be a small price to pay for getting him back again.

CHAPTER TWENTY-SEVEN

Renata awoke to Caleb shaking her. She groaned and braced for more demands that they take him home. "Go back to sleep, Caleb."

"Renata! Wake up!"

"No, it's time for sleep, Caleb. You have to give your body the rest it needs."

"Renata!"

She cracked her eyes open and could see that he wasn't wearing the sound processor portion of his cochlear implant. There was no point in talking to him, he couldn't hear anything she was saying. She put her hands, palms pressed together, against her cheek in a gesture to indicate sleep.

"Renata has to wake up!" Caleb insisted. His voice was a hoarse whisper. Renata wasn't sure whether it was because he was trying to keep quiet, or because he couldn't hear his own voice to modulate it.

Renata swatted him away. "Go to bed."

"Listen!" Caleb insisted. He put his hand flat on the wall and froze, his body language alert and concerned.

Renata frowned at this new behavior. She had no idea why his hand on the wall was so concerning. He needed to just relax and go back to sleep. Maybe he'd had a nightmare and it had left him with an unsettled feeling. Renata herself was feeling anxious, and the shorter she got on sleep, the worse it would get. She did *not* need to go off on a psychotic break while she was trying to look after Caleb.

"Go talk to Gabriel."

Gabriel was there to take some of the pressure off of her. He could do his part.

"No." Caleb grabbed Renata's hand and pulled it to the wall. "Listen."

Renata let Caleb press her hand flat against the wall.

"Listen," he repeated. He pointed at the ceiling.

Renata closed her eyes to focus on the sounds around her, and the suite overhead in particular. Once she and Caleb were both quiet, impressions started to trickle into her brain for processing. There were vibrations in the wall. A certain amount of vibration would be normal; the low, regular hum of the furnace fan that Renata's brain filtered out. The wind and weather outside. She felt a regular pulsation that she managed to match up with barely-audible footsteps overhead. There were faint voices, but Renata couldn't feel their vibrations in the wall. She could feel them walking around. A sharper vibration than the footsteps... a door closing, Renata thought.

Caleb was studying Renata's face. He nodded, knowing that she felt what he was talking about.

"What is it?" Renata asked, forming the words on her lips silently. If she could hear the neighbors' voices, they could hear hers.

"People," Caleb filled in. "Men in boots." His eyes went up to the ceiling as if he could see them. "Walking around."

Renata felt sick. Her heart beat fast.

"Where's Gabriel? Get your sound processor on, Caleb. We're going."

Caleb let go of Renata's hand and disappeared out the bedroom door. Renata felt for her shoes and pulled them on. She had left everything packed in her backpack in the TV room, so she didn't need to gather anything else.

In the main room, Caleb was connecting the sound processor and wrapping it around his ear. Renata gave Gabriel a brisk shake and he startled instantly awake.

"What is it?"

"There are people upstairs," Renata hissed. "It's three in the morning and there's people walking around opening and closing doors."

"Cops?"

"Maybe. We're bugging out."

Gabriel straightened. He reached out and grabbed his own backpack. Renata saw that he'd slept with his shoes on. She grabbed her own bag. Caleb had his sound processor back in. He picked up his backpack.

"What to do?" he asked urgently.

"There's a secret way out," Renata said. It was one of the reasons she had picked the safe house. On the surface, it was a perfectly normal, one-bedroom rental suite. But there was more to it. "This way."

She led them away from the door that led up the stairs to the back door of the house. Instead, she went through the narrow, slatted door into the furnace room. A big, modern-style furnace was the only thing immediately apparent. But there had previously been a much older coal-fueled furnace or boiler, which was still tucked away behind the furnace, and there was space for coal to be piled up for use. And the feature that had sealed the deal for Renata: old plank steps that led up to a door that had been used for coal deliveries. Not a coal chute that they would have to wriggle up through, but a door they could just walk out of.

From the outside, it blended into the siding of the house, and there were only a couple of feet between the house and the fence. When it had been built, the house had been on a big property, probably a farm, but when the land had been developed it had been subdivided, and there was no longer enough room for a wagon to pull up to the side of the house to refill the coal supplies. Only someone who had squeezed behind the modern furnace into the coal room would know that there was a door on that side of the house.

Renata led the boys around the furnaces and up the stairs, pulling out her phone to shine its light on the steps so no one would trip and fall. They were all skinny, so getting around the furnace was not a problem. At first, Caleb balked at the sight of the ancient stairs in the dark room. But Renata wasn't giving him any choice.

"You want the police upstairs to take you away?" she demanded in a low voice. "You remember what happened last time?"

Caleb hesitated, but eventually, he followed Renata gingerly up the stairs. Gabriel brought up the rear, also shining his phone light. Renata slid the bolt back and slowly turned the knob. She had lubricated the hinges before they had moved in and the door opened with barely a whisper. Renata led them out into the yard, along the fence, sheltered from view by scratchy berry bushes. Even if someone had been watching for anyone to come out the hidden door, they would have had a difficult time seeing the teenagers in the dark.

At the back fence, there was a garbage pass-through, where aluminum garbage cans could be filled from the inside of the yard, and emptied by garbage men into the garbage truck on the alley side. The metal cans had been replaced by big plastic garbage and recycling bins that were too tall for the little garbage niche and instead stood as sentinels down at the other end of the fence, near the garage. Renata took the boys through the garbage pass-through and then quietly down the alley, away from the house.

———

Sleeping rough with Caleb meant *not* sleeping. Gabriel tried to talk Renata into going to sleep in the tent without him, while he kept an eye on Caleb, but Renata was too keyed up to even try.

The thought of how close they had come to being discovered, the police upstairs, moving through the house, bound to go down the stairs and search the rental suite in just minutes, had Renata so hypervigilant that for the second night in a row, she was going to end up with next to no sleep.

"You use the tent," Renata told Gabriel. "See if you can convince Caleb to go back to sleep with you."

Gabriel did his best to talk Caleb into going back to sleep, but Caleb had decided that they were now going home and would have none of it.

"Go see Mom and Dad," he insisted. "Gabriel can sleep there. Renata can sleep there. Caleb sleep in his room."

"We can't go see them yet, bud," Gabriel said patiently. "They are going to court tomorrow. If they can show the judge that they've done everything DFS said they had to do and that none of DFS's evidence was ever any good, we might get lucky."

"Go home now."

"No. But maybe soon. See what the court decision is tomorrow."

"Then Caleb not sleep." Caleb folded his arms across his chest stubbornly.

Gabriel rubbed his scratchy eyes. He was used to going without much sleep, but even on those days when he didn't get a lot of time for sleep, he could usually relax and rest, something that he could not do when he had to watch Caleb and make sure he didn't take off to go home.

They agreed to split up in the morning. Renata had already been spotted with Caleb, so she couldn't afford to be seen with him again. She would find other billeting arrangements for them in case the court case didn't go the direction they wanted it to, and Gabriel would keep Caleb fed and entertained until they knew one way or the other.

Gabriel had a feeling that he'd gotten the short end of that stick. But Renata had already had to deal with Caleb by herself for a couple of days. It was time for her to get a break.

CHAPTER TWENTY-EIGHT

Judge Dee-Dee rarely sat in on cases that were heard by other judges. She had enough of her own cases to hear without trying to pick up additional hearings. But she had reasons for wanting to sit in on the case being heard in Judge Cameron Wickham's courtroom, so she had her clerk clear her schedule for the time of the Hibbert case and found a seat in the spectators' seating.

Wickham wisely closed the hearing to media, not wanting a spectacle. The results were bound to make it to the local news, of course, but that didn't mean they had to be right inside his courtroom. Wickham looked slowly around the courtroom to see if there was anyone else he should exclude, and his eyes stopped for a minute on Judge Dee-Dee.

They didn't spend a lot of time together socially. They both went to the big events such as Christmas parties, fundraisers, elections, but they didn't golf together or meet for private lunches. Judge Dee-Dee had no idea if Judge Wickham even golfed. She didn't.

Regardless, he was bound to have heard of her previous involvement in cases that had involved Renata Vega, Gabriel Tate, and their Underground Railway for kids who had been medically kidnapped or otherwise wrongly apprehended by DFS. Some of the stories had blown up in the media, and that meant that most of the judges would prefer not to have any cases that involved the Underground Railway on their dockets.

Wickham tapped his pen on his desk a few times, considering Judge Dee-Dee's presence in his courtroom, then he continued to examine the other spectators. He addressed a few of them, finding out what their interests in the case were, and eventually the observers were whittled down to just a few. He didn't challenge Judge Dee-Dee's right to be there or ask her about why she was interested in the case.

Judge Dee-Dee sat back in her seat and got as comfortable as the wooden bench would allow. The room was called to order, the case announced, and Wickham started with the preliminaries.

Caleb was not in the courtroom, but it was not unusual for the children being discussed to be absent from the courtroom. Wickham had doubtless heard the hoopla surrounding Caleb's disappearance. Nevertheless, proceedings went on as if everything were routine.

Andrew Searle was called to testify and presented his case, not quite calling Wes and Riley Hibbert abusers deserving of prison sentences, but coming pretty close. The Hibberts' lawyer, Martha Hawkes, stood up, straightened her petite black blazer and skirt set, and began attacking the case.

"You mention that you had reason to believe Mrs. Hibbert might be an alcoholic. What were your reasons for that?"

"We do have a positive drug test," Searle shot back. "That test shows that Mrs. Hibbert has habitually consumed copious amounts of alcohol over the months prior to testing."

"Is that a pre-screen or a gas chromatograph confirmed test?"

Searle was brought up short. "Baby Best has been performing these same tests for us for decades. Hundreds of child custody cases have been determined based on their results."

Hawkes looked at Judge Wickham, who glared down at Searle. "You didn't answer the question."

"Technically, I suppose this could be called a pre-screening test, but as I say, they have been used many times before…"

"But you didn't get a gas chromatography to confirm it."

"No."

"And you're aware that Baby Best's results have been thrown out of evidence previously because of these issues."

"And other judges have chosen to accept them," Searle countered.

Judge Dee-Dee knew that was not quite true. Hawkes made a notation on her legal pad and let the silence draw out for an uncomfortable length of time.

"Mrs. Hibbert then volunteered to wear a SCRAM anklet, didn't she?"

"Yes, she did."

"SCRAM, for the information of the court, stands for Secure Continuous Remote Alcohol Monitor. It is a device that has been used to ensure that convicts on parole or probation comply with their no-alcohol rules. Did Mrs. Hibbert have a SCRAM installed by an expert?"

"She did."

"And you have no evidence that she attempted to tamper with or alter the results of the monitor?"

"No. I'm sure someone has probably come up with a way to get around the devices, but…"

"But you have no evidence that she did."

"No."

"And how much did Mrs. Hibbert drink during the monitoring period?"

Searle took a drink of his water. "None," he admitted after a lengthy pause.

"No alcohol?"

"No. None."

"And how would a person who was previously consuming sixteen to eighteen drinks a day fare when stopping all alcohol cold turkey?"

"I'm not an expert in alcohol rehabilitation…"

"But you are experienced enough to know that a raging alcoholic who is completely cut off would experience symptoms of alcohol withdrawal."

"Yes, of course."

"How did Mrs. Hibbert seem to you during her first few days wearing the monitor?"

"Like I said, I'm no expert…"

"Did you notice any tremors? Delirium? Severe mood swings? Seizures? Any symptoms at all?"

"No. I didn't."

"And to your knowledge, could hair products containing alcohol account for a false positive in the hair strand test performed by Baby Best?"

"Yes. There would be no way of knowing whether the alcohol came from an external source."

"Did you examine Mrs. Hibbert's hair care products?"

"No. I didn't check any of the cosmetic products in the home."

"Did you *ever* examine *any of* Mrs. Hibbert's hair care products?"

Searle reconsidered his answer. "Mrs. Hibbert did show me a hair spray she claimed to have used that was 70% alcohol."

Hawkes nodded slowly. "So let's go back to my original question. What were your reasons for believing that Mrs. Hibbert was an alcoholic?"

"There were a number of signs observed in her newborn that were red flags for consuming alcohol during pregnancy. And we don't have any proof that she *didn't* consume alcohol during her pregnancy."

"What were those symptoms?"

"Low birth weight. Irritability. Poor sleep, poor feeding, delayed milestones. Seizures. What is referred to as Failure to Thrive."

"Did Caleb test positive for drugs or alcohol when he was born?"

"No. To my knowledge, no such tests were run."

"Have you had an opportunity to review a recent test that was done of Caleb's cord blood by a private laboratory?"

"Yes."

"Was it positive for any congenital infections?"

"Yes. It was positive for toxoplasmosis."

"And what are the symptoms of a baby born with an active toxoplasmosis infection?"

"I'm not sure..."

Hawke brought out a heavy medical tome and showed it to Searle, who read the name and publication details into the record.

"Would you turn to the flagged page, please?"

He did so.

"Looking at the list of possible symptoms of congenital toxoplasmosis, do you see any of Caleb's symptoms on that list?"

Searle was silent, reading through it. "Yes."

"Can you read them out as you notice them?"

"Low birth weight, vomiting, feeding problems, seizures, hearing loss, jaundice, neurological deficits..."

"So many of those symptoms that you recognized as red flags for alcohol abuse could also be symptoms of a congenital infection such as toxoplasmosis."

"Apparently. Yes."

"So to sum up… there is no proof that Mrs. Hibbert is or was an alcoholic, and Caleb's symptoms at birth could be explained by his congenital toxoplasmosis?"

Searle shifted uncomfortably. "There were other concerns."

"Such as?"

"Caleb had been hoarding food. That is a very strong indicator of neglect. A child who has not been properly fed, who is underweight like Caleb, hoards food because he doesn't know when he's next going to be able to get a meal. Or because he has Reactive Attachment Disorder and does not believe his parents will provide the necessaries of life."

"Did Caleb hoard anything else?"

"He had a number of collections, which I would consider to be unsanitary. Another reason that the Hibbert home was not a good environment—"

"Are you aware that persons with autism might tend to collect esoteric items?"

"As could anyone."

"And that people known colloquially as 'hoarders,' who may collect things to the level that their health is endangered may have a form of OCD?"

"Sure. Of course. But Caleb isn't an old cat lady. He's a young teen."

"Are you aware that almost half of those who are diagnosed with OCD test positive for toxoplasmosis, compared with only nineteen percent of healthy controls?"

"No."

"Was Caleb diagnosed with OCD?"

"No, he was not."

"Had it been discussed?"

Searle considered for a moment. "Yes, it had been discussed."

"And why was he not diagnosed with OCD?"

"Because of his autism diagnosis. His psychologist wanted to give it some more time before deciding whether it was part of his autism or a separate disorder."

"And as you read, neurological disorders are higher in patients who test positive for toxoplasmosis."

"Yes."

"Including autism."

"It doesn't say that here," Searle challenged, thumping his finger down on the book. His chin lifted triumphantly.

"There have been some studies," Hawkes said, pulling several reports from her desk. "Would you like to review them?"

"No… I'm willing to accept that neurological disorders could include autism."

"Did you have other concerns about the Hibberts?"

"His mother often posted personal information about the family, which could put Caleb in danger, and could indicate that she was seeking attention because of his medical issues. This is an indicator for factitious disorders—"

"But you're not suggesting that everyone who overshares on social media has factitious disorder…"

"Of course not."

"How did Caleb contract toxoplasmosis before he was born?"

Searle stared at her as if she were crazy. Judge Dee-Dee had to admire Hawkes's persistence. She was a bulldog with the facts she'd been given.

"From his mother," Searle said.

"Riley Hibbert had toxoplasmosis and passed it on to her unborn son?"

"Yes, of course."

"And were you aware that women with toxoplasmosis have been shown to display personality changes that include more worrying and anxiety, as well as a greater tendency to be outgoing and to trust others?"

It was Judge Wickham who challenged Hawkes this time. "Hold on. That can't be true. Where is this stuff coming from?"

Hawkes pulled another series of reports from her rolling briefcase. "I have a briefing memo and the studies that have been done, if you would like to review them."

Wickham looked dubiously at the volume of paper. "I'm going to reserve the right to review those before I make a ruling. This sounds like something out of a science fiction novel. Are you sure toxoplasmosis isn't actually an alien invader from another planet?"

Hawkes looked at him. She looked down at her papers and then back up at him. "No, your honor."

Her deadpan expression was spot on, and Judge Dee-Dee had to restrain herself from laughing aloud at the effect. Embarrassed, Judge Wickham looked at his watch.

"Can we speed this up a little? I believe most of the salient points have been made…"

"Were there any *other* concerns by DFS?" Hawkes asked.

"There certainly were. There were a number of indicators of domestic abuse, including cuts and bruises on Caleb when the police picked him up. I would also point out that at the time he was not dressed properly for the weather and that his cochlear implant was not functional."

"Did anyone other than the Hibberts confirm that Caleb sometimes self-harmed or showed risk-taking behavior?"

"Yes."

"Did Caleb show any fear of his parents?"

"No, but abused children have been known to be coached not to show any obvious signs."

"Did anyone other than his parents confirm that he had a combination of sensory defensiveness and sensory-seeking behavior? Which means that he sometimes sought out stimulation that you or I would have considered painful, and that he found other normal sensations, such as wearing pants, to be painful?"

"Yes."

"Did his teacher or anyone else suggest that his cochlear implant was often non-functioning?"

"No."

"He usually wore it and was able to understand speech and hear other sounds around him?"

"As far as our investigation was able to determine, yes."

Hawkes gave a long sigh. She looked at the judge and down at her watch.

"And did you have any other concerns about Caleb?"

"His mother claimed to have been involved in several traffic accidents, which is another red flag for domestic abuse. His father admitted to coming from an extremely abusive home."

"Were you aware that people who test positive for toxoplasmosis have a higher rate of traffic accidents?"

Searle looked at the judge, rolled his eyes, and shook his head slightly. "Your honor… this toxoplasmosis sounds like black magic. Is the Hibbert family going to contest that every issue that DFS identified is because of toxoplasmosis?"

Judge Wickham readjusted his glasses on his nose, looking down at the briefs that had been filed and the notes he had made. "I have yet to see any compelling reason Caleb should be kept from his parents. I see that DFS recommended parenting classes and a Safety Plan, which the Hibberts have complied with. Is there anything else you'd like to bring to my attention?"

"His father," Searle repeated, "he comes from an abusive home. It's a well-documented fact that abuse victims have a tendency to become abusers—"

"But it is not a given. And they have taken your recommended parenting courses to make sure they have been given all of the necessary tools."

"Unlike the father's brother Kris," Hawkes spoke up, "who was given custody of Caleb in spite of the fact that he came from that *same* abusive home and had *no* parenting experience or education."

Judge Wickham took his glasses off and folded the arms in. He laid them on the desk in front of him. Judge Dee-Dee recognized this as the ritual of a judge who had made up his mind and was ready to make a ruling.

"I believe that the Hibbert family has complied with all of DFS's recommendations and that DFS has failed to find any convincing evidence of abuse, neglect, or danger to Caleb."

Searle's face flushed red, but he made no protest. The courtroom was silent. Not a person moved as they waited for the judge's ruling.

"It would appear that the red flags in this case were, in fact, red herrings. I direct DFS to return Caleb to his parents at the earliest possible opportunity."

"That's rather difficult when DFS doesn't know his whereabouts," Searle muttered.

Judge Wickham looked at him. "I assume that DFS will be cooperating with the police to find the boy and return him safely home."

Searle said nothing more.

CHAPTER TWENTY-NINE

Gabriel glanced over at Caleb to make sure he was still occupied with the computer game on the library computer. He didn't like to resort to video games, but Caleb was otherwise intractable, refusing to do anything he was told, constantly repeating that he wanted to go home.

Gabriel looked back down at his phone, willing it to ring. Even just a text. Something to indicate that there was news. He jumped when it vibrated in his hand. He swiped the button and put it up to his ear.

"Yeah?"

"It's Katt," she said unnecessarily. "I just got a call from Carmel."

"And…?"

"Judge Dee-Dee sat in on the hearing and gave her a call…"

The anticipation was killing Gabriel. He didn't care how they got the result of the hearing, all he cared about was the result.

"They ruled that Caleb be sent back to his parents."

"Hallelujah!" Gabriel stretched his head back, gazing up to the ceiling. "Finally!" He blew out his breath. "We need a place to return him to. Somewhere the police won't be watching for us, because I don't want to be detained for questioning. How about the school? There's a playground just down the hill."

"Okay, I'll pass it along. What time?"

Gabriel looked at the clock in the wall, calculating how quickly they'd be able to get there by bus. "Let's say… two hours. That should be long enough for us to get Caleb there. Tell Riley and Wes to come alone. I know they can't control whether they're followed, I'll try to be out of the way."

"Do you want me to tell Renata too?"

"Yes."

"Okay. Talk to you later, Gabe!"

Gabriel disconnected the call and looked at Caleb. "Hey, Caleb. Want to go see your mom and dad?"

———

Caleb was sitting on a swing when his parents pulled into the empty parking lot beside the playground. He jumped off and promptly tripped, landing face-down in the sand. He quickly jumped back up, and brushed himself off as he took a few steps toward them in an awkward run. Riley and Wes jumped out of the car and hurried toward him. They met halfway, all reaching out and pulling each other into an embrace, so that the three of them clutched in a tight huddle.

Gabriel and Renata were too far away to hear the words that were exchanged, and Gabriel felt that was probably the right thing. It was a private moment for them, one that Gabriel and Renata had the opportunity to observe, but didn't need to be a direct part of. It was one of the rewards of what they did. There was no fame, no fortune; the families they helped couldn't pay them back for reuniting them. The Hibberts were comfortably middle-class, but many of those that they helped were barely making ends meet, another reason DFS liked to remove children from the home. A family who couldn't provide the necessaries of life couldn't be allowed to raise a child.

Renata moved. Gabriel looked over at her. She held her hand over her eyes, like she was trying to press away a headache.

"Hey. Are you okay? Are you not feeling well?"

"No." Renata's voice had a catch in it. "I'm fine. I'm just… thinking."

Gabriel studied her, worried. "Thinking about what?" He put his arms around her and she melted against him. Gabriel wasn't sure what was wrong, but holding her had apparently been the right choice. "It's okay," he whispered. He couldn't know that everything would be okay, but he'd learned that such words helped, even when he couldn't know the enormity of the problem. He just held her, waiting for her to talk to him or to pull back away. Renata dropped her hand, turning her face up toward him.

"I'm just thinking of Elena." Her eyes opened and he could see tears filling them. She whispered, "My mommy."

Gabriel tried to swallow the lump in his own throat. He gave her a squeeze.

"I know," he said. "I know."

EPILOGUE

Caleb was walking through the empty house, flapping his hand rapidly beside his face. Riley had known that it would be hard for him, but she wanted to give him the time he needed to be able to come to terms with the loss of his childhood home. He became very attached to objects and she knew that he wouldn't want to give up the house any more than he wanted to give up any of his other treasures.

"Did you take pictures of it?" she asked, taking her phone from him. "Every room?"

"Yes," Caleb nodded jerkily. "Every room."

"Then you can take it with you wherever we go. You won't have to forget it."

Riley heard the door open and Wes's shoes tapped hollowly over the hardwood floors. "Everybody ready to go?"

Riley gave Caleb a hug. "We're ready," she answered for both of them.

She was careful not to betray her anxiety about leaving the home that they had loved for fifteen years. Caleb had never known any other house. She needed to be strong for him.

"Caleb will come back," Caleb offered.

"No. Caleb will not come back. We are going on a new adventure. You're going to like our new house."

"Caleb and Mom and Dad."

"Yes. All together. We don't have to live apart anymore."

Caleb nodded. He smoothed his eyebrow and took deep breaths, calming himself. Riley gave him another squeeze.

Moving out of state meant leaving their DFS record behind. They could start fresh somewhere else, in another part of the country. Nobody would know about what had happened. Riley had taken down her blog and had shut down all of her social media accounts. There would be no more sharing their family's challenges with her online friends.

It wouldn't be easy, but they would do everything they could to stay under the radar of Social Services in their new state.

They would do everything they could to stay a family and never be torn apart again.

Did you enjoy this book? Reviews and recommendations are vital to making a book successful.

Please leave a review at your favorite book store or review site and share it with your friends.

Don't miss the following bonus material:
Sign up for mailing list to get a free ebook
Read a sneak preview chapter
Other books by P.D. Workman
Learn more about the author

Sign up for my mailing list at pdworkman.com and get Gluten-Free Murder for free!

PREVIEW OF PAIN

CHAPTER ONE

Hannah curled up into herself, arms wrapped around her middle, knees up to her nose, the pain taking over her body. It started in her stomach and spread outward until her whole body was racked with pain. She couldn't stand the covers pulled over her or the air moving in the room. Every sensory input hurt from head to toes.

She held her breath for as long as she could, hoping to make herself pass out. But eventually, her lungs and diaphragm insisted that she had to breathe, and she took a deep gasp of air that sent more pain blasting through her.

How could air hurt?

Tears coursed down Hannah's face. She sniffled and shuddered, unable to find a breathing rhythm that didn't hurt. She wanted to change her position, but she couldn't unclench her body.

Tess moaned and rolled over in her bed. Hannah tried to call out to her.

"Tess. Tessa… please…" Her voice was tiny and she knew there was no chance of waking Tess up. When Hannah was assigned to wake everyone up in the morning, Tess was the hardest to get out of bed. Not just because she was stubborn. She slept like the dead.

"Tess. Wake up." Hannah tried to be louder, but her voice was barely a whisper.

Tess rolled over again. Then she propped herself up on her elbow, looking in Hannah's direction in the dark.

"Hannah?"

"Get Mom," Hannah begged.

Tess didn't move right away. She stared in Hannah's direction as if she weren't sure what to do. It wasn't like it was the first night that Hannah had the pain. And they both knew that there was nothing Fae Glover could do about it. Hannah should just go back to sleep and let Fae sleep so that she could get to work in the morning.

Hannah continued to cry. Eventually, Tess swung her legs over the edge of the bed and padded across the cold floor to the door. Hannah could hear everything, every creak of the house, every time Tess took a step with her bare toes. Tess's knock on Fae's bedroom door.

"Mom? Mom, Hannah wants you."

"What? Tess?" Fae's voice was heavy with sleep. Hannah felt guilty waking her up, but she needed her mother at her side. She couldn't just go back to sleep.

It didn't take Fae long to rouse. She was used to having to get up in the night to take care of sick children. She was a mother. She entered Hannah's room and went to her bed.

"Hannah? What's wrong?"

Hannah couldn't speak. It just hurt too much. She had used up all of her energy in waking Tess up. She just sobbed in response to Fae's query.

"Oh, baby," Fae said softly. She sat down on the edge of Hannah's bed.

The mattress depressed under her weight and the whole bed rocked, making Hannah shift position and try to brace herself from rolling into Fae. She cried out with the pain that sliced through her belly like someone had kicked her in the gut. She didn't know how she was supposed to stand it. How could anyone live through anything that hurt so much? Every time it happened, she was sure they would figure it out this time. The doctors would find some cancer eating away at her internal organs, or a hole in her stomach, something that would explain the incomprehensible pain. And then maybe they'd be able to fix it. Or maybe they would just be able to tell her in hushed tones how much longer she had to deal with it.

You only have three weeks to live, and then it will all be over. The pain will be gone.

"Mommy," Hannah cried. She sounded like a baby instead of a grown-up twelve-year-old, but she didn't care.

Fae stroked her head. Her broad fingers caressed Hannah's even cornrows, bumping up and down across them. It hurt. Everything hurt.

"Make it stop," Hannah begged.

"Shh. It will pass. Do you want me to sing you a song?"

Hannah didn't want a song. She wanted something to take away the excruciating pain. She didn't answer, and Fae began to sing.

She didn't have a great voice. It wasn't a singing voice that made people stop and take notice, their hearts soaring with wonder. It was just a mom voice. The same voice that had spoken to Hannah from the time she was conceived. She knew it from her mother's womb, from the cradle, ever since she could remember being sick or sad. Fae sang a lullaby that she had sung to Hannah when she'd been sick with strep throat. When she smashed her finger in the car door. When Hannah was sad about Tess starting school, leaving Hannah the only one still too young to go to school.

But it didn't take the pain away.

It didn't make the rigid muscles relax so that Hannah could go to sleep and have pleasant dreams.

It made no difference at all. It was just one more thing that irritated her and made the pain grow, just like Fae's strong hands with their blunt fingers stroking her hair and rubbing a circle on her back.

"Don't touch."

Fae withdrew her hand. "I'm sorry, baby. It will go away, honey. It won't last forever."

"I need to go to the hospital."

Fae sighed. Hannah knew she didn't want to. She wouldn't be able to go to work the next day if she had to stay with Hannah at the hospital all night. And like every other time, the doctors would say that there was nothing physically wrong with Hannah. The pain was just in her head.

"Can't you rest here?" Fae asked. "They'll just send you home tomorrow anyway. Isn't it better to just be in your own bed? You know how much it hurts to drive."

Hannah sobbed, unable to catch her breath. She knew she was on the edge of hyperventilating. Her heart beat too fast and hard. It hurt with every thump.

"Mommy…"

"Okay. Okay, I'll take you." Fae sighed again. "Let me go get dressed and wake up Trevon."

Hannah tried to keep the panicked sobs under control. But she felt like she was having a heart attack. She'd seen people have heart attacks on TV, and her pain was far worse than the middle-aged white men who clutched at their chests and fell dramatically to the ground. She wished that she could just have that one little pain and it would all be done. The men on TV never suffered as she did.

She awaited the day when she would just collapse and the light would go out of her and she wouldn't have to deal with the pain anymore.

She could hear Fae getting dressed, picking up her keys and her hand-bag, and going across the hall to the boys' room to wake up Trevon and explain that she was taking Hannah to the hospital. Hannah didn't know why she even bothered. Why not just let Trevon sleep? He would know what had happened when he woke up in the morning and Hannah and Fae were not there.

But Fae woke him up and explained it to him and turned on his alarm so that Trevon would wake up in time to get everyone ready for school.

Then, finally, she returned to Hannah's room.

Fae knew there was no point in trying to get Hannah dressed. It would hurt too much, and then at the hospital they would just have to undress her again to get her into a hospital johnny so that the doctors and nurses could examine her and tell her that there was nothing wrong.

Fae slid her arms under Hannah's back and behind her knees and hefted her up. Hannah cried out with the jolt of pain.

She was too heavy for Fae and knew she should walk to the car under her own power, but she couldn't. If she tried, she would just collapse and Fae would end up having to carry her or to call an ambulance. And an ambulance ride was expensive. A trip to the emergency room was more than they could afford as it was. They had accumulated all kinds of hospital bills that Fae could not pay, but the hospital couldn't turn them away. Not when Hannah was in a crisis. They had to treat her, even if they couldn't pay.

Hannah clung to her mother, not wanting to be dropped, wishing it would ease Fae's burden even though she knew logically that holding more tightly wouldn't make Hannah any lighter. She sobbed into Fae's neck, smelling her sweat and deodorant, the sleepy scent of her.

Fae was staggering by the time they got to the car. She put Hannah down on the freezing cold pavement in her bare feet to unlock the door, and Hannah slid into the seat. Her feet burned as she swung them into the car and pushed them into the gravelly floor mat to try to warm them up again.

Fae went around to the driver's side and got in. She looked at Hannah as she slid the key into the ignition. "Are you sure? Are you going to be okay with me driving?"

It was the only way she was going to get to the hospital. Even if they called for help, she would still need to ride in the ambulance, and that was much worse than the car. The ambulances rocked and seemed to have no suspension. Hannah would be clinging to the gurney and screaming in agony by the time they reached the hospital.

Hannah gave her mother a quick nod. She folded her body over her arms, hunching down under the dash to try to shrink the pain.

"You can't drive like that," Fae admonished. "You need to sit up, and you need to wear your seatbelt."

Hannah couldn't. She just couldn't.

But Fae didn't put the car into gear. She waited for Hannah to listen and obey. Hannah sobbed wildly, but Fae wouldn't relent. Eventually, Hannah managed to force herself back up into a proper sitting position. Fae reached across her to grab the seatbelt. She pulled it across and buckled it.

Then they were on their way to the hospital.

CHAPTER TWO

Mrs. Williams looked over the class as they settled into their assigned seats. Hope Glover was late or absent again. A couple of other children were not yet there. Avi, she knew, was down with the flu, and she probably wouldn't be back until the next week. George had a family trip of some sort that had been arranged ahead of time, with book work assigned for him to keep up with the class in his absence.

"Kaitlyn. Sarah. Time to settle," she admonished when the girls didn't stop chattering. The girls looked at her, rolled their eyes, and with a few facial expressions and small motions, promised each other they would finish their very important conversation later.

"Everybody get out your books," Mrs. Williams told them. "I want to see your work."

Even though most of the children completed their work on home computers, she still required them to print the work out and insert physical copies in their binders. It helped to keep the haves and the have-nots on an equal footing, all with binders rather than computers in the classroom, taking notes and doing their classwork by hand, required to hand in physical copies of the homework assignments.

With groans and exchanged glances, the students pulled out their binders to find their assignments or tried to come up with an explanation as to why they hadn't finished it. She generally knew which ones would not be done.

Hope Glover burst into the room, backpack swinging on her shoulder, wearing a hoodie speckled with snow, testifying to the fact that she had come straight in from outside without stopping at her locker first. There were no outside clothes allowed in the classroom, but that meant jackets and hats, not sweatshirts, which could just as easily be inside clothes. Mrs. Williams frowned, not just because Hope was late, but because a hoodie wasn't warm enough for the weather.

Hope's hair hung in unkempt locs around her face. Mrs. Williams hated dreadlocks, but she knew better than to complain about them. If she did so, she would be accused of racism, of being prejudiced against the girl's culture and natural black hair. But Mrs. Williams still hated the matted, smelly things.

"Hope, please sit down quietly and get your book out," she advised. "You know you're late."

"I'm sorry," Hope said immediately. "I was trying to get out in time, but Mom's at the hospital again with Hannah, and Trevon was hogging the shower. I had to take care of Tess and everything…" She rolled her eyes and shook her head, playing for pity. "Everything is so disrupted when someone has a medical emergency, you know…"

Mrs. Williams gave her a hard look. It wasn't the first time that Hope had used her sister's health as an excuse. It simply wasn't acceptable. "Hope. You're a big girl. You can look after yourself."

Hope's fourteen-year-old lip started to quiver. She looked up at Mrs. Williams with a hurt look.

"I do look after myself," she insisted.

Getting close to Hope, Mrs. Williams highly doubted the girl had gotten her turn in the shower. She smelled rank. She had a red blob of jam on her shirt. When she saw Mrs. Williams looking at it, she licked her finger and tried to scrub it out. That only ground it into the fabric. After a moment, she gave up. She ducked her head and rifled through her backpack looking for her binder. Mrs. Williams suspected her of stalling. The girl was hoping that Mrs. Williams would get impatient and go on to the next student. But she didn't. While the rest of the class whispered, Mrs. Williams stood there waiting. Hope eventually pulled her binder out of her bag and put it on the desk. Again, she fiddled and stalled, waiting for Mrs. Williams to go on. Mrs. Williams didn't move. Hope opened to the proper section in her binder and stared down at it as if it were something completely foreign to her.

"I… uh… I did the work."

"Where is it?"

"I… I couldn't print it. There isn't any ink in the printer and I couldn't get to the library to print it there. So… I…"

"You know you need to print it."

"Yeah, I know."

"Stay after school today."

Hope's lip was trembling again. She bit it and didn't say anything, staring down at her book shamefaced.

Gabriel and Renata rolled up their sleeping gear and packed away the small tent. They both looked around carefully, watching for any trouble. The other homeless sleepers were starting to stir as well, gathering their belongings to leave before the police came along to roust them. The police ensured that the homeless were gone before the morning commuters started to put in an appearance. It was still dark out, and it was too cold for sleeping rough.

"We should have gone south," Renata muttered, even though she knew they had been over the topic many times already. They had talked it to death.

They should have moved south for the warmer winter weather, but that would require more money. And every time they started to build up some savings for bus fares, something would happen. Someone in the underground network would need them, a job that only they could do. Or the price of Renata's formula would go up and she didn't have any other options. Anything else would put her in the hospital, and they couldn't afford to be seen. Even though as far as they knew DCFS and Dr. De Klerk were not actively looking for them, if they popped up on the radar, they might become targets again.

Gabriel looked at Renata and didn't say anything about her complaint. They'd been over it enough times that she knew exactly what he would suggest. They could stay with Carmel or someone else in their Underground

Railway. There were plenty of people who were ready and willing to help them.

But that was too dangerous. Even staying overnight when Renata had been sick last had felt unsafe. She hated for anyone to know where they were. What if DCFS threatened to take Carmel away from her mother unless they revealed where Gabriel and Renata were? People could be turned. Renata couldn't put her trust in anyone, no matter how loyal they had been in the past.

Motels were too expensive to use them for more than a night or two when it was too cold to survive outside. And Renata had enough experiences with shelters to avoid them like the plague. Unless they really, really had no other choice for survival.

"How are you doing?" Gabriel asked Renata. "We'll go to the coffee place and warm up?"

Renata nodded. Her fingers were stiff with cold just from tying up her bedroll. Her joints ached from sleeping on the cold ground. Once it got to a certain temperature, there was no way to sleep comfortably. Not unless they had arctic gear. And they didn't.

"I'm fine."

Gabriel nodded. He watched her for a moment, analyzing whether she was telling the truth.

"Let's keep moving," Renata suggested.

They made their way over to the sidewalk, getting the kinks worked out, both alert for any sign of anything out of place. In the early morning, they were far less likely to be harassed by drunks or gang members who thought that a mixed race homeless couple made good sport. Her Hispanic features and Gabriel's black skin made people stop and look at them wherever they went. It might be the twenty-first century, but old prejudices ran deep and, in a population that was predominantly white, they attracted too much attention. People assumed that they were romantically involved, and she couldn't blame them. She and Gabriel *were* very close and, when they shared a tent or a room, people made certain assumptions.

The friendly 'open' light was on in one of their favorite coffee shops. Renata breathed a sigh of relief when they entered and the warm air hit her face. She looked around for anyone who might have caused them any trouble in the past, but saw only friendly faces. She and Gabriel kept to themselves, but they were there often enough to be recognized as regulars. A comforting, yet risky situation.

"I'll see you in a minute." Renata went into the ladies' room, which she knew they kept unlocked, and ran warm water for her formula. She preferred the premixed to the powder, but when the temperature was so cold, it turned into a block of ice. Even if it were only slushy, it would make her too cold inside. It would be hours before she stopped shivering. So she had to make do with mixing her own.

Once she had mixed a bottle, she joined Gabriel at his table in the corner and, unbuttoning one button on her shirt, connected her feeding tube to the formula bottle and started her breakfast. She pulled her coat back over the bottle to keep herself warm and to shield it from the eyes of people who would stare or be disgusted that she would dare to use a feeding tube in public. As if a discreet tube into her stomach were more revolting than touching and masticating her food.

———

Pain, Book #5 of the *Medical Kidnap Files* series by P.D. Workman can be purchased at pdworkman.com

facebook.com/pdworkmanauthor

twitter.com/pdworkmanauthor

instagram.com/pdworkmanauthor

amazon.com/author/pdworkman

bookbub.com/authors/p-d-workman

goodreads.com/pdworkman

linkedin.com/in/pdworkman

pinterest.com/pdworkmanauthor

youtube.com/pdworkman

www.ingramcontent.com/pod-product-compliance
Lightning Source LLC
Chambersburg PA
CBHW061256210726
48293CB00003B/992